Praise for Tammy L. Grace,

author of The Hometown Harbor Series and the Cooper Harrington Detective Novels

"This book was just as enchanting as the other. Hardships with the love of a special group of friends. I recommend the series as a must read. I loved every exciting moment. A new author for me. She's fabulous."
—*Maggie!, review of Pieces of Home: A Hometown Harbor Novel (Book 4)*

"Tammy is an amazing author, she reminds me of Debbie Macomber… Delightful, heartwarming…just down to earth."
— *Plee, review of A Promise of Home: A Hometown Harbor Novel (Book 3)*

"This was an entertaining and relaxing novel. Tammy Grace has a simple yet compelling way of drawing the reader into the lives of her characters. It was a pleasure to read a story that didn't rely on theatrical tricks, unrealistic events or steamy sex scenes to fill up the pages. Her characters and plot were strong enough to hold the reader's interest."
—*MrsQ125, review of Finding Home: A Hometown Harbor Novel (Book 1)*

Killer Music is an award winning novel, earning the 2016 Mystery Gold Medal by the Global E-Book Awards

Finally Home

Tammy L. Grace

www.tammylgrace.com
Facebook: https://www.facebook.com/tammylgrace.books
Twitter: @TammyLGrace

Published in the United States by Lone Mountain Press, Nevada

ISBN 978-1-945591-03-7 (paperback)
ISBN 978-1-945591-04-4 (eBook)
FIRST EDITION
Cover design by Alchemy Book Covers
Interior Formatting by Polgarus Studio
Printed in the United States of America

ALSO BY TAMMY L. GRACE

Cooper Harrington Detective Novels

Killer Music

Deadly Connection

Hometown Harbor Series

Hometown Harbor: The Beginning
(FREE Prequel Novella)

Finding Home

Home Blooms

A Promise of Home

Pieces of Home

Dear Readers,

Welcome back to Friday Harbor! Find a comfy spot and delve back into the next book in the Hometown Harbor Series. I love surrounding myself with these characters...they seem like old friends. *Finally Home* (Book 5) picks up where the fourth book ended and features Kate's story. She's the woman who came to the island and opened Alexander's, the art and antique shop.

I recommend you read the series in order for the most enjoyable experience. In case it's been too long since you've made the trip with me to Friday Harbor, I wanted to refresh your memory with a quick summary of each book. **Be advised there are spoilers so don't read any further if you haven't yet read Books 1-4.**

*Spoiler alert: The first book features Sam and her move to Friday Harbor after finding herself divorced at fifty years old. She opens a coffee shop and bakes delicious pies. She discovers comfort surrounded with new friends and falls in love with Jeff and they end up married.

The second book focuses on Linda, the local florist. *Spoiler alert: She and Sam's best friend, Max work together on Sam and Jeff's wedding. She suffers a broken ankle and Max tends to her injuries. Jeff is the victim of a horrific accident resulting in a traumatic brain injury shortly after returning from his honeymoon with Sam. While Sam keeps a vigil at Jeff's bedside, Linda and Max fall in love.

The third book, *A Promise of Home,* has a touch of Christmas and features Regi. *Spoiler alert: She moves to the island shortly before her 40th birthday in an attempt to fulfill a youthful promise she and her high school sweetheart, Cam, made with each other. Regi's journey is littered with disappointment in the form of her mother and brother, coupled with a tragedy involving her daughter, Molly.

Regi ends up falling for Nate and this book ends with their wedding. Two new characters, Kate and her best friend, Spence, are introduced in *A Promise of Home*. Kate is in her early sixties and opens an art and antique shop. Regi's tumultuous relationship with her own mother causes her to seek the guidance of Kate.

In the fourth book, *Pieces of Home*, Ellie's story unfolds. *Spoiler alert: She's had a difficult childhood and was taken in by her aunt and uncle after her parents disowned her. She's grown up working hard at the local bakery and eventually takes over the business.

She's faced with several challenges, including a serious medical diagnosis and a career change. She also discovers her birth daughter is ill and in need of a transplant, which sends Ellie on a quest to reconnect with her high school boyfriend. Sadly, Ellie is unable to find a donor and the teenaged girl succumbs to her illness. In addition to this tragedy, her beloved uncle dies.

Through all of this, she connects with the new owner of the winery, Blake. He gives her a new job and they begin to fall for each other. The last scene of this book is after her uncle's funeral when she receives a surprise visitor at her door—the father she hasn't seen in almost twenty years.

Fix your favorite beverage and settle in for another escape to Friday Harbor where you'll catch up with your old friends and learn more about Kate in *Finally Home*.

Happy Reading,

Tammy

P.S. If you enjoy reading whodunit mysteries on the cozy side, check out my Cooper Harrington Detective Series. I'll be starting the third book in this series soon. The first book, *Killer Music: A Cooper Harrington Detective Novel* is a Gold Medal Winner in the 2016 Global E-Book Awards. It, along with the second book, *Deadly Connection* is available at Amazon in print and electronic formats.

These books are set in Nashville, Tennessee, and feature Cooper "Coop" Harrington, an irresistible bachelor detective, who lives with his wealthy aunt. Coop's faithful friend and assistant, Annabelle and his loyal golden retriever, Gus, both lend a hand during his investigations.

"Those we love can never be more than a thought away…for as long as there's a memory, they live in our hearts to stay." —Author Unknown

Chapter One

A light breeze ruffled Kate's silk robe. She tucked the soft blanket under her chin. The air held the clean smell of morning and the sky promised another perfect day. The pleasant aroma of fresh coffee drifted from the kitchen while she absorbed the peaceful view from her back patio. Kate's slippered feet rested on the soft cushion of the outdoor ottoman. She closed her eyes and drank in the quiet, interrupted only by the sounds of birds chirping.

The scrape of a mug against the glass table stirred her from the edge of sleep. "Here's your coffee, hon," said Spence, taking a chair next to her.

She smiled at him and took a sip, cradling the warm ceramic. "Good morning. Are you packed for your trip?"

He nodded. "Yeah, I'm all set. I should be back in a couple days, maybe less."

She yawned and took another swallow, "Mmm, thanks for the coffee."

He gave her hand a gentle squeeze. "You didn't sleep well again?" he asked.

She crinkled her nose. "I woke up early and couldn't get back to sleep, so I read until it started getting light and then came out here."

He put his hand atop hers. "If it's any consolation, this should be my last trip, at least for a few months."

She smiled. "Don't worry about me. This time of year I always get a bit sad. It's harder to keep my thoughts about Karen in the background. Mother's Day is always hard and so close to her birthday." She focused on the plants along the fence, eyeing the new rose she had planted in honor of Karen. In keeping with tradition, she planted a rose on Karen's birthday. It had broken her heart to leave her huge rose garden behind at her house in Seattle, but with Linda's encouragement, she had decided to carry on with honoring her daughter. This year's was a beautiful Queen Elizabeth, a stunning perfect pink rose. It joined the other, a gorgeous Peace. When Kate moved to the island, all it took was mentioning her habit of planting a yearly rose in memory of Karen and Linda was at the house staking out an appropriate garden and readying it for planting.

The yard had some attractive plants along the fence and rather than disturb them, Linda created a new garden for the roses near the patio. There was enough space for the next twenty years. This year Spence had added an engraved garden stone bearing a quote about remembering those we love. She gazed again at the healthy green foliage of the plant, already arching toward the sun. "Mitch is planning a visit soon, so that's good news."

"I know he was sorry he couldn't be here for Mother's Day."

"It's okay. I have to work through these feelings." A fat tear fell from her eye and plopped onto her robe.

"I'm sorry, Katie." He squeezed her hand. "I've got to get a move on to get the ferry. Are you going to be okay?"

She nodded. "I'll be fine. I'm just wallowing a bit. I've got a busy day to distract me."

He bent and kissed her before disappearing into the house. She heard his footfalls and then he hollered out to her as he left. The front door banged shut and the engine of Spence's car came to life. She listened to the tires roll out of her driveway and shut her eyes again.

She breathed in the perfume of her lilacs in bloom and felt her shoulders relax. She smiled as she rested, remembering her sweet daughter and the happy times of Karen's life. Her mind, like a reel of old film, flicked through the memories of birthdays and celebrations with both Karen and Mitch. She purposely stopped the playback before Karen's college years.

The gentle warmth of the sun touched her face and she opened her eyes to the bright morning. The sun had risen bringing the unadulterated light found only in the beginning of a new day. Kate gathered her cup and went inside to ready herself for her work at Alexander's. Her eyes rested on the giant bouquet of flowers Mitch had sent her for Mother's Day. It was withering and needed to be tossed, but she plucked a few of the dead blooms and let it be for another day.

* * *

All signs of sadness had been wiped from her face by the time Kate walked into town to open her shop. She flicked on the lights and flipped her open sign around, propping the door to take advantage of the weather. She stowed her things upstairs in her office and caressed a photo on her desk of a young Karen and Mitch.

The tourist season didn't officially begin until Memorial Day, but the past few days had been busy with island visitors. Late yesterday she had sold two paintings and busied herself wrapping and boxing them for shipment.

"Good morning, Kate." Sam poked her head in the open doorway and waved. "I brought you a coffee."

Kate turned from the wrapping counter. "What a sweetheart. I had a cup at home but would love another. I got up too early today."

"I came in early to bake and am heading home now. Just popping over to the hardware store to see Jeff."

A group of four women entered the store and Kate moved to greet them. "I'll catch up with you later. Thanks for the coffee." Sam gave a nod and scooted out the door.

Kate was never alone the entire morning. Customers came and left with their purchases until it was past lunchtime. Kate's stomach grumbled prompting her to call in an order for lunch.

She was surprised when Blake came through the door a few minutes later. He held the takeout bag in front of him. "I was getting lunch to go and told them I'd drop yours by on the way."

"That was kind of you. You should join me."

He glanced at the time and shrugged. "I could do that. Ethan's at the winery, so I can spare some time."

She retrieved some plates and they sat down in the backroom. "How's Ellie?" she asked, opening the containers.

"She's still shell-shocked, I think." He swallowed a bite of his sandwich. "She's been so sad about her uncle and then when Ted showed up like that…I think it's overwhelming."

"Is her father planning to stay long?"

Blake shrugged his shoulders. "Not sure. I think they're both playing it by ear. I told her to take some time off and spend it with him." He finished a bite and shook his head. "I'm not sure I could handle seeing my dad after twenty years of no communication."

"I'm sure her emotions are running the gamut," said Kate, spearing a forkful of salad. "She's had a rough few months."

"That's the truth." He finished off his sandwich. "Where's your partner in crime?"

She smiled. "Spence had to go to Seattle. He has to testify at a trial, but will be back in a few days."

"I guess that comes with the territory, huh?"

"Afraid so. His retirement didn't halt the wheels of justice. He'll have to go back periodically until all his cases are prosecuted." She gathered the empty containers and wiped the table. "I'll be glad when he's home."

"We'll have to get together when he gets back and when Ellie's feeling up to it." He made his way to the door. "If you need anything, let me know."

As Blake stepped through the door, Nate hopped from his delivery truck, carrying boxes. "Hey, Kate, I'll stack these behind the counter."

Blake greeted Nate with a firm hand on his shoulder and a nod as he made his way back to his own truck.

Nate stacked the boxes next to the wrapping counter and hustled back to the truck. He returned with a beautiful arrangement of white roses. "I was at Buds and Blooms and Linda said these were for you. I offered to drop them since I was coming here."

Kate's eyebrows rose and her smile widened. "Those are stunning." She took the glass vase and set it near the register.

Nate grabbed his electronic signature pad and jogged to the door. "Catch ya later, Kate."

She plucked the card from the bouquet. *Miss you already, Katie. Love, Spence.*

She held the card to her chest and inhaled the sweet aroma of the tight buds.

The afternoon was quieter with only a scattering of customers, but right before closing time, business increased. Two couples on vacation, who were avid collectors, explored every nook and cranny of the shop and amassed a large number of purchases.

As she was ringing up the orders, the phone rang. She snatched the receiver and continued to work on the order. "Alexander's, how may I help you?"

"Kate, it's Sherrie at the Haven. I hate to bother you but wanted to catch you before you closed today. There's a guest here, a woman, who knows you."

"Really?" Kate's eyes scanned the shop and she saw the foursome deep in conversation in a corner of the store. "Who is she?"

"Maggie Fields. She arrived yesterday." Kate sucked in a breath and said nothing.

"Kate, are you there? Do you know her?"

Kate's mouth went dry and she stammered, "Uh, sorry, yeah. It's, um, been a long time."

"She asked about you and mentioned you. She seemed hesitant to contact you. It may not be my place, but I wanted to let you know she was here. You're welcome to come out and visit with her."

Kate furrowed her brow. "What —"

She was interrupted by a tap on her shoulder. The woman stood inches from her and said, "Excuse me, I've got a question about this piece."

"Sherrie, I'll have to call you back. I've got some customers. I'm sorry." She hung up the phone and turned to the woman asking about a clock.

It took all of her mental fortitude to focus on the shoppers. They were in a buying mood and she wanted to give them her attention, but the thought of Maggie Fields in Friday Harbor was mind-blowing. She pushed the mystery to the back of her mind and ran two large credit card sales through the machine before she closed for the day.

She tallied the register and sunk into the sofa in her office, contemplating what would bring Maggie to the island. She hadn't seen her in almost twenty years. At one time they had been best friends—inseparable. That had all changed after Karen's death.

She shook her head. Maggie had drudged up the sad memories she had been working so hard to forget. She let out a long breath and rested her head against the back of the couch. "What are you doing here, Maggie?" she whispered.

Chapter Two

After closing the winery, Blake drove by Ellie's house on his way to the marina. He slowed, scanning the street for Ted's car. He didn't see it, so made the turn into Ellie's driveway.

He rang the bell and heard Oreo barking. Ellie opened the door and gave him a smile and motioned him inside.

"Sorry to barge in. I was thinking about you on my way home."

"You're a pleasant surprise," she said, hugging him. "I was sitting outside. Come and join me."

She brought him an iced tea and folded herself into the outdoor couch. "Did you have a busy day?"

He shook his head. "Not really, just getting things ready for the season." He took a long swallow and added, "How's your dad?"

"He's okay. We drove around the island today. I think he's trying to figure out what he's going to do. At times he seems resolved to a divorce," she shrugged, "but I think he's afraid to be alone." She let out a heavy sigh. "Other times he acts like he's going to go back to her. I'm not sure what to think."

Blake didn't say anything and petted Oreo while Ellie continued to talk about her new relationship with her dad. "We talked about him moving closer to Ceci. That way he could be around her and the kids. He's afraid of change. I think that's why he stayed with Mom all these years."

"I saw Max today and he offered to take your dad golfing."

"That would be great. He needs to do something to relax. I'm trying my best to be nice, but when we get to talking about the past, I sometimes lose it. I blew my top today and told him I thought he was a coward for not standing up for me against Mom."

"I think it's healthy for you to tell him what you think and how you feel."

She sipped her tea and nodded. "We're taking a break from each other tonight." She pursed her lips and gazed at the yard. "I dreamt of him returning for me for so long, but my attitude goes from cheerful to outrage within minutes."

"You've got twenty years of emotions you're dealing with. I think it's understandable."

She smiled and gripped his hand. "How about you stay for dinner?"

"I could be persuaded." He squeezed her hand and gave her a wink with his captivating eyes.

As she prepped in the kitchen, her cell phone rang. She rushed to wipe her hands and poke the screen. "Hey, Dad," she answered.

"You've got to be kidding me." The rise in her voice prompted Blake to vacate his deck chair and come through the door. "You understand she's manipulating you again? Like she always does."

Ellie's cheeks reddened and her voice went up an octave. "Don't let her do this to you. You have to put your foot down and make her realize you're not going to be part of her circus anymore. We talked about this."

She rolled her eyes and shook her head. "We're just getting ready to eat. I think you should call the police and let them deal with it."

Ellie pounded her hand on the counter and the bowls she was using slammed together with a loud clang. "I'm not being coldhearted, Dad. I'm being a realist. You're being naïve if you can't see through her antics." She let out a breath. "I'll talk to you later."

She punched the screen and flung the phone down on the counter. Blake's eyebrows rose in question. "You okay?"

She nodded and went back to whisking the marinade for the chicken. Her hand whipped the liquid into a vortex. Blake watched for a few minutes and then with a gentle touch, placed his hand on hers to stop the action. "Tell me."

She poured the marinade into the bag of chicken and pulled it closed with enough force to make the zipper whine. She plopped onto a chair and said, "Mom called threatening to commit suicide."

"Whoa, is that something she's done before?"

Ellie smirked. "Apparently. Dad told me she had done that before when I was a kid." She gripped the kitchen towel she held and twisted it one way and then the other. "From what he said, whenever he got stern with her or didn't come to her defense, especially when it came to me, she would threaten to kill herself."

"Did she ever actually take steps?"

Ellie's face contorted. "Puh-leeze. She didn't have to. Dad would conform and do whatever she wanted to console her. We talked about it at length these last few days. I really thought he understood it was a manipulative tactic she used."

A lone tear squirmed down her face. "In his twisted logic, he thought he was protecting me when he sent me to live with Uncle Bob and Aunt Ginny. He wanted to keep me away from her. He confessed he was worried what she would do to me and then as I got older, what I might do to her."

"I'm not downplaying how horrible I think it was that he banished you from your home, but I think you were better off with your aunt and uncle. They loved you and gave you a happier life than I think you would have had with your parents."

She nodded and wiped her eyes with the dish towel. "I know that in my head. My heart is the problem."

He gripped her hand. "Would you rather be alone?"

She shook her head. "Let's have dinner. You start the grill and I'll make a salad." She gave him a swift kiss and added, "I feel better when you're with me."

They put dinner together and ate on the deck, enjoying the peaceful sounds of Ellie's backyard. The phone rang as they were finishing the meal and Ellie glanced at the screen. "It's my dad," she said, rolling her eyes.

Blake busied himself by clearing the table and doing the dishes, giving her some privacy. When he finished he fixed two mugs of tea and took them outside. He found her nestled on the couch by the fire pit, petting Oreo. He handed her a mug and sat next to her, placing his arm around her shoulders.

"He said my sister is going to drive over to Mom's tonight. Dad's going to take the first ferry in the morning and go home."

"Is he coming back?"

She shrugged her shoulders and took a sip from her mug. "Who knows? Once he's around her, he'll probably change his mind and fall back into his old habits."

He squeezed her close and she rested her head against him. "I'm sorry. I know this has to be stressful."

"I'm so conflicted. Part of me is so happy to have my dad back, but I know I can't let myself get too comfortable. He could disappear just like that." She snapped her fingers. "I can't, for the life of me, figure out why she has such a hold on him."

"They've been married a long time," he said.

"I don't think it's some deep love. It's more like a habit or obligation."

"I take it he didn't call the police?"

She shook her head. "He thought they might lock her up and she would be embarrassed." She took another long drink of tea. "That's exactly what needs to happen so she stops this nonsense."

She leaned forward and put her mug on the table. "I'm coming back to work tomorrow. I need something productive to do. If Dad decides to come back, he'll have to work around my schedule."

She snuggled back into position and Blake kissed the top of her head. "Works for me."

* * *

Blake was already at the winery when Ellie arrived for work. Oreo bolted from the car to join Blake and the crew working outside and Ellie settled into her desk. Event requests had been arriving daily and she had to turn a few away due to conflicting reservations. They were booked every weekend through the summer season and even had a few weddings into October.

As she plotted the information on her event template, she sighed. "We've got to get some extra help." She finished adding the latest bookings and turned to tackle the stack of papers in her basket. Her sorting of invoices was interrupted by the phone.

"Island Winery," she answered.

"It's Izzy, Ellie. How are you? I didn't expect you back."

"It's my first day and I'm doing fine. Blake's outside, but I can have him call you."

"That would be great. I wanted to let him know I'd be there Friday. I should be there around six, just in time for him to take me to dinner." Her warm laugh made Ellie smile.

"Sounds great. I didn't know you were coming, but I'll let him know."

"He'd been talking about how busy he is and with the season starting in a few days, I told him I could come and help out."

"I'm thrilled you'll be here. Where are you staying?"

"Blake said he'd get me a room."

"Nonsense. You can stay with me. Rooms are way too expensive this time of year. I've got plenty of space and would love the company."

"Oh, I don't know. I don't want to cramp your style or be in the way. I know you've got a lot on your plate right now, Ellie."

"Honestly, I'd welcome the distraction and return to normal."

"What about your dad? Isn't he staying with you?"

"No, he's staying in town and he's leaving today. I'm not sure if he'll be back, but if he returns, we'll figure it out. Sam's house is huge and so is Linda's, so there's plenty of room for guests if things change."

"Make sure Blake's okay with the idea. I don't want to intrude. We'll figure things out when I get there tomorrow."

"Sounds great. Can't wait to see you, Izzy. We'll meet you at the ferry dock and take you to dinner."

She disconnected and finished sorting through her paperwork, managing to pay all the invoices before the morning ended. She heard the front door open and turned to see Blake filling the doorway. "Hey, how about lunch?" he asked.

"Do we have anything here?" she asked.

He gave her a sheepish grin. "No, when you're not around I don't take the time to shop and make lunch. We'll have to go to town."

They locked the door and hopped in his truck. "Izzy called this morning. She's arriving Friday in time for dinner. She said you can give her a call."

"Oh, good."

"I told her she can stay with me. Rooms are too pricey now."

Blake turned to her. "You don't need to do that. She's going to help me, so I booked her a room at The Haven."

"I called Sherrie and un-booked it. I love having Izzy around and you don't need to waste your money on a room."

"But—"

She interrupted him with her palm raised. "No, I'm not listening to anything you have to say about it. She's staying with me. That's final. If my dad comes back, we'll figure something out. Got it?"

He nodded and grinned, but kept his eyes on the road. "Got it."

They opted for a quick lunch at Soup D'Jour. Blake reserved a dinner table at Lou's for Izzy's arrival while Ellie went to the market. They spent the afternoon preparing the winery for the weekend kickoff of the tourist season.

Ellie checked her phone throughout the day for messages from her dad or Ceci but never heard from either of them. She shut down her computer and as she was locking the door Blake came around the corner of the building with Oreo in tow.

"Are you outta here?"

She nodded. "Just finished. How about you?"

"I think we're ready. I need to concentrate on the tasting room tomorrow and we should be set for the weekend." He moved closer to Ellie and shifted a tendril of her hair from her cheek. "Since it's one of our last nights to be alone, I was thinking I could come by, have dinner, and hang out. How's that sound?"

She smiled. "Sounds like the perfect way to end a day."

Chapter Three

Kate's day had been filled with activity, leaving her little time to contemplate Maggie's sudden appearance. She went home exhausted and spent a few minutes talking to Spence before she collapsed in bed. The funk of Mother's Day and Karen's birthday still lingered as she contemplated getting ready for work Thursday morning. Bouts of insomnia led to tearful nights followed by ruthless fatigue. This had been Kate's pattern the last few weeks.

Kate paused at her Victorian dressing table, running her palm over the smooth mahogany. She slid her hands over the antique pewter urn that stood atop the set of small drawers. She let her fingers glide over the cool metal and trace the engraved roses that circled it. Contrary to what many thought, having Karen close by comforted Kate.

Today as she touched the urn that held all that remained of her sweet girl, she choked on a sob. Karen would have been forty years old. It seemed like she had only died, but it had been twenty years. Kate shuddered as she thought of that horrible day and begged her mind to wander to happier times. It was so hard to explain to others how the loss of Karen still plagued her.

A mother just didn't get over it. The constant agony had eventually subsided, leaving a residual ache in its place. She didn't think of Karen each day like she had for years. The pain had diminished and like an old injury peaked only at certain times. Not when it rained or the weather changed, but at anniversaries, birthdays, and other pivotal events where the absence of her daughter was intense.

Truth be told, she often wondered if that wasn't part of the reason she didn't want to marry Spence. She loved him more than she had ever loved Jack. It wasn't a question of love or fear of commitment that held her back. It wasn't Mitch. He loved Spence and the feeling was mutual. No, when she forced herself to go there, she understood. It was the overwhelming sense of loss she knew she would feel without Karen there to celebrate the day.

Kate was sure Spence suspected as much. He didn't pressure her and told her he understood. He knew her struggle with grief and only wanted her to be happy. She removed her hand and whispered, "I love you baby girl."

She blotted her cheeks and dabbed her eyes. She glanced at the clock and let out a gasp. She tugged open the drawer that held her cosmetics and rushed to get ready. She forced her mind to shift from Karen to Alexander's and all the work she had to do at the store.

Nate's mom, Lulu, had agreed to work Friday and Saturday and as Kate doctored her dark rimmed eyes, she was reminded of the need to find additional help for the store for the summer season. Lulu, with her knowledge of the island and refined taste, was the perfect fit for Kate's shop. She usually worked a couple of days a week and took items from the store as payment. Kate swept the mascara wand across her lashes and sighed. "I've got to find someone else who can work a few more days a week."

She enjoyed the short walk to the harbor and stopped by Harbor Coffee and Books for a latte on her way. She perched in her office and used the time she had before opening the store to draft an ad for a clerk. She jotted on a notepad and scratched out and reworked it several times. She shook her head as the many clocks in the store chimed, signaling the end of her alone time. She left the pad and scurried down the stairs to unlock the door.

The streets were bustling with tourists who had arrived in advance of the Memorial Day weekend. The browsers kept her busy. Sales were few, but she had been occupied all day, answering questions and visiting with vacationers. She had foraged in the fridge and had time for a few bites of lunch, but was starving by late afternoon. As she was contemplating takeout for dinner, the door chimed and a woman approached the cashier area. Kate stuffed the menus back into the drawer and turned to greet the woman she hoped was the last looky-loo of the day.

"Welcome to Alexander's. How…" Kate sucked in her breath. Her eyes met those of the woman. "Maggie?"

The woman nodded. "It's me. Sherrie told me she called you, so I thought I might as well come and see you."

Maggie's face was fuller than Kate remembered, but she recognized her eyes. Her hair was very short and almost white. A start contrast from the last time she had seen her old friend. Kate studied Maggie, taking in her delicate frame. Kate's brow creased, "What are you doing here?"

Maggie shrugged. "Just visiting. Remembering happier times here." She turned and glanced around the space, fingering some of the antique picture frames on a dresser. "You have a lovely shop. You've always had such an eye for decor, Katie."

"I like it here. It's a slower pace on the island."

"I'd like to take you to dinner if you don't have plans."

Kate felt her heartbeat quicken and her mouth went dry. She stammered, "Uh, well, I don't know if that's a good idea."

Maggie's lips were pursed and Kate noticed a sheen in the woman's eyes. "I know I don't deserve it, Katie. Please let me treat you to dinner. For old time's sake." Maggie reached for Kate's hand and Kate flinched at her touch. "I have some things I need to tell you."

Kate looked away and wished for another group of browsing tourists to interrupt the encounter from her past. She had spent so much of her life with Maggie. Karen and Kaitlin were the same age and the two families lived a few houses apart. It had been a wonderful time of her life…until that horrific day over twenty years ago.

"Okay, Maggie. Where do you want to go?"

"Your choice. You'll know the best spots."

Kate flipped her closed sign over and made a quick call to Lou to request a quiet table. She told Maggie to look around while she closed out the register. Kate hurried through the motions of printing out her daily report and doing her deposit. She stuffed everything in a bank bag in her purse and doused the lights in her office.

She found Maggie admiring some of the artwork displayed on the wall. "All set. We can walk to Lou's. He's reserved us a spot."

Kate locked the door. "This is still one of the most beautiful places on earth," said Maggie, as they strolled along the harbor.

Kate nodded, her mind reeling with images from the past. She and Maggie picnicking with the kids, taking them to movies, visiting the park, and the time the two women had treated themselves to a weekend getaway to the San Juan Islands. Maggie had been like a sister. She had never imagined her life without her best friend by her side.

Kate led Maggie to a secluded table and the waitress produced menus. Kate's hunger had disappeared, replaced by a queasy feeling in her stomach. She had been dreaming of crab cakes before Maggie had come through her door. She opted for a bowl of soup and Maggie did the same. Kate sipped her iced tea, waiting for Maggie to spill whatever was on her mind.

"I didn't know you lived here until I saw your shop. I came for a visit, just to relax in the peaceful surroundings. I saw your store and the name and knew it was you, but Sherrie confirmed it."

"I haven't thought of you for more than a decade, Maggie. I used to think of nothing else. After we lost Karen and then when Jack left me, I ached for our friendship. I felt so betrayed...by you...by the world. I can't believe you're sitting here now." The edge in Kate's voice revealed the anger she had held for so long.

"I deserve whatever you can throw at me. I was a complete fool. A monster really. You should have been given my support and loyalty. I'm more than ashamed of how I treated you."

"It's a pity it took you two decades to figure that out." Kate's knuckles were white from gripping her glass.

"I know that now. That's why when I saw your shop, I knew I had to see you. I have no excuse, Katie. I've been a horrid friend and I'm sorry."

"Where's Frank?"

Sorrow filled Maggie's face. "Frank passed away not long ago. Heart attack."

"I'm sorry to hear that. I didn't know."

"He had divorced me about a year ago and then died a few months later."

Kate gasped. "I had no idea. I'm sorry. I know how hard divorce can be."

Maggie's eyes fell to the napkin in her lap. "I know you do. That's what I kept thinking about. I know how awful I was to you when Karen died. And then Jack. What I did is inexcusable. I need to apologize for that...and so many things."

"It was a long time ago. I've tried to move forward and stop myself from looking back. The past is too hard."

Maggie's eyes glistened and she dabbed at them with her napkin.

"I'm so sorry, Katie. I should have never judged you."

Kate gave a slight nod. "How's Kaitlin? Is she still in Seattle?"

Tears flowed down Maggie's cheeks and she shook her head. "No, she's gone."

"Where is she living now?"

Maggie grabbed another napkin off the table and blotted her face. "She's dead, Katie. My baby girl is gone."

Kate's hand flew to her chest as the waitress arrived with their soups. Kate's hand shook as she moved to shove the bowl away. "Oh, my gosh. What happened?"

"She and her fiancé were in an accident. They both died in the wreck. It was at night and they went off the road. We didn't find them until the next day. They were in thick trees."

"Oh, Maggie. This breaks my heart. I know there's nothing that can take away the utter despair of losing a child." She reached for Maggie's hand. Her old friend held on with a fierce grip.

"I know and I apologize for what I did to you. I should have never ever said the things I did about you as a mother. I had no right to even begin to think you could have done anything to prevent Karen's death. I was beyond stupid. I'm so sorry, Katie."

Kate felt hot tears sting her eyes. She swallowed the lump in her throat and took another sip from her glass. "I couldn't believe it at the time. I felt so alone. I never thought you would abandon me like that. After all that, I didn't expect to see you again or dream I'd hear you apologize."

"It's entirely too late. I know that now." Maggie released Kate's hand and gripped her own glass of tea. "I ridiculed you for losing your daughter. I betrayed you and then wasn't there for you. Jack ran out on you and Mitch. Then the same thing happened to me. Frank left because I became so despondent over Kaitlin. I couldn't function."

Kate sighed. "I know that feeling all too well. How are you now?"

Maggie shook her head. "Not great. I'm still struggling." She gulped from her glass. "How's Mitch?"

Kate smiled through her tears. "He's wonderful. Living in Olympia and doing well. He'll be coming for a visit this summer."

"I'm glad you have him, Katie. Truly, I am." She took a spoonful of soup. "You should eat a bit."

Kate shook her head. "I don't think I can right now." She ran her finger down her glass, making a stripe in the condensation. "To say I'm overwhelmed would be an understatement."

Maggie ate almost all of her soup. Kate sat in silence, thoughts of the past fresh in her mind. Lou interrupted the twosome when he arrived at the table. "Kate, do you not like the soup? I'll get you something else."

She looked up, her cheeks still wet in spots. "Oh, no. I just lost my appetite."

He glanced at Maggie, noting the crumpled napkins in front of her and her blotchy face. "I'm sorry to disturb you two. I hope everything's okay." He gave Kate's shoulder a squeeze. "You let me know if you need anything. I'll send something home with you for later."

Kate patted his hand and nodded. She used another napkin to dab her face and tried to wipe away the smudges of mascara under her eyes.

As soon as she stashed her mirror back in her purse, Regi walked by the table. "I thought that was you, Kate. Nate and I are having a bite to eat. From my angle, I couldn't see you were with someone. I was going to ask you to join us. Sorry to interrupt you."

"Not to worry. This is Maggie. She was a…neighbor of mine long ago. She's visiting the island and surprised me today."

"How delightful." Regi reached across the table and shook

Maggie's hand. "I'm Regi and that's my husband, Nate." She leaned and pointed to a table across the restaurant.

"Regi and Nate were married in December. She's a secretary at the high school. They're two of my best friends here."

Maggie nodded and smiled. "You couldn't ask for a better friend than Katie."

Regi's eyebrows rose. "Nobody calls her Katie, except Spence, of course. You must be old friends." She smiled and turned her attention to Kate. "Speaking of Spence, Nate said we need to do dinner when he gets back. How about this weekend?"

"Sounds terrific. Thanks, Regi."

She said her goodbyes and returned to her own table. Maggie gave Kate a quizzical look. "So, Spence?"

Kate lips curved into a smile. "Yes, he and I are a couple now. He retired and moved here recently."

"How wonderful for you. He's always been such a great friend to you. I'm so happy you two are together." She winked and added, "He's the one for you. I could see that even when you were married to Jack. Spence adored you and his devotion to you never wavered."

Chapter Four

In the excitement of Thursday, Kate had forgotten about posting her advertisement for summer help. She hadn't slept well after getting home from dinner with Maggie. The flurry of emotions made her uneasy. She was relieved when Spence called and they chatted late into the night. He was stunned to hear Maggie was on the island. He promised to be home in time for a late dinner on Friday.

Friday morning Kate was running later than normal. Her mind felt foggy from lack of sleep and too much activity. She found the deposit in her purse and dropped it at the bank before stopping for a caffeine fix on the way to the store. She ducked into Sam's and opted to snag something yummy for breakfast, along with her favorite coffee. Lou had sent her home with an order of crab cakes and some of his signature lobster mac and cheese, but she hadn't eaten it last night.

She glanced at her watch and shrugged. She had a few minutes to sit and enjoy her breakfast. Sam was in the back baking but took the time to deliver a buttery croissant and a caramel macchiato to Kate. She took a chair next to Kate and said, "How's it going?"

"I'm glad it's Friday. That's about all I can say at this point." Kate took a sip from the fragrant brew and sighed. "I needed that. I've got to wake up this morning."

"Were you up late visiting with your old friend?"

Kate's eyes widened. "Uh, no, not really."

"Regi was in this morning on her way to work and said she ran into you last night."

Kate nodded as she chewed a bite of the flaky pastry. "She did." Kate took another sip of coffee. "Truth be told, I haven't spoken to or seen Maggie for almost twenty years."

Sam's forehead crinkled. "Wow. I guess you guys lost touch?"

"You could say that. It's a long and…painful story. We had a falling out. She's here on vacation and noticed my shop. She was kind last night and apologized. I agreed to have lunch with her tomorrow." Kate glanced down at her plate. "I'm not sure why."

"Sounds like you need to work through a few things. I wanted to invite you and Spence to a barbecue at our house on Monday for Memorial Day. Are you guys free?"

Kate smiled and her eyes sparkled. "We are and we'd love to come."

"Stop by anytime after noon. It's casual. We don't have a set time yet." The door chimed and a hoard of people stepped inside. "The onslaught has officially begun," said Sam, hurrying back to the kitchen. "I've got to get all my pies done for the weekend."

Kate finished the rest of her breakfast and took the coffee to go, along with a second one for Lulu. Her helper arrived a few minutes before opening. "Good morning, Kate. Are you ready for a busy day?"

She handed Lulu the coffee. "It's been busy all week and from the crowds on the sidewalk, I'd say we're in for a hectic day."

True to her prediction, they were swamped with business throughout the day. Kate heated up Lou's provisions from last night for their lunch. They scarfed it down between customers. During a short afternoon lull, Kate had time to put the finishing touches on her advertisement. She gave it to Lulu to get her input.

"This looks great and as I'm reading it, it reminded me I have to tell you something. I need foot surgery and I saw the specialist last week. I was hoping to put it off until after summer, but he tells me I can't wait. So, long story, but I'm scheduled for surgery in about three weeks. I'm afraid I'll be out for two months, at least." She handed Kate the paper. "I'm so sorry to do this to you, especially in the summer."

Kate felt her neck tighten. "Don't worry about it. Concentrate on taking care of yourself. I'll figure something out." She hurried upstairs to post the ad on a few online sites and also printed a copy to put on the door. She emailed it to Ellie, Linda, Jeff, and Sam, along with Nate and Regi, hoping they might know someone.

She heard the door chime several times and rushed downstairs to help Lulu with the current mob of tourists. By the time the day ended, Kate's feet were sore and her neck ached. She wished Lulu a good night. "I'll be in tomorrow after lunch to help. I'm glad we're closed on Sunday and Monday. We could use the rest."

"Take your time tomorrow. I'll be fine and the customers will have to be patient." Lulu gave her a wave as she went through the door.

Kate tallied the register and her eyebrows rose when she scanned the daily total. "Whew, I knew we were busy, but that's almost a record." She completed the deposit and locked the shop. After she dropped by the bank she made her way to the beach and sat on the low rock wall, gazing at the harbor, waiting for Spence. She had already reserved a table at Big Tony's, knowing how much he loved pizza.

As she waited, thoughts of Maggie drifted through her mind. She took solace in knowing Maggie felt bad about how she had treated her after Karen's death. At the same time, she wasn't ready to give up the resentment she carried. She knew Maggie could never do or say enough to heal the wound she had left on Kate's heart. Years ago she had decided to let go of her feelings for Maggie and by feelings, she meant all of them. Love, friendship, hate, anger, disappointment. She left all of it with the pain Maggie had caused. Now with Maggie here, it was proving difficult to forget.

She wasn't sure there was much to add to their conversation from last night, but it seemed important to Maggie that Kate join her for lunch. "What else can she possibly say?" Kate whispered, as she checked the time and opted to wait at the restaurant.

Kate ordered an iced tea and did some people watching while she waited. She didn't have a view of the landing, so she couldn't watch for Spence. She was worried he may have forgotten about their pizza date when she saw him hurrying to her table.

He smiled and gave her a wink as he approached. She rushed to him and wrapped her arms around his neck. "I've missed you so much."

He laughed and kissed her. "My goodness, I've only been gone a few days. That's quite a welcome, Katie."

He linked his arm in hers as they made their way to their seats. They snuggled next to each other in a booth at the back of the restaurant and Kate rested her head on his shoulder. "I want you to know how lost I feel without you. I can't imagine my life without you in it. You, my sweet man, are my everything."

He gave her a quick kiss on the head. "I feel exactly the same. I love you." The server arrived with their salads and wedges of warm dough slathered with butter and parmesan.

Kate couldn't resist the aroma of the fresh baked cheesy wedge and tore off a piece. Spence groaned as he took his first bite. "I've been looking forward to this all day." Kate filled him in on her unexpected visitor and the last few days.

He finished his salad and said, "It sounds like Maggie's visit has dredged up a lot of old memories. Are you going to be okay?"

"I was already feeling vulnerable, with Karen's birthday and Mother's Day. Maggie showing up put me over the top. I never imagined I'd see her again. I had shelved her to the dusty recesses of my mind. I thought I was over the horrible feeling of betrayal and loss. My friend should have been there for me and when she wasn't, my world fell apart. I never understood how she could be so cruel."

"Do you think her apology was sincere?"

She nodded. "Oh, yes. It was heartfelt. I'm trying to decide if she ever would have apologized to me if she hadn't lost Kaitlin and Frank. It sounds petty, I know, but I don't think she would have given me another thought."

Spence put his hand atop hers. "Sometimes it takes a tragedy to make people understand what's important."

"I'm going to lunch with her tomorrow and then that's the end of it. I can't keep reliving the past. I need to stay focused on now and look forward. I don't do well when I look back."

"It's going to be fine. We'll get through this Maggie situation like we've gotten through everything else." He brought her hand to his lips and kissed it.

"I didn't even ask you about the trial. How did it go?"

"I think it went well. The jury is out, but the prosecutor promised to call me when they had a verdict. He feels confident and I didn't have any trouble with the defense attorney. It's a strong case."

"Good, I'm glad. I hope you don't have to go back soon." Kate boxed up the remaining portion of her wrap.

"Let's go for a walk around the harbor and pick up some ice cream at Shaw's," suggested Spence.

"How can you think about ice cream after all this?" She gestured to the empty plates on their table.

"We'll walk it off, I promise." He winked as he helped her from the booth. They strolled arm in arm around the harbor and surrounding streets. She told him about Lulu's foot and trying to find a helper while they took in the gorgeous evening.

The perfect weather and Spence's strong shoulder made Kate forget about Maggie and the memories she brought with her. As they walked, Spence said, "I have a surprise I brought home."

She lifted her head from his shoulder and gave him a quizzical look. "What kind of surprise?"

"You'll see when we get home. Promise me you'll keep an open mind."

Her brows furrowed. "Hmm...now I'm nervous." She tugged on his hand. Let's get going. I want to see whatever this is."

Spence parked the car, took Kate by the hand, and led her to the door. "Okay, now I realize I should have probably talked to you before I did this, but it was sort of a spontaneous decision and one I had to make right away."

"Oh, my goodness, just let me in to see."

He opened the door and went through, leading her to the backyard. "There it is." He pointed to a beautiful golden retriever stationed on the patio. "Her name is Roxy."

Kate's eyes widened and her mouth hung open, but she said nothing. She turned and looked at Spence and then looked at the dog.

"I know it's a big commitment, but I've missed having a dog and Roxy just retired from the department. I got her for a dollar. Her handler died—natural causes. Roxy is almost eight, so they decided to retire her. She's a great dog. Well trained and won't be any trouble. Plus she'll be great company."

Spence opened the door, gave a quick motion and Roxy came through looking up at her two new roommates. Kate let the dog sniff her hand and then stroked her blonde almost white coat, admiring her long feathers on her legs and belly. One look into Roxy's sweet brown eyes was all it took for Kate. She knelt down and said, "Welcome to your new home, Roxy."

The dog raised her paw and covered Kate's hand. "Looks like we have a deal," said Spence. "I already talked to Jeff and he's going to install a dog door for us and outfit us with everything we need for Roxy. He wants us to bring her over to play with their dogs."

Kate noticed the dog's slender build and thick fur. "What was she trained for?"

"She was an explosive detection dog. She's in great shape and is well behaved. She'll be no trouble." He stroked the dog's head. "If she doesn't work out, I'm sure I can get one of the guys at the precinct to take her."

Roxy leaned her head into Kate. "Ah, she's a sweet girl. I haven't had a dog since the kids were growing up."

Spence put his hand atop hers. "I figured Roxy deserved a nice retirement and she's about our age, so it should work out perfectly."

Kate grinned and gave him a quick kiss. "Where is she going to sleep?"

Spence stood and waved his hand. "I picked up all of her stuff. She's got a plush bed, her food, toys, and the works." He pointed and said, "I set up her bed in the corner of the living room. We can move it somewhere else if you want. They said she was used to sleeping near the door of the house. They think she enjoys the job of guarding it."

"That works for me. We'll see how she does."

"I can get her acclimated over the next few days. I think she'll prove to be a great addition to our home."

After lavishing Roxy with attention, Spence gave her the command for bed and they watched her trot over and nestle into her fluffy perch. They turned off the lights and made their way down the hall.

Kate's eyes struggled to stay open as she watched television. She slept away the stress of the last few days, resting in Spence's arms.

* * *

Saturday morning Kate slept late. She was an early riser by nature but had not budged from her spot in the large bed. Even when streaks of morning light filled her room, her eyes remained shut.

Spence crept out of bed and got ready for the day. He was making breakfast when Kate appeared, her hair tousled, wrapped in her silky robe. "I can't believe it's so late. You should have woken me."

"I think you needed the rest. Do you want some breakfast?"

She eyed the makings spread on the counter and glanced at the clock. "I better not. I'm meeting Maggie at eleven." She poured a cup of coffee. "I'm going to grab a shower."

By the time she returned, Spence had tidied the kitchen and was engrossed in the newspaper, Roxy at his knee. Kate poured another half cup of coffee and settled in her chair with her tablet. She saw an email from Sam, who suggested Kate contact the University of Washington and use them to try to find a student in art history who might want a summer job.

She also had a handful of notifications from the ad postings. She scanned the applicants, noting none had any experience with high-end retail. Most were all food service workers. She shook her head in disappointment.

She navigated the UW website and sent an email outlining her quest for a summer helper, choosing to term it as a paid internship. She knew it was late in the game to be looking for a student, but hoped someone would answer her next week.

She finished scanning emails and checked herself in the mirror. Spence came up behind her and embraced her. "You look lovely." She wore a plum airy cardigan over a plum sleeveless blouse and gray pants. Her signature silver jewelry and fashionable sandals completed her look.

She gave Spence a kiss and squeezed his hand before leaving. "Wish me luck."

"You'll do fine. I'll stop by and see you this afternoon. Regi and Nate want to do dinner tonight at their place. Does that work for you?"

"You bet. I'll see you soon, sweetie." She bent and nuzzled Roxy's neck. "See you later. You keep an eye on Spence."

She elected to walk, enjoying the exercise and the freedom of not having to deal with parking downtown. When she arrived at the Front Street Café she dashed into the ladies room. She felt hot from the walk in the sunshine and knew she was nervous. She ran cold water and fanned a moist towel in front of her face, willing the redness to disappear.

She found her way to the hostess station and realized she was still early. She inquired about Maggie and the hostess led her to a table. Kate's eyes widened when she saw Maggie and another woman seated at the table with a toddler between them.

"Oh, Katie, hello," said Maggie. "I'm afraid time got away from us."

"I'm a bit early."

"Janette, this is my old friend, Kate." Maggie bent to kiss the baby on the forehead. "And this sweet girl is Emma."

Kate shook Janette's hand and cooed at the little girl.

"We'll see you back at the house," said Janette, scooping up Emma and slinging a large diaper bag on her shoulder.

Maggie waved at the baby and Emma waved back. "I didn't realize you were staying with someone. Did you leave The Haven?"

"Just today. I rented a place here on the island. I was staying at The Haven until it was ready. I got the key this morning."

Kate took a sip of water. "I'm confused. I thought you were just visiting."

"I was, but I like it here and was looking to rent a place somewhere. Here is as good as anywhere."

Kate's brow creased. "What about your house?"

"I sold it. I was ready for a change." The waitress interrupted them and took their orders.

"So Janette is…?" asked Kate.

"She's Emma's nanny and helps me around the house. Emma's my granddaughter."

Kate choked on her water and coughed into her napkin. "Don't they call that burying the lead?"

"I had intended for Janette and Emma to be gone by the time you arrived. I was going to tell you. Sorry, I'm flustered." Kate noticed her old friend's hand tremble as she gripped her glass of water.

"I have a lot of things I need to tell you." Maggie reached for Kate's hand and held it.

Chapter Five

Izzy drove one of the last cars off the ferry and eased her way onto the street in search of a parking spot. Blake and Ellie were sitting on the deck at Lou's watching the activity below and spied her car inching along Front Street. Blake hurried down the stairs and jogged alongside her car.

He gave her a goofy wave and she rolled down the window. "Where am I going to park? Is everyone from the city here or what?"

He dashed around the car and hopped in the passenger seat. "Yeah, it's crazy. He directed her to the back of what used to be Sweet Treats, where he and Ellie had parked the truck. "The bakery's closed now so after hours we use their spots back here when parking is nowhere to be found."

They made their way back to Lou's and joined Ellie at their table. Izzy greeted her with a hug and welcomed the glass of iced tea waiting for her. Lou made a point of stopping at the table and engulfed her in a quick embrace. "I'm glad you're back with us. We can always use another beautiful woman in our midst."

Izzy laughed. "You're quite the charmer, Lou. No wonder you're so busy."

Lou gave her his signature grin and was called away for a kitchen issue. "I think he's smitten with you," said Ellie. I've never seen him light up like that."

Izzy smiled and took a sip of her tea. "I think he's an accomplished flirt." She plucked a piece of bread from the basket on the table. "He's sweet and harmless."

They lingered over dinner and discussed the winery and the busy summer it would bring. "I was talking to Mom and Dad before I left. I told them I might decide to stay for the summer and they were fine with the idea. What do you think, Blake?"

Her brother's eyes widened. "Really? That would be terrific. You're sure you could be away from home that long?"

Izzy nodded. "I can handle things via the computer or phone. If I need to go back for a day or two, it would be doable. I'm in the mood for a change of scenery, not to mention the bonus of keeping an eye on my little brother."

He grinned and turned to Ellie. "She means bossing me around. She loves it."

"I think it would be great. You're the perfect person to help us." She gave Izzy's hand a squeeze. "Kate is also looking for help at her store. If you're interested, I know she'd love to have you."

Izzy's eyes widened. "That could be fun, depending on the schedule." She took a long swallow from her glass. "So, I'll need to find a place to rent for the summer."

Ellie gritted her teeth. "That could be a problem. We can talk to Nate's dad and see if he can help find something. The island fills up in the summer. You can stay with me until you find a place, so don't worry."

"That's kind of you, but only if you're sure. I don't want to be a pain."

"You're always a pain, Izzy. Why change now?" Blake said with a laugh and a smile.

Izzy rolled her eyes and continued talking to Ellie. Lou stopped by the table to check on things and deliver complimentary desserts.

"Guess who's going to be here all summer?" said Ellie, raising her brows toward Izzy.

"That's great news," said Lou. "Another perk of the season."

They lingered over dessert and Ellie texted Nate to get the ball rolling on finding Izzy a summer rental. She also sent a message to Jeff and Linda, since they knew everyone on the island and might know somebody with a vacant house.

After Blake helped Izzy cart her things into Ellie's house, the threesome stayed up late visiting around the fire pit. Oreo sprawled out with her head on Ellie's lap. Blake yawned and said, "I've got to get going. You girls get some sleep." He bent and kissed Ellie and gave Izzy a pat on the head.

After Blake left, Izzy held up a bottle of wine she had brought from the family vineyard. "Join me in a glass?" she asked.

"I probably shouldn't, but I'll give it a try. I'm not much of a wine aficionado."

Izzy busied herself in the kitchen, uncorking and pouring. She swirled the beautiful magenta liquid in the glass and presented it. "First," she said, "admire it. Look at its color." She held it up to the light in the kitchen.

"It would make a great toenail polish," said Ellie.

Izzy rolled her eyes and smiled. "It's gorgeous. Now we sniff." She breathed in the aroma. "What do you smell?"

Ellie sniffed again. "Fruity, a bit floral. Pleasant, maybe spicy."

"Take a sip and let it roll over your tongue. Close your eyes and think about all the individual tastes."

They each took a sip. "So, what did you taste, Ellie?"

"Um, berries, I think, plus something different."

"This is our Syrah. You were right about berries. It's got a rich blackberry presence and florals, as you said. After you swallow, you might taste something like a smoky flavor, plus black olives."

"That's it. That's what it was." Ellie smiled and took another small sip.

"It's a lovely wine. One of my favorites." The two left the kitchen and gathered around the fire on the patio. "We'll spend the summer learning about wines."

Izzy drank another full glass of wine while they chatted about the island, Ellie's dad, and the winery. "I'm sorry you've had to deal with such a tense situation on the heels of your uncle's death. I'm sure your stress level is high. I don't want to add to it by being here," said Izzy.

Ellie slid her glass to Izzy and switched to water. "Not at all. This is great fun for me. I've been so isolated with working nonstop at the bakery my whole life that I haven't had time to build many friend relationships. I've been less stressed since I went back to the winery this week. It keeps me busy and I spend less time worrying about my dad."

"Good for you. I've learned the hard way you can only control one person and that's you. The rest...kids of a certain age, spouses, parents, siblings, whatever...you can't do anything but give your advice and opinion. It's up to them."

Ellie watched the flames dance and nodded. "I've decided to concentrate on my own life. I've got great things going on with a new job I love, a new house, and Blake. I've never had this much to be happy about. My dad will make his own choices and if I'm not a part of his life, that's the way it will be. Like you said, I'm responsible for me."

"I hope he decides to be part of your life and from the sounds of it, leaving your mom seems like the best option for him. It's hard to make a big change like that after so many years, even if it makes logical sense. From what you say, your mom suffers from some deep psychological issues and has pegged you as an enemy. Your brother's life doesn't sound healthy either. It appears she's impacting everyone around her in a negative manner. She could benefit from some professional help."

Ellie smiled and chuckled. "That's a diplomatic way of saying she's bat shit crazy."

Izzy shrugged. "Too many years of delivering harsh news in a tactful manner. It's the lawyer in me."

Ellie glanced at her phone and said, "It's late. I've got to get to bed." She saw a message from Jeff and scrolled the screen. "Hey, Jeff says he knows a couple who just finished a studio cottage on their property and want to rent it. He's going to call them tomorrow and put you in touch if it's available."

"Wow, that was fast."

"I always say this island had the Internet long before the technology was invented."

Izzy laughed as she helped Ellie clean up and douse the lights. "You sleep as long as you like. Come to the winery whenever you're ready. Oreo and I will be there by nine."

Izzy gave her a hug goodnight and headed for the guestroom.

* * *

When Izzy awoke she found coffee brewed and a box of pastries on the counter. In bold marker on the pink box Blake had written, *Love you, Izzy.* She smiled and chose a sinful eclair from the box, poured a cup of coffee and took both outside to the patio.

While she was enjoying the garden view, her cell phone rang. It was Jeff letting her know that the cottage he told Ellie about would be available in less than two weeks. He had spoken to the couple who owned it and lived on the property. They were willing to show it to Izzy now and rent it to her for the summer if she liked it.

She jotted down the address and phone number and thanked

him. Based on what Jeff said about the likelihood of finding another option, she decided to set up a time to see it immediately. She arranged for a visit in the afternoon before taking a shower and setting out for the winery.

She found Blake and Ellie in the office when she arrived. After explaining about the cottage, Blake offered to tag along with her when she went to check it out. He tasked Izzy with unboxing and pricing the wine that had been delivered from the family winery in Yakima.

Izzy worked with Ellie to make sure the inventory was entered and attached price tags to the bottles before displaying them in the main room. Ellie fixed them lunch before the pair left for the rental.

The cottage was less than a mile from the ferry landing and the property had a lagoon in the backyard. Blake drove down the long driveway and saw an older, but well-kept home. He and Izzy waited several minutes for a response to his knock on the front door. A man with almost shoulder length gray hair greeted them.

Izzy put forth her hand and introduced herself. "This is my brother, Blake."

The man shook their hands. "Great to meet you. I'm Doug. Eileen, my wife, is out now, but I'll show you the place." He led them around the main house on a driveway path. It circled the house and diverged. He gestured and said, "You can drive down here and there's an area for parking right next to the cottage."

As they followed the grassy path, the cottage came into view. "We built this over the last year. We have enough property and thought we could get a little extra income from renting it out to tourists. Jeff helped me get all the materials and gave me a lot of good advice."

He led them to the two steps leading up to the front door. "It's small. Just over eight hundred square feet, but has all the essentials." He unlocked the door and ushered them in. "We're not quite done with some of the finish work, but will be in about two weeks."

Izzy took in the cozy space and the large window overlooking the lagoon. "Nice view," she said, wandering through the small living room to the tinier kitchen. There was a mosaic-topped table in the kitchen and the normal appliances. Not much counter space, but enough room for a toaster and coffee maker.

The furnishings were in place and covered with plastic. The bedroom had built in bookshelves and cubbies to make the most of the small footprint. A modern bathroom was next to the bedroom and consisted of only a shower, no tub. She noted the fireplace in the living area and the hardwood floors. The bedroom had a door leading to the deck that wrapped around the water side of the cottage. A small table and chairs sat on the deck outside of the kitchen area.

Doug pointed out the wireless connection and promised cable television along with a hot tub and grill on the deck. He left them alone to peruse the area and asked them to come up to the main house when they were done.

"What do you think?" asked Blake.

"It's tiny, but I don't need anything big. Just a place to sleep and have simple meals. It's great that it's furnished. I only brought my personal essentials. I wish it had an office, but I'll have to make do."

"Being brand new is appealing. If you're not concerned about the size, I think it's great. You're close enough to town to walk if you wanted. I don't see any issues."

She put her arm through his. "Let's go sign some papers and write a hefty check."

Chapter Six

Kate was more frustrated than she had been when Maggie first appeared. Before they finished lunch, Maggie had to leave. She told Kate she wasn't feeling well and needed to get home. Janette had taken the car with Emma, so Kate called her a cab, explaining there was only one on the island. She waited with her on the bench outside the café. Maggie stepped into the bright yellow car and said, "I'll get in touch with you later when I'm feeling better."

Once Maggie was on her way home, Kate hurried to work. She found the shop full of customers and Lulu at the register with a line of buyers. She tossed her things in the backroom and helped Lulu work her way through the patient group of tourists.

Izzy came through the door as a couple of ladies left with their purchases in tow. She found Kate at the counter. "Looks like you're keeping busy," she said, as Kate finished wrapping package.

"Izzy, it's wonderful to see you back on the island."

"Ellie tells me you're in the market for some help. I've decided to stay for the summer and help Blake out, but could probably squeeze in a day a week here, if that would help. I could use a few things for my new place, so we could work out a trade," said Izzy, taking a look around the store. She explained she had just rented a small cottage and could use some things to make it her own.

"That would be wonderful. I know how busy the winery is on

the weekends, so talk it over with Blake and let me know what day works best for you. I'm closed Sundays and Mondays."

"I'll get back to you, but think Tuesday or Wednesday should work. I don't have to be at the winery all the time, only to help out for events and busy weekends. I'll be in touch." She gave Kate a quick hug on her way out the door.

Kate was still behind the register when Spence showed up, an hour before closing time. He wandered through the store and made his way up to Kate's office to wait for her.

With the last sale rung into the register, Kate hurried to the door and locked it, flipping over the closed sign. "Go on home, Lulu. I'll close down."

"I'll see you at Nate and Regi's tonight. I'm going to go home and rest my foot for a bit." Lulu gathered her purse and limped out the back door.

Kate bundled the money and receipts and made her way upstairs. "You had another busy day, huh?" asked Spence, perched in a chair with a book.

"It's nonstop." She began the task of reconciling her daily report, chatting as she organized the credit card transactions. "So, Maggie delivered a bombshell today." She tallied the totals and finished her record-keeping. "She's got a granddaughter. Kaitlin had a baby, Emma. The little girl was only a couple of months old when Kaitlin and her fiancé were killed in the wreck. He wasn't the father of the child. Maggie doesn't know who the father was. Sounds like Kaitlin was running wild and got into some trouble."

"Wow, wasn't she a bit old to be behaving like a teenager?"

"That's what I thought. From what Maggie said, Kaitlin hadn't made much of her life. She dropped out of college and got mixed up in drugs and the party life. Once she got pregnant, she turned her life around and met this guy and they were going to make a go of it."

"That's a shame. Poor little girl."

"I know. Maggie didn't feel well, so we cut lunch short. She told me she has more to share. Oh, and by the way, she's renting a place here on the island. She told me she sold her house and was looking for a change and decided to stay here."

Spence frowned. "That sounds like a rather spontaneous decision."

Kate nodded as she stood behind her desk, cleaning it off and filing papers away. "I know. I can't imagine doing that. She's got a young lady named Janette with her who helps her around the house and serves as a nanny." She closed her desk drawer and plopped on the settee. "The whole thing is weird."

"So, she's got custody of Emma?"

"Yeah, she and Frank adopted Emma after Karen's death. That's the only time she looks happy—when she talks about Emma."

"She probably keeps Maggie going. Sort of like when you lost Karen but knew Mitch needed you."

Kate looked at her hands and nodded. "Yeah, but I can't imagine raising a baby at my age. Talk about tired. No wonder Maggie looks so worn out."

"We better get going. I'd like to get to Nate and Regi's early and talk to him about a fishing trip."

She laughed and gathered her things. "By all means. I'm sure Nate will be delighted to oblige."

They started down the stairs when Kate stopped. "Where's Roxy?"

"Oh, I dropped her off at Regi's on my way here. She and Murphy are playing in the yard."

"They didn't mind another dog, huh?"

"Not at all. Wait until Roxy meets the rest of the gang. I don't think she got to play much, so this will be fun for her."

"How'd she do?"

"Actually, she's a bit timid when it comes to other dogs. I think it's because she mostly worked and her owner didn't have other dogs."

They maneuvered through the roads, thick with tourists, and made their way to the house. Spence had stopped by the bakery and picked up a dessert to contribute to the gathering.

Nate greeted them at the door. He and Spence retired to the patio to discuss fish and check on the dogs, while Kate helped Regi in the kitchen. Kate deposited the cake on the counter and asked Regi if she could help her.

Her feet were thankful when Regi insisted Kate sit at the counter and enjoy a glass of wine while she finished things in the kitchen. Kate took a sip and sighed. "It's been a long week."

"I was sorry to hear Lulu has to have foot surgery. I know you depend on her."

Kate nodded. "I know. The timing isn't great, but I should have gotten around to getting help anyway."

"I'm committed to Sam one day a week, but I'd be happy to help out. I could probably squeeze in a little time," offered Regi.

"If I get in a real bind, I'll call, but you need to enjoy your summer. Izzy stopped by today and she's going to be here all summer. She offered to help one day a week, so that's a start."

Regi put the salad in the refrigerator. "Nate told me the same thing about relaxing. I haven't had a summer off since I started working at a school years ago. I've always found a summer job. Now that we have a house and Cam is footing the bill for Molly's education, I don't need the extra work." She shrugged and poured herself a glass of wine. "I'm conditioned to stay busy. I'd be bored hanging around here."

"My advice would be to take advantage of the freedom. Cut back and take some time for yourself. You deserve it. Maybe just work two or three days a week."

Regi smiled. "That's sensible. Sort of the best of both worlds. I'm not working the weekends, so Nate and I can spend some time together."

Soon Lulu and Jack arrived and the group gathered on the patio. As soon as the meal was done, Lulu gripped her husband's hand. "I'm sorry to cut the evening short, but my foot is killing me. I need to get home and rest." Her pale face grimaced in pain.

Nate and Jack helped Lulu to her feet and she winced when she put any weight on her foot. "I'm so sorry, Lulu," said Kate. "I don't think you should work this week. You need to rest your foot. I don't like to see you suffering."

"We'll see how it goes," Lulu said, her voice quiet. "I hate to dine and dash. Dinner was fabulous, Regi."

"Not to worry. Let me know if you need anything," said Regi, giving her mother-in-law a hug.

Nate followed his parents outside and helped Lulu get in the car. He came back in and shook his head. "I didn't realize how bad her foot was bothering her. She's always such a ball of fire."

"Good thing her surgery is coming up. I don't think she could wait much longer," said Kate.

They cleaned up the kitchen and gathered on the patio to enjoy slices of cake. Spence stuck to coffee and nodded to the wine bottle and wiggled his brows at Kate. "Go ahead and have all you like. I'm driving. You can relax a bit."

She smiled. "Just one more glass and then we better get going."

Regi poured and raised her glass. "To summer," she glanced at the dogs, "and to Roxy." Nate and Spence finished their cake and engaged the dogs in a game of fetch.

After a few more bites, Regi asked, "So how's it been reconnecting with your old friend, Kate?"

"She's the reason for the wine tonight." Kate sighed. "It's a long story, but we had been closer than sisters for much of my life. She was like a second mom to my kids."

Kate took a nibble from her fork and looked across the yard at the water. "When Karen died, Maggie…she just abandoned me. She blamed me for her death. Thought I should have known something was wrong."

Regi reached for Kate's hand. "I'm so sorry, Kate. How awful for you."

"It's been a shock to see her." A tear slid down her face and she dabbed at it with her napkin.

"You don't need to talk about it now."

"It's been a rough few weeks." Kate gave her a weak smile and turned her attention to the dogs running with the two men.

Spence returned to the table and left Nate to the wild antics of the two dogs. He put his hand on Kate's shoulder. "Are you ready to leave?"

She nodded. "I think so. Thanks so much for dinner, Regi. It was wonderful to visit and relax."

Spence called out, "Roxy, here girl." The dog immediately stopped playing and ran to Spence.

"I think we need to send Murph to the same school Roxy attended. She doesn't mind well." She laughed and watched Nate tumble on the grass with the ball of golden fur.

They said their goodbyes and headed back to town. Spence rested his hand on Kate's knee. "What's on the agenda for tomorrow?"

"Sleeping late sounds great to me. I need to work on finding a helper for the store, but outside of that, no plans."

"A lazy day will do you good."

Roxy lounged across the back seat, her eyes shut, content as Spence drove. When he glanced at Kate, he saw her eyes were closed. He grinned and took the long way home.

* * *

Sunday morning Spence took Roxy on a walk to the harbor and let Kate sleep. He picked up some donuts from the bakery and found Kate fresh from a shower when he returned.

She was on her computer and gave him a quick smile. "Here's an email from a woman who's interested in working at Alexander's. If she works out and I have Izzy one day, that would ease my anxiety over the store."

He led Roxy to her bed and joined Kate at the counter. "Sounds promising."

"She's moving to the island from Seattle. She's a nurse and plans to work one or two days a week at the hospital, but has an interest in art history and her friend works at UW and told her about my job posting."

"I think that's better than a student. Older people will be more reliable and apt to stay on, don't you think?"

She nodded. "I agree. Andi sounds like a good fit. That's her name, Andi Mitchell. She's retiring and slowing down. She bought a house in town. She's moving this weekend, so we can meet this week."

"I think Lulu needs to stay off her foot, so that would be great if you actually have a replacement. She won't feel as guilty leaving you."

"I know. Last night she looked like she was in such pain. I'll call her today and check on her."

"Maybe we ought to invite Andi to dinner tonight. You know how nice it is to have a home-cooked meal someone else prepares when you're tired from moving."

Kate rose from the chair and put her hands on the sides of Spence's face. "You are so smart." She gave him a quick kiss and said,

"I'll call her now and see if she'll come. What a wonderful idea."

He glanced at Roxy as Kate hurried to dress. "We never get tired of hearing how smart we are, do we?" The dog's tail thumped against the floor in agreement.

Chapter Seven

Spence volunteered to cook after Andi had accepted their invitation to dinner. Kate spent the day cleaning and organizing for the week ahead, thankful she was closed tomorrow. By the time the dinner hour rolled around, Kate had the house in order, complete with fresh flowers throughout and Roxy's toys in a stylish basket. The place was gleaming and the patio was set for company.

Andi was on time and Kate greeted her at the door. Roxy was busy in the backyard with Spence. "Hello, I'm so glad you could come, Andi."

The petite woman with a friendly smile extended her hand and presented a bottle of wine. "Here's my contribution. I can't thank you enough for inviting me. I don't have the energy to make a sandwich at this point."

Kate ushered her into the living area. "I'll put this in the kitchen and how about I get us some iced tea?"

"Sounds perfect." Andi sat on the sofa and a few minutes later Kate appeared with a tray of tea along with some appetizers.

"Oh, this looks yummy. I'm starving," said Andi, taking a small plate and a glass.

"We figured you'd be hungry and ready to put your feet up. Spence is grilling and we're going to eat outside. We have a new to us dog, Roxy. She's very well mannered, but let us know if you don't like dogs."

"Oh, I love dogs. That was a concern for me when I was looking for a house. I needed a yard for my old guy, Oscar."

Spence interrupted the conversation and introduced himself. "I'm grilling chicken and steak. It's your choice, ladies. I'll need to know how you like yours done, Andi."

Andi shook his hand and returned to her seat, sweeping her graying blond bangs from her face. "Medium works for me, but I'm fine with chicken, either is wonderful."

"It will be ready in about twenty minutes. You two just relax," said Spence.

"What a sweet guy," said Andi.

"He's the real deal. I've known him since high school. I'm divorced and moved here about eighteen months ago. Spence retired and decided to join me. It's been wonderful having him in my life full time."

The two women chatted about the island and Kate gave Andi tips on the best places to eat. They discussed the store and Andi's hospital schedule. Andi shared her love of art and decorating while she admired Kate's home and furnishings. "I would have loved to have made a career in that world, but my practical side kicked in when I was in college and I decided to be a nurse so I could earn a good living. As it turns out, it was a wonderful career, but I'm ready for a change."

Andi moved to some photos and said, "Oh, these must be your children. They're so cute."

Kate stood behind her and said, "Yes, that's Mitch and Karen. Mitch lives in Olympia and Karen passed away twenty years ago."

Andi gasped, "Oh, I'm so sorry. I know how hard loss can be." She met Kate's watery eyes. "I lost my husband two years ago."

The two women embraced, tears spilling onto their cheeks. "That pain never goes away. I'm so sorry to hear about your husband," said Kate.

Kate guided them to the sofa. "That's the main reason I'm moving. I just couldn't stay in our house any longer. Everything reminded me of Chad. I had to get out of there." Her knuckles turned white as she gripped her glass of tea.

"I understand that feeling. Memories are a mixture of happiness and sadness, with a large helping of regrets." Kate took in Andi's pale face and her gunmetal blue eyes, leaking slow tears. She patted her hand and added, "A new place and a new start will do wonders."

Andi nodded and took a tissue from the side table. "I sure hope so." She wiped her eyes and sniffed. "Chad was killed in Afghanistan. He was a Major in the Army."

"Oh, Andi, that's horrible," said Kate. "I know there are no words to make it less painful."

Andi continued to blot her face. "I didn't mean to come over and blubber to you. I keep thinking it will get easier."

Spence poked his head around the corner and said, "Dinner's ready, ladies." He pretended not to notice the pile of used tissues in Andi's lap and her red-rimmed eyes.

Kate left Andi to compose herself and gathered the side dishes from the kitchen. Roxy greeted their guest with a few sniffs and received a pat on her head. She retired to her outdoor bed, while the threesome gathered at the table.

Kate steered the dinner discussion to the job at her store and Andi's schedule at the hospital. Andi would be working Mondays as a nurse and was open to whatever schedule Kate needed at the store.

"Why don't you get settled this week and if you're up to it, you can start on Friday and see if it will work out for you? Our busiest days are on the weekends, but during the summer, it's always busy. I've got a friend who will be on the island for the next few months and she's going to work one day, I'm hoping you can work Thursday through Saturday. I can help when we're busy but will come and go. We're closed on Sundays and Mondays."

Andi took a sip from her wineglass. "That's doable for me. I need to keep busy, so having three days off a week is plenty."

"Once Labor Day hits, it will slow down and I'll most likely have to cut you back to Friday and Saturday only."

"I'm flexible. I've got a retirement from my career in Seattle, so I'm okay. I sold our house and am simplifying my life." She chuckled and added, "That's the plan, anyway."

Spence asked about her new house and she explained it was a few blocks from the harbor. "It's on the small side but it's perfect. It's been remodeled and has a new deck, plus a large yard for Oscar."

"If you need any help, just say the word. I'm usually free and know some strong guys who could lend a hand with anything you need," offered Spence.

Andi's eyes twinkled. "That's so kind of you. The movers got everything of size moved in, so I'm working on the small stuff. I need to get organized and do some grocery shopping and get the lay of the land."

"We'll introduce you to Max. He's a doctor who's semi-retired but agreed to work at the hospital a few days a week. He's a great guy and a top-notch cardiovascular surgeon," said Spence.

"That would be great. I've got an appointment on Wednesday to do all my paperwork and get ready for my first shift next Monday. I'm working in the ER."

"As it happens, we know the ER Chief there, Dr. Sean Doyle. He's a great guy. I'm sure you'll like him."

"You two are quite connected for only being here a short time."

Kate smiled. "We've been lucky enough to be embraced by a wonderful group of friends who have lived here a long time, some all their lives. It's a small island and the people are welcoming. Max actually convinced Sean to move here and accept the position at the new hospital. It's a lovely facility."

Kate gave Andi a quick rundown of the group she and Spence had come to think of as family. She explained about Jeff and his family owning the Harbor Resort along with Cooper Hardware and Sam coming to the island and finding her second chance with Jeff. She told Andi about Linda's beautiful nursery and her flower shop and explained that Max had come for Sam's wedding and he and Linda hit it off and he decided to move to the island.

"How about I meet all of you Wednesday morning for coffee at Sam's place?" said Spence. "She bought Harbor Coffee and Books and makes the best pies you've ever tasted. I could go with you to the hospital and introduce you to Max. He works on Wednesdays."

"That sounds wonderful. Does nine o'clock work for you?"

They made a plan, which included Kate joining them on her way to work. As the sky began to fade, they indulged in dessert and coffee. They were treated to a lavender and gold streaked sunset, with the promise of many more summer evenings to come.

Spence offered to drive Andi home since she had opted to walk through town. Kate outfitted her with leftovers and a warm hug and watched as Spence drove away. Kate looked up at the darkening sky and gave a nod. "She's gonna work out, I can feel it."

* * *

Sam and Jeff had decked out their house for a traditional Memorial Day barbecue. The yard was filled with dogs, running and tumbling over each other. Kate and Spence arrived and added Roxy to the mix. She was wary at first, but soon assimilated with the others and was playing and frolicking with the rest of them. The golden retriever seemed to take a liking to Zoe, perhaps sensing a long lost sister, and hung close to her side.

The women helped Sam in the kitchen and then joined the men on the deck to soak up the gorgeous view of the water and watch the entertaining dogs on the grass below. The table was covered with a variety of appetizers and finger foods. Nate made his way to the food and piled a plate high. "So, what are you boys up to?" asked Sam.

"Just finalizing a plan for another fishing trip." His eyes brightened when he discussed their next great water adventure. Max joined the group, giving Linda's shoulders a squeeze while he perused the array of snacks.

"I hear fishing is in your future," said Linda, looking up.

"Yes, we've got a plan. Spence has been itching to go and this group doesn't need much of a push to get them on the water."

"Did Spence tell you about Andi? She's a nurse and will be working at the hospital and hopefully for me," said Kate.

"Oh, that sounds good. He didn't mention it yet, but the dominant topic has been fish." Max piled some chips on his plate.

"We had her over for dinner and to discuss working at Alexander's. She's a lovely woman who lost her husband not long ago. She's looking for a fresh start here."

"I know that feeling. I hope the island brings her as much happiness as it has me." He gave Linda a quick peck on the cheek. "The best move I ever made."

"We're meeting her for coffee Wednesday at Sam's and then Spence is going to bring her over to meet you at the hospital."

"I've got a better idea. How about I meet all of you for coffee? That way I'll have more time than just squeezing her in at the office."

Kate smiled. "That would be wonderful. I'm sure she'll fit right in at work, but it would be nice to have you show her around. She's working the ER." They made plans to meet at Sam's before Max rejoined the fishing experts.

Ellie and Blake arrived with Izzy, prompting Jeff to light the grill.

Izzy made the rounds to receive hugs and congratulations on her summer residency. While Jeff cooked, the ladies carted out dish after dish and set up the tables so they could all sit together at one huge square.

Spence and Blake made sure the dogs were fed and after their afternoon of nonstop play, they passed out on the cool grass. Jen and Sean arrived late, toting a selection of desserts from the bakery. They squeezed around the table as Jeff delivered two heaping platters of meat, fresh from the grill.

The chatter subsided long enough for Max to give a toast to summer, friends, and the beauty of their surroundings, along with a warm welcome to Izzy. Food was passed amid the laughter and conversations around the table.

The fishing trip was finalized for next weekend. Kate told the group about Andi, her new helper and a part-time nurse. Izzy filled them in on her new cottage and thanked Jeff for his suggestion. Nate and Regi updated them on Lulu's surgery, which had been moved up and would take place tomorrow.

As soon as the last pink gilded ribbon of light sunk into the sea, Jen and Izzy offered to take care of the clean-up duties. Sam and Linda plated the dessert options while Jeff and Blake started the fire pit. The group moved closer to the beach, listening to the water lap against the shore and watching the sky grow ever darker.

"I'm inviting all of you ladies to my house next weekend. While the guys are fishing, I think we should have a movie marathon," said Linda. "Everyone can bring something to eat and we'll have our own weekend of fun."

"Sounds like they're going to leave Friday afternoon, the last day of school, so count me in," said Regi. One by one the ladies committed to the idea.

"Since Friday is a workday, why don't we meet for dinner out to kick-off the weekend? We can do the rest of the meals at my house," suggested Linda.

"Since one of my favorite things is lists, I'll volunteer to make a list of food and snacks and email it to you guys," said Sam.

"I'll make a reservation at Lou's for Friday night," said Kate. The group agreed on a time that would work for everyone before the party broke up for the evening. One by the one the dogs were matched with their owners, while Sam and Jeff made sure Zoe and Bailey stayed behind.

Jeff grabbed Sam's hand and led her back to the fire pit. "Let's just sit here and enjoy this."

She tucked her head into his shoulder as they snuggled together. They glanced up at the stars sprinkled across the ink colored sky while listening to the soft rhythm of the water against the beach and the sporadic crackle of the fire. "Another perfect night with my favorite person," said Sam.

Chapter Eight

Kate had a busy Tuesday and only had time for a few bites of the lunch Spence delivered. She finished the daily paperwork and saw her cell phone blinking. She scrolled through it and found a message from Maggie. She apologized for cutting their lunch short and wanted to set up a time to meet and continue their visit.

Kate sighed as a variety of options shuffled through her mind. Part of her wanted to forgive Maggie and rekindle their old friendship, while another part warned her to keep her distance and avoid digging up old wounds. Whether or not she accepted Maggie back in her life, the curiosity surrounding her story beckoned Kate's interest.

She sat back in her chair and surveyed the office she had come to love. It was a haven, a safe place far away from her old life and pain. She admired her favorite items displayed throughout and glanced at the photo of Karen on her desk. She wiped a lone tear from her eye and dialed.

Kate suggested Maggie come to the house for dinner on Wednesday. She knew she could count on Spence to cook for them. An after work meal also gave Kate the ability to use the excuse of being tired to cut the evening short.

As was his habit, Spence greeted Kate at the door with a kiss and a tall glass of iced tea. She perched on the patio while he finished putting dinner together. They chatted about Maggie's upcoming visit and Spence assured Kate he would handle dinner and then go visit one of the guys. He placed the last dish on the table and joined Kate for their meal.

She took a bite of his lemony pasta dish. "Delicious." She reached across and put her hand on his. "I'm lucky to have you. I'm so glad you joined me here."

He gave her a broad smile. "Katie, I can't imagine my life without you. I'm beyond happy here on the island with you. I want the rest of your life to be the best and I promise to be by your side and do all that I can to make you happy." He took her hand and kissed it.

"I'm the luckiest gal in the world," she said, giving his hand a squeeze.

* * *

Wednesday morning Spence and Kate met Andi at Harbor Coffee and Books. They arrived first and snagged a table in the corner. Andi came through the door as they were taking their first sip. They waved at her as she made her way to the counter.

Sam hurried to greet her, extending her hand. "I'm Sam and you must be Andi. Kate's told me you'll be helping her. I'm so happy to meet you."

Andi smiled and gripped her hand. "Well, thank you. I'm excited to be here and so glad Kate and Spence suggested meeting at your shop. You'll be seeing a lot more of me. I'm addicted to coffee." She placed her order and dug into her purse.

Sam told her to keep her money. "As a welcome to Friday Harbor, it's on the house. Just come back and see us."

Andi took her coffee and pastry and joined Kate and Spence. "She's a sweetheart, isn't she?" said Andi, nodding to Sam.

"That she is. One of the nicest women on the island," said Kate.

They chatted about Andi's progress on her house and the influx of tourists in the streets until Max arrived. He ordered a drink and joined them. "Sorry, I'm a few minutes late. You must be the new nurse I've heard so much about. I'm Max Sullivan," he said, extending his hand.

Andi introduced herself and thanked him for meeting. "I'm looking forward to seeing the new hospital. I've heard great things, but did all my research and communications online or on the phone."

"You'll love it. It's state of the art and filled with great people. I understand you'll be working with Sean in the ER. He's a great guy. He's there this morning and I told him we'd stop by."

Her eyes twinkled. "That sounds great. I'm looking forward to a new job and with it being only one day a week, I'm hoping things work out with Kate." She raised her brows at her prospective employer.

"I'm sure it will. I'll show you the ropes Friday and we'll see what you think. Speaking of, I better run and get to work." She slipped out of her chair and gave Spence a quick kiss.

The threesome finished their breakfast and Spence left Andi in the capable hands of Dr. Sullivan.

* * *

Wednesday Kate closed the shop a few minutes early and hurried home. She found a note from Spence. Dinner was ready and he and Roxy were visiting Nate and Regi. Kate looked at the clock and dashed to change into jeans. She popped the veggie flatbreads into the oven and retrieved the pitcher of fresh iced tea.

The doorbell rang and she greeted Maggie with her best smile. "Welcome, please come in. We're going to eat on the patio if that's okay?"

"Sounds wonderful," said Maggie, her eyes roaming the space as she followed Kate to the kitchen. "Your house is lovely, Katie. I hate that you had to cook for us after working all day."

"Ah, Spence was sweet enough to do all this for us tonight. He's made us some veggie flatbreads and a yummy grilled chicken salad. I haven't found dessert yet, but knowing him it will be something tasty he picked up at the bakery."

Maggie perched at the counter while Kate cut the flatbreads. She asked Maggie to carry the tea and they made their way outside. "Oh, this is a great spot. Just the right amount of shade for the evening," said Maggie.

"It's peaceful out here. One of my favorite morning rituals is to have coffee outside."

They filled their plates. "How's Emma doing with the new house and the move?"

Maggie's eyes lit up as she told Kate about dipping Emma's toes in the water and watching her at the park. "Janette takes her exploring somewhere while I nap each day."

"Are you still feeling under the weather?"

"I'm getting better each day. It's peaceful here and that helps." She took a bite of the flatbread. "Delicious."

As they ate, Kate let her mind wander to happier times. She and Maggie had eaten hundreds of meals together. They had taken the children to parks, the zoo, the ocean, and thousands of story hours at the library. As Maggie chatted about Emma, Kate saw the young mother she knew so long ago. The woman with wavy blond hair, piercing eyes that advertised her intelligence, and the soft smile with a huge laugh that contradicted her petite size.

Kate listened as Maggie filled in the gaps of the last twenty years. "I got breast cancer fifteen years ago. At the time, I thought it was the worst chapter of my life. Little did I know there was something even crueler."

Kate's hand went to her chest. "Oh, Maggie."

"It took over a year and lots of treatments, but I beat it. It was awful and I felt horrible much of the time, but I survived." Maggie's eyes filled with tears and she dabbed at them. "Surgery, chemo, radiation. The chemo was the worst. Debilitating much of the time. I can't…"

Kate patted Maggie's hand. "I'm sorry I wasn't there for you then."

A sob erupted and Maggie drew her napkin to her face. "The only reason you weren't there was because of me. You have nothing to be sorry for."

Kate watched Maggie's chest heave and her back twist. Her guttural cries sounded like a wounded animal. Kate was at a loss. She knelt beside Maggie and patted her back, whispering, "It's okay. It's okay."

"No, Kate. It's not," she blubbered. Maggie took a few long breaths. "I'm sorry. I need to go."

"Are you sure? Are you okay to drive?"

Maggie nodded as she eased herself out of the chair. "I'll be okay. I just need to get home."

"I can drive you," said Kate, following Maggie to the front door.

She wiped a sheen of sweat from her hairline. "No, no. I'll be okay. I'll call you tomorrow. I'm sorry, I guess I'm not feeling as well as I thought."

Kate tried to help Maggie outside, but Maggie waved her away. Kate frowned as she watched Maggie stumble into her car. Kate stood on the sidewalk and lifted her hand as the car drove away, but Maggie didn't return her goodbye.

She shook her head and returned to the house where she kept busy cleaning up the dinner dishes and storing the leftovers. She sent Spence a text and told him the coast was clear. After the kitchen was tidied she took a glass of wine outside and plopped into her favorite chair to analyze her visit with Maggie.

She heard the door open and the sound of Spence talking to Roxy. The pair joined Kate outside. Roxy put her snout on Kate's lap and received a thorough neck scratching.

"You guys are done early. Did you use your excuse and cut the evening short?"

Kate shook her head. "Maggie got upset and said she had to go."

Spence grabbed a ball and tossed it across the yard as he slipped into his chair. "What made her so upset?"

Kate rehashed the visit, explaining that when Maggie began talking about having breast cancer fifteen years ago, she began to melt down. She took a sip from her glass. "She said she didn't feel well and she looked a bit ill. I guess it was too much for her."

"She's dealing with lots of difficult memories. As hard as it is for you, I think she's having an even worse time. She's acknowledged her fault in ending your friendship and the pain she caused you over Karen. I think she's trying to make amends."

Kate nodded as she petted Roxy. "I never thought of it that way. Maybe it's too overwhelming for her to think about. Not to mention the death of Kaitlin. I know the constant pain that brings." Kate leaned her head back and closed her eyes. "I'm not healed from Karen's death. I never will be. Maggie's dealing with that, along with the loss of Frank, Emma, a move, plus her apparent guilt in rehashing our relationship."

Spence put his hands on her shoulders. "Memories can be powerful. Especially tragic ones."

* * *

Kate didn't sleep well and went to work early to finish typing the daily procedures for Andi. She wanted to make sure everything was documented and easy to follow for Andi's first day tomorrow. While she was putting the pages in a binder, her mind wandered to Maggie. Although she hadn't thought of her old friend for years, she hated to see her so distraught. She thought about calling her, but didn't have much time to chat and didn't want to cause Maggie further distress.

She finished the binder and cleared her desk. She had a few minutes before the store opened and hurried outside to grab a coffee at Sam's. Sam was busy putting some freshly baked pies in the display case when Kate breezed through the door. The scent of baked sugar, cinnamon, and fruit permeated the air and tempted those waiting at the counter. The line was long and Kate glanced at her watch.

After Sam closed the case she greeted some of the other customers in line on her way to Kate. She whispered, "What can I get you. I'm on my way out, but I'll make your drink. I know you have to be open in a few minutes."

Kate whispered her order and with her eyes, Sam motioned to the deck outside. Kate made her way to the outdoor space, which was congested with tourists. She waited a few minutes, taking in the calming scene of the harbor. The air was filled with the fragrance of the bushes in bloom along the deck. She felt a tap on her arm and saw Linda.

"Hey, are you playing hooky?" asked Linda.

Kate laughed. "No such luck. Just sneaking in a coffee before I open. I've been there for hours working in the office."

"I'm on a quick break myself. It's a beautiful day and we're busy with lots of flowers today."

"Speaking of flowers, could you send a cheerful bouquet to an old friend of mine today?"

"For you, of course." She took a notepad from her apron pocket and wrote down the order. Kate described the house and gave her the street name, although she didn't know the house number. "I'll figure it out, not a problem."

Sam appeared with a drink for Kate and one for Linda. "I saw you out here and thought I'd better rescue you from the mob of tourists in line. You two have a great day and I'll see you for dinner Friday." They both tried to pay her and she refused and waved them away as she went back inside.

"What a sweet lady," said Kate. "Each day I'm reminded of what a great decision I made to move here. I don't ever want to leave."

Linda put her arm around Kate's shoulders. "We're lucky to have you. I'll get this order delivered today."

The two women waved goodbye and headed back to their respective businesses. Kate had another demanding day and by closing time she was exhausted. Spence had stopped by with lunch and a quick visit from Roxy. He kept the dog in the backroom and relieved Kate for a few minutes so she could scarf down a couple of bites.

At the end of the day, she trudged upstairs and finished her daily report and deposit. She picked up her phone and saw she had a message. It was from Maggie, thanking her for the flowers and apologizing for her emotional outburst. To make amends she wanted to treat Kate to lunch on Friday.

Kate blew out a breath that ruffled her bangs. "I'm not sure I can take another meal with Maggie." She put the phone in her purse and headed home. She arrived to find Spence and Roxy waiting on the patio with dinner.

She discussed Maggie's invitation with Spence while they dined on grilled salmon. "It's Andi's first day, so I hate to risk a complication. At the same time, I know Maggie's in pain and I don't want to make her feel worse by putting her off." She continued to voice the pros and cons of the lunch date.

By the time Spence had twisted her arm to join him in a cupcake for dessert, she had made up her mind. "I'm going to go ahead and have Maggie come to the shop for lunch. I want to be close by in case Andi needs help, plus I'll be able to keep the meeting short in case it ends like the others."

* * *

Friday morning Kate picked up a selection of pastries and coffee on her way to work. Andi arrived a full thirty minutes early and greeted Kate with a warm smile. Kate showed her the backroom and the storage cabinet for her personal belongings. "I picked up some treats to celebrate," she said, offering her a coffee and opening the box from the bakery.

"Oh, I shouldn't," said Andi. "But, I will." She smiled and made her selection. While Andi nibbled, Kate went through the binder, going over the opening procedures and how the cash register worked. Andi followed Kate to the counter and learned how to run a credit card sale.

Andi shadowed Kate as she pointed out various items and explained the general layout and the way her inventory and pricing worked. "Add my cell and home number in your phone so you have it. If ever you have a problem and I'm not here, just call me."

Kate gave her a key to the store and showed her how the locks worked on both doors. "Upstairs is a loft with my office." She pointed to a tasteful sign at the base of the stairs. "No customers up there. You shouldn't need to hassle with traipsing upstairs either. All the daily reports sheets are in this binder. You can fill them out and do the deposit and drop the bag at the bank after you close."

Kate opened the door and the day began with a group of women in a shopping mood. As they were wrapping their items, Kate said, "I forgot to mention. I have a friend coming by for lunch today.

We'll be in the backroom. If you need anything or have a question, feel free to interrupt at any time."

"Will do. I brought a lunch today, so I can eat whenever it works." Andi finished adding a gold ribbon to the bag she was working on and presented it to Kate. "How's that?"

"Perfect. You go ahead and finish these and I'll help the next group at the counter."

They worked together with ease. Kate found Andi to be competent and excellent with the customers. They had a lull in traffic during the lunch hour and Kate suggested Andi take a break and eat. "I asked my friend to come around one-thirty, so I'll take my break then."

Sales were steady, but not overwhelming and when Maggie arrived, Kate felt confident Andi could handle things for an hour. Andi was busy ringing up a sale and Kate caught her eye, giving her a hand signal that she'd be in the backroom.

Kate led Maggie to the makeshift break room and helped her unpack the takeout boxes from Soup D'Jour. "Katie, I'm so sorry I've been such a basket case. I guess I'm not as strong as I thought I was." She took a chair and took the lid off of her soup.

"Not to worry. I'm sure you're overwhelmed with the move and whatever bug has you under the weather. It's not as easy to bounce back at our age." Kate smiled and sniffed her soup. "This potato soup is one of my favorites."

"All their soups are delicious. I have Janette go there daily."

"How's little Miss Emma doing?"

Maggie smiled. "She's a happy girl, luckily. Janette takes excellent care of her. She's got her own room with all her toys and familiar things in the house, so she's better than we were at the bed and breakfast. Just need to get her back in a routine."

"I'm sure she'll settle in. I'm always amazed at the resilience of children." She paused and took a bite of her salad. "I wish I had their ability to adapt. It took me a long time to recover from Karen's death. Honestly, I'll never be over it, but it was several years before I didn't think of her each day."

Tears formed in Maggie's eyes. "I know exactly what you mean. I'm struggling with that, not to mention Frank. Even though we were divorced, it's different with him gone. He could have helped with Emma, but now…"

"One thing I've learned is that you're stronger than you think. I didn't think I could go on, but I knew Mitch needed me. It seemed like a demand I couldn't face at the time, but looking back it was good to have a purpose. A reason for getting out of bed. A reason to keep from crawling in a hole and never coming out."

Maggie sniffed and wiped her nose. "My problem is everywhere I step, there's a new hole ready to swallow me."

"Emma's a darling. I think focusing on her will be your key to moving forward. She's lucky to have a grandma like you in her life."

Tears fell from Maggie's eyes. "She's the love of my life, which is what makes this situation so hard right now."

Kate frowned. "What do you mean?"

"The cancer's back, Katie. I'm dying."

Chapter Nine

Kate felt like she was in a trance the rest of the day. Spence stopped by with Blake on their way to the marina, but she didn't have time to tell him about Maggie. He was in a hurry to meet the rest of the guys for the fishing trip and she was busy with customers.

She and Andi worked together to finish the afternoon and she oversaw Andi as she closed out the register and prepared the daily report and deposit. Kate pronounced the day a success and promised to see Andi in the morning.

She went home to check on Roxy before heading to Lou's to meet the girls for dinner. She didn't feel like a gathering but had been looking forward to spending time with her friends. She would obsess about Maggie if she stayed home.

She fixed Roxy's dinner and gave her the command to eat. Being a police dog she had been trained to eat only when given a specific phrase. This one happened to be German. Spence had explained it was to protect the dog from being fed poison. The added bonus was Roxy never begged or seemed interested in food until she was told to eat.

"I'll be home soon, Roxy. You be a good girl," Kate said, as she left the dog in charge and hurried to the car.

The ladies were already seated at an oversized table in the back when she arrived and squeezed into a chair next to Regi. Lou insisted on serving them himself and brought Kate a glass of iced tea. "I've got some complimentary appetizers coming out for you ladies and then I'll take your orders."

They made their selections and the discussion turned to weekend activities. Jen was organizing pedicures for them, Linda had downloaded a number of movies, and Sam had the food and snacks handled.

"Izzy's providing wine and I'm making some desserts as well as cinnamon rolls for Sunday morning," said Ellie. "We won't be able to get to Linda's until around six tomorrow after we're done for the day."

"We'll have dinner at seven and with the three bedrooms, plus the loft, we have plenty of room for anyone who wants to sleep over, including dogs," said Linda. "So bring your jammies when you come for dinner, in case you decide to stay."

Regi noticed Kate was quiet and preoccupied. She passed her the plate of crab cakes and said, "Are you doing okay?"

Kate blinked her eyes several times. "Sorry, just lost in thought. It's been a day."

"How was your new helper? Andi, right?"

"She's terrific. A quick learner and does a great job with the customers. She's going to fit right in."

"Oh, that's good news. Lulu will be relieved. She told me to thank you for the flowers, by the way."

"Tell her not to worry and just get better. I'll have to stop by and say hello to her next week."

"So, what happened today to put you in such a funk?"

Kate explained about Maggie's lunch visit and her cancer bombshell. "We didn't have a chance to discuss much after she told me the cancer was back. She's convinced she's dying. It's a dreadful situation."

"That's an unbelievable amount of stress. I'm sorry to hear about her being ill on top of everything else."

"With her diagnosis, I thought she would have chosen to stay in the city. I know our new hospital is great, but I'm sure she'd have easier access to treatments and specialists there. I'll have to chat with her more this weekend."

They were interrupted by Lou, delivering the entrees. Kate picked at her plate and left early, promising to see everyone at Linda's on Saturday. On her way home, she dashed by the market to get the ingredients for the fruit dish she was taking to Linda's.

* * *

Kate's Saturday was hectic. She got up early to make the dip for the fruit tray and made sure all the fruit was washed and readied what she could. She planned to rush home and slice the rest of it before dinner, to assure it was fresh.

The shop bustled with customers all day and she and Andi were kept busy helping browsers or wrapping orders. During the chaos, Andi asked if she could put a small painting on hold. "I love this scene of the island and I have the perfect spot in my new place for it."

Kate looked at the tag and said, "How about I give it to you at cost? You get a discount anyway, but I'll let you have it for what I paid. Consider it a housewarming discount."

"Oh, that would be wonderful. That's so kind and generous."

Kate stashed it behind the counter and made a note of the cost in the receipt book. In between customers, Kate took a quick break in her office to check her cell phone. She saw a text from Spence telling her all was well and a voicemail from Maggie.

She punched the button and listened. She gasped when she heard Maggie tell her that Janette had left due to her mother having a fall and needing her help. "I'm sorry to ask, but being new, I don't know much about the island. I need some help with Emma and need to find someone reliable soon. I'd be grateful for any leads you can dig up for a nanny." Maggie's voice was weak and she sounded miserable.

The bell sounded on the door and she heard the chatter of customers. She let out a sigh and made her way downstairs to help Andi. Closing time arrived and Kate let Andi do the paperwork and then checked it over.

"Looks great, Andi. Thanks for a terrific day."

"Oh, it's been fun for me. Doesn't even seem like work. I'll see you Thursday," she said, gathering her things.

Kate wished her a happy first day at the hospital and set about closing the store. She noticed Andi had left the bag with her painting behind and grabbed it before heading home.

She changed clothes, fed Roxy, and gathered her overnight items. She finished her fruit tray and loaded Spence's car with everything, including the dog and her bed. "I'm not sure if we'll stay the night or not, but just in case, we'll be ready," she said to Roxy.

Looking at her watch she saw she had enough time to drop the painting by Andi's. She parked in front of the cottage and made sure the windows were down for Roxy before she hurried to the front door. She knocked and didn't get a response. She could see the lights were on and knocked a bit louder.

Kate noticed Andi's blotchy face and red-rimmed eyes when she opened the door. "Oh, Andi, I'm sorry to disturb you." She held up the bag. "You forgot your painting."

Andi let out a muffled sob. "Oh, how nice of you. Sorry, I've been feeling a bit down." She opened the door and motioned Kate inside.

Kate hesitated, but couldn't resist Andi's sad eyes. "I can't stay but a minute." Oscar, Andi's retriever mix, greeted Kate with a nose to her knee. Kate rubbed Oscar's head and he wandered away to his bed.

"I didn't want to take the painting until I paid for it, but thanks for coming by with it."

"I'm not worried about it." Kate looked around the space and noted the tasteful décor and furnishings. "Your home is lovely."

"I decided to embrace the whole island living theme, hence the painting."

"It will be perfect here." Kate looked at Andi again. "Are you going to be okay?"

"I miss having Chad here. I wanted to share my day with him. I know it's crazy, but I still talk to him sometimes. I told him how much I liked you and your shop."

Kate put a hand on Andi's shoulder. "I understand talking to someone who's gone. Believe me. I'm glad you enjoyed your day, but I'm sorry you're having a rough night."

"I'll be okay. It's hard to be alone sometimes."

Kate's eyebrows rose. "How about you come with me tonight? I'm meeting a bunch of girlfriends for a potluck and movie marathon. You'll love them. I promise."

"That's kind, but I hate to intrude. I'll be okay."

"I insist. Come on, it'll be fun and you'll meet some new people. Max's wife, Linda is hosting. The guys are all fishing."

Andi gave her a small smile.

"I'm taking our dog, Roxy, with me. Linda has it set up so we can stay overnight. I'm not sure about that yet, but I'm prepared."

"Oh, I don't think I want to stay overnight and Oscar has had enough upset with the move."

"Follow me out there and leave whenever you want. I know you'll love the group. If it's not your thing, just stay for dinner and leave."

Andi grinned and fluffed her hair. "Okay, let me repair my face a bit and I'll follow you."

Kate waited a few minutes, talking to and petting Oscar, while Andi got ready. She sent a quick text to Linda and Sam explaining she was bringing Andi. When Andi reappeared, Kate described where Linda lived and made sure Andi was right behind her when she made the turn to Linda's.

Andi carried the fruit tray while Kate held Roxy's leash and led her around the house to the yard. She found the group of dogs playing and Roxy trotted over to join her new friends. Regi was throwing brightly colored rings and the dogs were focused on catching them.

Regi waved at Kate and jogged over to greet her. Kate turned and introduced Andi. Regi babbled with ease and pointed out all the dogs, naming them along with their human counterparts, while Kate took the fruit tray inside.

She found Linda in the kitchen, surrounded by Sam and Jen, busy getting the dishes arranged on the counter. "Hey, I got your text and explained about Andi, so everyone knows."

"I called Ellie and told her. She and Izzy will be here in a few minutes," said Sam, taking the fruit tray from Kate.

"Oh, good. She's feeling a bit down and I didn't want her to be alone. She lost her husband a couple of years ago and is feeling sad and missing him tonight. She's a lovely person. I'm sure you'll like her."

They heard the chatter of Regi's voice before she came around the corner with Andi. All of the ladies introduced themselves while Regi added the name of each of their dogs, as the women welcomed Andi.

The bell rang, announcing Izzy and Ellie, who had to make several trips to cart in all the goodies. Izzy made a beeline for Andi and extended her hand, "I'm a newbie here just like you." She explained who she was and how she came to be on the island. "I'm here for the summer, helping at the winery. You'll have to come out one day for a tour."

Andi smiled and chose a glass of a golden white wine Ellie offered from a tray with several varieties. Oreo had followed Ellie into the house and Andi noticed the sweet border collie, bending down to pet her. "Oh," said Ellie, "I need to take her outside. Do you have a dog?"

Andi told her about Oscar and offered to escort Oreo to the yard. Oreo found her friends and rushed to the grass to join in the fun. Andi sat in one of the chairs on the patio and soaked in the gorgeous view.

Kate found her as the sun was beginning to set, leaving a sparkling trail of gold atop the water. "Great place to end the day, huh?"

Andi turned. "Marvelous. I've been watching the dogs. I should have brought Oscar. He'd have fun with them."

Kate took a seat next to Andi and showed her the plate of food she had gathered. "Go on in and fill a plate. We're going to eat outside."

The women chatted and laughter drifted from the kitchen to the patio, where one by one the women gathered. Jen slid into the empty chair next to Andi. "I'm so glad to meet you. Sean said Max brought you by the other day."

"I'm excited to start work Monday. Dr. Doyle and I know many of the same people from the city. I'm fortunate to be able to keep nursing an active part of my life, while officially retired."

"He's always busy and happy to have an experienced nurse. He has had several rotate through, most of them still in school, so he's thankful to have someone more permanent and with all your knowledge." Jen took a quick bite and added, "You should come tomorrow and have a pedicure with us."

"Oh, I'm not sure that's in my budget at the moment."

"No, no, I should have explained. I own the salon and I'm treating everyone to pedicures tomorrow. It's part of our getaway weekend we planned. I'd be happy to have you join us."

"That's so kind of you. I don't want to take advantage of Kate's invitation tonight."

Jen gave her a warm grin. "Trust me. You're not horning in or taking advantage. It'll be fun and it's relaxing. This is a great group of women. Give us a chance, you'll like us."

Andi's eyes widened. "Oh, I can tell you're all wonderful. I'm having a fun time getting to know all of you. It's not that."

Kate took the other chair next to Andi. "Glad you met Jen. If you need someone to do your hair, she's a magician."

"I'm trying to convince Andi to have a pedicure with us tomorrow," said Jen.

"Oh, you must come," said Kate. "It's the ultimate."

The rest of the group overheard the attempts to convince Andi to join them in pedicures and were relentless in their cajoling. Andi laughed and said, "Okay, okay. I'll go."

The women clapped and laughed while Linda started the fire pit. The bright flames shot through the cool colored glass. "Oh, so pretty," said Kate. She collected some dishes and made a trip into the house, followed by Andi.

"I should probably get going and check on Oscar. He's still not quite adjusted to the new place."

"You're welcome to bring him and stay over if you want."

"I didn't think I would, but a big part of me would like to. I just want Oscar to get more acclimated before I introduce him to a whole bunch of dogs and a new place. I'm afraid he'd be overwhelmed."

"I understand. I was worried about Roxy with the others, but they've all become quite the group of friends. You could come back in the morning for breakfast and bring him. It would only be a few hours and then you could drop him back home when we go into town for pedicures."

Andi helped Kate put the dishes in the dishwasher. "That sounds like a smart plan. I'll come out in the morning and see how it goes. He's a gentle guy. I worry about him. He's had a tough time adjusting."

Linda bustled in with another load of dishes and retrieved Ellie's desserts. "Oh, you girls are the best. Thanks for cleaning up."

"I've had a wonderful time, Linda. It's been great to meet all of you and you have a gorgeous place." Andi glanced at Kate. "I need to get home, but Kate's convinced me to come back tomorrow for breakfast and bring my dog, Oscar."

"We'd love to have you." Linda plated up selections of the cakes Ellie had made. "You should have a piece of cake before you go. Ellie makes the best."

Andi helped Linda carry plates to the patio and joined the group around the fire. "Mmm, yummy. This is as delicious as I remember," said Regi, taking another bite of Ellie's chocolate mousse cake.

Jen said, "The vanilla with the strawberry filling is terrific, Ellie."

"I miss baking, so this was fun," said Ellie, as she forked a berry into her mouth. "Being a diabetic takes all the pleasure out of the eating part, but I'm glad to see you guys are enjoying them."

Andi finished her small piece of cake and said, "I've had a wonderful time meeting all of you. It's been great fun, but I need to take off. I'll see you in the morning."

One by one the women stood to give Andi a hug goodbye. Kate walked her out and said, "I'm so glad you came tonight. We'll see you and Oscar in the morning."

The lights from the pathway reflected off Andi's wet eyes as she moved to hug Kate. "Thanks for inviting me. You were right. I needed this." Kate gave her a tight squeeze and watched as Andi maneuvered between the cars and drove down the driveway.

Chapter Ten

After a long night of movies, most of the women slept late. Kate had opted for bed after the first movie, *The Age of Adaline*. She woke at her usual time. She had claimed one of the guest rooms and saw Regi and Jen sprawled on the couches in front of Max's big screen television when she padded to the kitchen. She started the coffee brewing and per Ellie's instructions, put the cinnamon rolls in the oven.

With that done, she coaxed the dogs outside and fed them, making sure she told Roxy to eat. After their speedy breakfast, they took off to explore the yard. She tiptoed through the living area and found the coffee ready and perched at the counter to savor a few moments alone.

Sam joined her in the kitchen, making herself a cup of tea. "Morning," she whispered as she took a chair next to Kate.

"Sorry if I made too much noise," said Kate, checking out the window to look for Andi.

"No, I've been up for an hour or so. I was reading until I heard signs of life out here."

Kate took a sip from her cup and glanced at the two still sleeping on the couch. "When they're older and wiser like us, they'll go to bed earlier and make sure they get an actual bed."

Sam chuckled as she fetched her brewed tea. "How's your old

friend, Maggie? Is she settled in her house yet?"

Kate let out a breath. "I had lunch with her Friday. I've actually had a couple of meals with her and none of them went well." She summarized the abrupt endings to their visits and Maggie's revelation about her daughter's death, her divorce, and her granddaughter. Kate admitted she never expected to see Maggie again after the tumultuous end of their friendship when Karen died. "I'd written her off long ago and now she's back in my life. Then Friday she tells me her cancer is back and she's dying." She shook her head and took another swallow from her cup. "I'm not sure what to think and need to talk to her and get more facts."

"Poor woman. I know this can't be easy for you, Kate."

"To top it off her nanny had to leave because of a family emergency, so Maggie's looking for someone. Do you have any ideas?"

Regi came around the corner. "I smell coffee and baked goods. What ideas are you looking for, Kate?"

"Oh, Maggie's nanny for her granddaughter had to leave for a family emergency. She needs someone to help with Emma."

"Hmm, how much time?" Regi poured a cup of coffee and took a seat.

"I'm not sure, but Maggie's ill, so I suspect almost full-time. Janette was living with them."

Regi frowned as she took a sip. "Well, I'm off for the summer so I could help out. I can't live there, but could help with the little girl."

The light shifted through the window and caught Kate's attention. "Here's Andi." She hurried to the door before Andi could knock and led her to the grassy yard. The dogs were interested in Oscar and gave him a good sniffing. After that ritual, they pronounced him a member of their club and he scampered along with the rest of them.

"Well, that was easier than I thought," said Andi, watching as he trotted in between Zoe and Roxy.

"Come in. We've got coffee ready and the cinnamon rolls are baking."

They climbed the stairs to the house and found the kitchen filled with women and the couch vacant, meaning Jen had risen. "We're either getting ready for the day or visiting over coffee. Take a seat and I'll get you a cup."

Izzy had joined the other two and was at the counter sipping coffee. She gave Andi and Kate a wave. Sam and Regi scooted down and made room for Andi at the counter. "How's Oscar?" asked Sam.

"Seems to be fitting in just fine," said Andi.

"We were discussing Kate's friend, Maggie. She's ill and has a baby granddaughter to care for after her own daughter died. Now her nanny has left," said Regi, as the buzzer sounded on the oven.

They heard Ellie say, "I'm here. I'm coming for the rolls." She rushed by and grabbed the potholders before sliding the pan out of the oven. The inviting scent of sugar and cinnamon wafted through the kitchen.

"Those smell out of this world," said Andi.

"Wait until you taste them," said Regi. "They're epic."

"I've got to let them cool before I frost them, so we'll have to wait a bit," said Ellie, fanning her hand over the pan.

"Are you serious about helping out with the baby, Regi?" asked Kate. "That's a substantial commitment."

"I'm not sure I'm up for full-time, but I could definitely do it a few days a week. I'm only working one day a week at Sam's. Nate and I promised each other we'd keep our weekends free for activities, but I'm up for Tuesdays, Wednesdays, and Thursdays until she finds a permanent nanny."

"What's wrong with your friend, Kate?" asked Andi.

"Cancer. She had breast cancer years ago, but she said the cancer is back and she doesn't have much hope."

"I worked in oncology for years. If there's anything I can do, let me know."

Kate nodded. "I'll keep that in mind. I'm going to visit with Maggie in the next few days and try to get a few more details. If anyone hears about a good nanny, let me know. I'll relay your offer, Regi."

Linda came through the garage door with a handful of flowers. "Oh, good, you're all up and at 'em. I've been doing my gardening and visiting with the dogs." She arranged the fresh flowers in a vase and placed it on the dining room table. "Breakfast smells wonderful."

Ellie was mixing frosting and Kate retrieved the leftover fruit while Sam and Regi set the table. Fresh from the shower, Jen joined the group. "I see I'm just in time to do nothing," she laughed and helped herself to coffee. "I stayed up way too late."

"You've got perfect timing," Ellie said, blowing her bangs out of her eyes and finishing off the icing.

They gathered at the dining table and in between bites of the luscious cinnamon rolls, the discussion about Maggie's predicament continued. "Megan is home for the summer. She'll be working at the coffee shop, but is always looking for extra money. She could probably take a few days a week," said Jen. "I'll ask her and see what she thinks."

"I know Maggie would feel more comfortable if it was someone I knew, rather than someone she finds online. That would be wonderful if Regi and Megan could handle it."

Sam said, "I've never had children, but I can help out if there's ever a conflict. I can also work around whatever Megan decides to do."

"When I visit Maggie, I'll give her the options and see what she thinks. Thanks for your willingness to help. I can't offer much of my own time, but I'm also willing to fill in when needed, especially Sundays and Mondays," said Kate.

"Well, we better hit the road and get our feet pampered. I think the guys plan to be home by four this afternoon," said Jen, gathering dirty dishes from the table.

"Max texted and said we could grill part of their catch tonight, so plan to come back for dinner," said Linda.

The dogs were gathered and loaded into cars, except for Zoe and Bailey, who stayed to keep Lucy company. Jen had the salon ready and two of her staff on hand to man the pedicure stations. Sipping on frozen drinks from Sam's shop during their treatments, they learned more about Andi's loss of her husband.

"It was his last tour. He'd been in the service and then in the reserves. It had been his whole life, but he was looking forward to being done. I was so worried about him and thankful he would be done and home for Christmas. That was the plan anyway. He was killed by an IED right before Thanksgiving two years ago. It was my worst nightmare."

"You know how you see in the movies when the uniformed guys come to tell the wife her husband is dead? It's a million times harder when you see them coming to your door. I wouldn't answer it and kept screaming at them to go away. I sort of folded up and collapsed. They went and got my neighbor to stay with me. It was the hardest day of my life."

Tears dotted the cheeks of the women as they listened to Andi's story. She brought a tissue to her own eyes and said, "I was convinced I was going to die. I didn't think I could live without Chad. It had always been the two of us and then he was just gone. I'm still not over it."

"Where's your family?" asked Kate.

"My parents live in Florida. They came and stayed for several weeks. I have a sister in Pennsylvania, but she's got her own life and family. Chad's parents are in Arizona. They had a horrific time. They worshiped Chad and came for a few days, but I think it was too hard for them to see me. I limped along, trying to get through the days. I had to work until this year for retirement, so kept that goal in my mind." Her voice cracked and she took a sip of her drink. "Once I did that, I wasn't sure what was next. I was so focused on one day at a time, I hadn't thought about what I would do when I could retire."

"You don't have any children?" asked Sam.

She shook her head. "No. After several miscarriages, we quit trying. So, nothing to keep me in the city. I thought leaving the house and all those memories would be the right move, which brought me here. Now, I'm not sure. It's a good feeling to be starting over, but I still feel lost and alone without Chad. I've always been self-reliant with him being away so much, but still had him to talk to and we always decided big things together. It's not the same now."

Kate reached for Andi's hand. "I think he'd be proud of you. It takes nerve to move to a new place and start over, as you say." She glanced at Sam. "You're in good company. Sam moved here to start her life again and so did I. Regi came here looking for one thing and found something better. I think you'll find what you need here."

The women nodded in agreement. "I've lived here since I was a child and can tell you I wouldn't trade it for anywhere. Not only is it beautiful and peaceful, but we've got a wonderful and caring community. My family is gone, but I'm lucky to be surrounded by all of this," said Linda, looking at each of her friends.

"I couldn't agree more. I've had a tough year, to say the least. I couldn't have endured all the loss without these women," said Ellie. "It took a lot of courage to leave and come here. I know you can do this, Andi."

"And when you feel like you can't, you call one of us," said Regi. "I came here not knowing anyone. Just like you. I was lucky enough to meet these wonderful ladies and they helped me survive some of the worst moments of my life. They'll do the same for you."

Amid the sniffling and tears, Izzy stood. "You all make me feel like home." There were a few laughs amid the crying as Izzy continued. "Andi, I've only been here to visit but can tell you these women are genuine and they mean it when they say they're going to be there through thick and thin. They've welcomed me and my brother. That's one of the reasons I wanted to stay for the summer. This place and these people make me feel better. I know they'll do the same for you."

Andi smiled through her tears. "I believe you. Thank you all so much for sharing and listening. I haven't talked to anyone about Chad for a long time."

Jen pronounced Andi's toes done and after the women admired each other's color choices, they helped Jen straighten the shop and get it ready for business tomorrow. Linda headed for the door. "We'll have dinner around six tonight. It'll be super simple, just fish and salad, plus any of our leftovers. See you then," she said, as the women made their way outside.

Chapter Eleven

Kate's new Monday morning habit was a hit with Roxy. Rather than spend time on the patio in the early hours, she hooked up Roxy's leash and they strolled into town. The beginning of daybreak provided enough light to see, but the sun had not yet risen. While the tourists were sleeping and with only a scattering of other early morning enthusiasts she and Roxy enjoyed the uninhabited sidewalks. The air smelled fresh and clean and the hint of salt became more prominent as they reached the waterfront. They departed from the path and stopped at the stone wall along a scenic area of the harbor.

Kate leaned against the cool rock, damp with dew. She rotated and swung her legs over the wall. She had a front row seat for the opening of a new day. As she waited, Roxy snuggled next to her and put her front paws on the top of the rock wall. Minutes later the celebrity of the morning's feature emerged. A golden glow filled the space between the water and the horizon.

The two of them watched in silence as the sun made it's way higher in the sky. A blanket of thin clouds overhead made for a gorgeous contrast of clear blue and gold. The clouds softened the brilliance, except for an opening where rays escaped and painted a golden ribbon on the water.

As the golden light filled the sky, activity along the street increased. Kate heard the squeal of brakes and chatter of shopkeepers. The smell of fresh-baked bread mingled with the spice of the peonies and alstroemeria in bloom along the storefronts. She gripped Roxy tighter. "Shall we finish our walk and get home?"

Roxy hopped down from the wall and waited for Kate to turn around and take her leash. They meandered through town and back to the house where Kate found the coffee brewed and filled her cup. She poured Roxy's breakfast in her bowl and went out on the patio to enjoy a few more minutes of solitude.

After getting a few household chores done, Kate called Maggie to arrange a visit. She offered to go to the market and pick up anything she needed on the way to meet for lunch. She jotted a list and after giving Spence and Roxy a kiss goodbye headed to the store.

After the market, she picked up an order at Soup D'Jour before driving to Maggie's house. She let herself in and made a few trips to bring in the shopping. She heard Emma squealing and followed the sound to find Maggie in bed with Emma playing at her side, babbling and saying a few words Kate recognized.

"I've got your groceries and brought us soup for lunch. Do you feel like getting up?"

"If you can take her for a bit, I'll take a quick shower and see you in a few minutes."

Kate held Emma and stopped by the changing table to give her a fresh diaper and a change of clothes. With Maggie's illness and Janette's departure all efforts in toilet training Emma had ceased. She took her into the living room and found a playpen full of toys and activities and placed her inside. Emma jabbered and played with her toys while Kate put away the groceries and did the dishes in the sink.

She gathered some cereal and applesauce and secured Emma in her high chair for brunch. The little girl gobbled up the dry cereal from her tray and slurped the food from her spoon like a greedy bird. "Ah, poor Emma. You were a hungry girl."

Maggie came into the kitchen and said, "Oh, thanks for feeding her. You're a lifesaver. I'm so tired this morning." She slid into a seat at the island counter.

"I brought some soups and salads for lunch if you're interested. I put the rest of the groceries away as best I could."

"Thanks, Kate. I'll write you a check."

"Not necessary." She gave Emma the last bite and wiped the baby's face clean. She plucked her from the chair and handed her to Maggie. "There's Grandma. She can hold you while I fix our lunch."

"How's my big girl?" she asked Emma, who responded with a smile and a hiccup.

"I spent some time with friends yesterday and explained your situation with Janette leaving. One of them, Regi, is a secretary at the high school and off for the summer. She volunteered to help watch Emma three days a week. She can't stay here all the time but has a lovely home where Emma could spend the days. Also, another friend has a college-aged daughter who would be willing to work on a schedule to watch Emma the other four days. She's only here for the summer break and looking to earn extra money. She could stay here at the house and watch her for you. Her name is Megan. Also, a couple of others said they could fill in during emergencies. So, not sure what you think, but that's what I came up with."

Tears formed in Maggie's eyes and she patted Emma on the back. "I can't tell you how much I appreciate this. I don't deserve your kindness." Tears fell down her cheeks. "I should have thought this through better before leaving and coming here without a support system."

Kate placed their plates on the counter and put Emma back in her high chair. She added some cheese and banana slices to the toddler's tray and sat down next to Maggie. "What was your plan?"

"I didn't have one. I just wanted to escape. I'm not sure how I thought it would work. I guess I thought Janette would handle Emma and I didn't think much beyond that."

"Are you having to travel back to the city to your doctor?"

She shook her head. "No, I'm done with doctors. The treatment wasn't doing much and I decided I can't go through all that again."

"What do you mean? You're giving up?"

She shrugged. "They said there's no cure. I can't beat it this time. It's spread too far. The result will be the same with or without the treatments and they make me too ill to take care for Emma. I had my last one before I came here, so I'm hoping I'll start feeling a bit better soon."

Kate felt her throat go dry. "There's nothing more for them to do?"

"The term end-stage doesn't do much to boost my hope. I could suffer more and maybe stretch my time by a couple miserable months, or I could skip that part and live until I die. I chose to live and enjoy the time I have left with Emma."

Kate glanced at the grinning girl tapping her fists on her tray and giggling. "I'm saddened you're in such a position to have to make that choice."

Maggie took another spoonful of soup. "I've come to accept it, sort of. If I think about it too much, it makes me crazy. I'm just taking it one day at a time."

"On that note, shall I bring Regi by to meet you and Emma? I'm thinking she could take Tuesdays through Thursdays and then Megan could handle the other days."

"That sounds terrific. As I get to feeling better, which should be next week, I should be able to do more. As time goes by, I'm sure I'll need more help, but for as long as possible, I'll do it myself."

Emma's head was nodding and slumping, signaling nap time. Kate took her from the high chair and said, "Looks like she needs a nap. I'll put her down. That will give you a couple hours to rest and then I'll bring Regi over later this afternoon."

Maggie planted a kiss on Emma's head as Kate cradled her. "She's the best thing I've got going right now."

* * *

After introducing Regi to Maggie and lining up Megan to visit at the end of the week, Kate spent Monday evening relaxing with Spence. He suggested dinner out at the Front Street Café. After their meal, they retrieved Roxy and took a long walk through town and along the harbor.

They took a break at the park overlooking the water and sat on a bench with Roxy at their feet. "I never get tired of this view. It's a powerful calming agent for me," said Kate. "Do you miss the excitement of the city?"

He gazed across the water and then into her eyes. "Katie, as long as I'm with you, I'll be happy anywhere."

She reached for his hand. "That's sweet, but I'm serious. You had such an exciting job, this has to be a bit boring."

"I'll admit there are times I crave the excitement of a new case, but I don't miss the absolute filth of humanity I encountered. There's a certain energy in a city, but I'm learning to adapt to the quiet here. I love the fact I can go fishing so often. We couldn't have asked for a nicer group of friends. I can honestly say I like each of them. I remember struggling to find couples we both liked when I was married, so I usually had my cop friends. It's easier to have common friends, especially ones with boats." He laughed and his eyes sparkled with mischief.

She smiled and squeezed his hand. "I agree."

Their conversation drifted back to Maggie. "Did she say what's she going to do about Emma in the long-term?" asked Spence.

"You mean if she passes away?" He nodded. "No, and I'm afraid to bring it up." She gave Roxy a rub behind her ears. "I feel like it's been a whirlwind with her. I hadn't dealt with our whole past relationship when all of this illness and drama came to the forefront. I feel horrible for Maggie and of course, worry about little Emma, but I'm trying not to get caught up in all of it. I hope things work out with Regi and Megan, but I feel myself becoming more and more anxious when I'm around Maggie and think about the future."

He put his hand around her shoulders and slid closer. "I know you want to help her, Katie. I understand the pull of emotions. I don't want to see you backslide. You've made such a happy new life here. I don't want Maggie's grief and her situation to erode all the good you have."

Kate nodded in silence. They continued to soak in the beauty of their surroundings while Roxy sighed and shut her eyes.

* * *

Tuesday morning Izzy arrived for her training day. Kate admired Izzy's skills. She was a natural with customers and didn't hesitate to introduce herself and guide people to things they might like. She did it all without seeming like a salesperson and didn't pressure them. She acted more like a consultant or personal shopper asking a few questions and showing them items to get a feel for their style.

Kate showed her the mechanics of running the register and where supplies were kept but didn't need to do much else. Izzy and Kate had a similar look and style and several of the customers asked if they were sisters.

At the end of the day Kate showed Izzy the daily report and without any real instruction, she completed it and the deposit. Kate checked it over and shook her head. "You're a marvel, Izzy. Perfect job and I love how you approach the customers."

Izzy gave her a grin. "I grew up selling wine in our family store, so I have decades of retail sales experience."

"Well, I'm impressed. You moved some pricey pieces today." Kate glanced at the boxes labeled and stacked on the counter. "We even have all the shipments ready for Nate in the morning."

"It was fun. I'm happy to help out." She retrieved her things from the back and added, "I'll see you next Tuesday. I don't have a super tight schedule at the winery, so if you get in a jam or something comes up and you need help, just give me a ring."

Kate gave her a key to the shop and showed her the alarm procedures before she followed her out the door. "On days I'm not here, just drop the deposit bag at the bank." She pointed down the street.

"Got it. I've got to stop by the market on my way to Ellie's. I'll catch up with you later."

Kate waved to Izzy as she headed in the opposite direction to the bank and then home. She took her time walking, enjoying the summer-like evening. She noticed an unfamiliar car in the driveway. She opened the door and heard Spence's voice coming from the patio.

She put her things away and wandered to the kitchen for a glass of tea. As she poured her drink, she heard a voice she recognized and smiled. "Mitch," she yelled, setting the pitcher on the counter and rushing to the door. "It is you," she said, hurrying to him.

"I wanted to surprise you," said her son, standing and hugging her.

"Wow, you sure did. I can't believe you're here."

"I bought a new car last week and finished things at work, so was in the mood for a road trip. Thought I'd drive up here and surprise you two," said Mitch.

"How long can you stay?" asked Kate.

"I thought I'd stay a couple of weeks. If that's okay?"

Spence had retrieved Kate's tea and touched the back of her arm. "Here, Kate, sit down," he pulled out her chair.

"Of course, stay as long as you want." She saw Roxy move to place her head on Mitch's knee. "I see you've met our newest addition."

He rubbed the dog's head. "She's terrific." Roxy settled at his feet. "I like this year's rose. Karen always loved pink. I remember you letting her pick out the paint for her room. It looked like a strawberry milkshake."

Kate smiled. "She had to have pink curtains and a pink bedspread. It was way too much, but it made her happy."

"Dad was a good sport. He never said a word, just painted it for her."

"She had him wrapped around her finger. He would have done anything for her." Kate's voice cracked and she took a sip of tea.

They both stared at the roses and Spence excused himself to prep for the evening meal. "Have you heard from your dad lately?" asked Kate.

"I talk to him every few weeks. Work has been hectic so I haven't had much time. I'll give him a call when I get home."

Kate nodded and finished the last of her tea. "How's he doing?"

"Okay, I think. He's never talkative. Usually, he says he's fine and asks me more about what I'm doing. I know he likes living where it's not so rainy all the time. I think the eastern part of Oregon agrees with him."

Spence returned with a platter and his cooking gear. Mitch filled them in on the political happenings at the Washington State Legislature while the aroma of their dinner grilling wafted in the breeze. He had a demanding job, but during the legislative session, it was gruesome. Sixteen-hour workdays were his norm, fraught with stress due to the antics of politicians. This year there had been a special session on the heels of the regular session, which had meant even more overtime and pressure.

Kate set the table and brought the side dishes out while Spence plated the steaks. Spence opened a special bottle of wine from Blake and the threesome sat down to a fabulous meal. Throughout dinner, Mitch regaled them with stories of gavel banging, naked protestors, and several all-nighters. He laughed and said, "That sums up the last several months of my life. What have you two been up to?"

Spence told Mitch about his recent trial in the city and shared highlights from his fishing trip. "Maybe we can squeeze in an outing while you're here?" he asked.

"That sounds great. I'd love a day out on the water." Kate stood and began clearing the table. "What about you, Mom? What's new with you?"

Her eyebrows rose. "Quite a bit, actually." Mitch helped tote everything into the house and he took over loading the dishwasher. She explained about Lulu's foot and hiring Andi and Izzy to help at the store as they worked on the cleanup duties.

Spence poked his head in the door to let them know he and Roxy were going for a walk. Kate perched at the counter. "Did Spence tell you Maggie's here?"

"He mentioned it, but didn't have time to tell me much."

He joined her in a cup of tea while she explained about Maggie's situation with Emma, Kaitlin's death, followed by Frank's, and her current terminal diagnosis. She told him about helping Maggie and finding Regi and Megan to watch Emma. "It's been overwhelming, to say the least." She cradled the warm cup in her hands.

"I can't believe she came here. Makes you believe in fate, huh?"

Kate shrugged. "I guess."

"If she hadn't come here, you would have never heard her apology or known about Kaitlin or what happened to Maggie. You might have read it in the paper or seen it somewhere and been shocked. Everything would have been left unsaid."

"I suppose you're right about that aspect. I like my life drama free and her presence brings anxiety." She took a sip. "I know that sounds selfish, but I put Maggie far far away long ago and I'm not sure I want to drag her out now. I feel such sadness for her, but I also dread seeing her."

"That's understandable. She reminds you of the worst time in your life. I get it, Mom. It sounds like you've done your best to help her. That's all you can do. I'm sure she doesn't expect you guys to go back to how you were."

"That's impossible." The snap in her response shocked her. She softened her tone and added, "It can never be how it was. I'm trying to forgive her. I sort of turned off all my emotions related to her years ago. It was easier that way. Now it's harder to ignore. I worry about her and Emma and know if things hadn't happened in the past, I would be doing all I could for her." She wiped a tear from her cheek. "It makes me feel guilty."

Mitch put his hand on his mom's shoulder. "You don't need to feel guilty. You could have rejected her, but you helped her."

She gave him a weak smile. "I'm glad you're here."

* * *

Spence wasted no time talking Nate into a fishing excursion with Mitch. Sam and Linda hosted a few dinners while Mitch was in town and made sure he had lunch partners each day Kate was working. Spence took a new consulting case for the department and kept busy on the phone and computer during the day. Mitch took Roxy for walks around town and usually stopped in to visit Kate at work. In the afternoons, he visited with Spence while helping him with dinner preparations. When they weren't enjoying evenings with friends, the threesome spent time outdoors on the patio, relaxing and conversing.

During one of these evenings, Kate said, "Izzy and Andi are going to cover for me so I have a couple of days off to spend with you. I'm sure you're getting bored by now."

"Not really. It's been nice to hang out and do nothing. I've been working so much, I'm enjoying the slow pace here."

"I talked to Ellie and she said we could come out for a tour of the winery one day. Thought we could play tourist and visit some of the sites and spend the day out and about."

Mitch nodded, "That sounds like fun. I'll drive us."

Spence treated them to a huge homemade breakfast the next morning and packed a cooler with some snacks. "I'm taking us to dinner tonight, so don't worry about getting home early. Lou's got a table and he'll hold it for us."

Kate thanked him with a kiss and left him in Roxy's capable care. Mitch had been climbing the ladder at work and with all his overtime pay had splurged on a sporty Mercedes convertible. He held the vivid blue door open and she sniffed, "Oh, smells like a new car. I love it."

He laughed and slid into the driver's seat. "It's a fun one. A bit impractical, but it's got a hard top, so it works in the wet weather."

"I think it's wonderful you treated yourself to something fun. Life is short."

He started the sleek car and followed the loop around the island. They stopped along the way to take in historical sites and scenic views. She showed him the alpacas and they drove by the lavender farm. They made a stop at Linda's nursery where Kate treated him to a garden fountain. He arranged the boxes it came in in the small car and they motored on to the winery. She ran her hand over the leather seats. "Now that I look at this car, I think Sam has one like it. You'll have to compare notes."

Ellie greeted them at the door of the winery, remembering Mitch from his last visit. Blake gave them a personalized tour, explaining the grapes and the process while driving them around the entire acreage.

People wandered throughout the property and the store was busy when they returned. "How about we break out our provisions and sit outside and have a snack?" suggested Kate.

They found a quiet corner table under the shade of the pavilion and nibbled on cheese and fruit, along with bottled iced teas. Mitch finished off a cracker and said, "I'm glad you and Spence are together. He's such a good man and treats you so well."

"He's one in a million. How about you? Any serious girlfriends in your life?"

He smirked. "I'm too busy to even think about a girlfriend."

"I hope you find someone who's kind and makes you happy like Spence does for me. Try not to work so hard that you're too busy to make a life."

"I hear ya, Mom. I know I'm not getting any younger. I sometimes can't believe I'm getting close to forty. I just haven't found the right one yet."

She patted his hand. "No pressure from me. It took me two tries to get it right. I hope you get it right the first time."

He adjusted his sunglasses and took in the view. "It's a pretty spot here." He grabbed a handful of grapes. "I went and saw Maggie the other day."

Kate's eyebrows rose. "Really?"

"Yeah, I didn't want you to feel like you had to go or worry about the visit, so decided to take a walk over there one morning."

"How did it go?"

"She was happy to see me. Quite emotional, but thanked me a bunch of times for coming to see her. She went on and on about how sorry she was about the past and the friendship she ruined."

"Yeah, that's what she's told me."

"I saw Emma. She looks a lot like Kaitlin to me. I think she's the sole source of Maggie's reason for living right now. She basically said as much."

"She wasn't specific, but her diagnosis is grim and she gives the impression she doesn't have long," said Kate.

He nodded as he set his tea on the table. "Yeah, it was a sad parting. She gave me a long hug. It was a forever kind of goodbye."

Kate blinked away tears. "I can only imagine her pain. To contemplate what's coming would be crushing. She has to be worried about Emma."

"Yeah, I know. We didn't talk much about that stuff. She wanted to know about my job and what I had been doing. She talked about Kaitlin and told me about Frank. It was hard for me to think of anything upbeat to say. I didn't stay long."

"It was kind of you to go see her. I'm sure it made her day brighter."

Blake interrupted them with a four-pack of wine bottles for Mitch to take home. "Oh, let me pay for them," he said.

"No, no, I insist. Take a taste of the island back home with you. You'll need it if you're surrounded by politicians all day. In fact, you may want to join our wine club." Blake gave him a shoulder squeeze along with a chuckle. "Glad you stopped by while you were visiting your mom."

Kate repacked the cooler and tossed their garbage while Mitch and Blake chatted. A large crowd walked by on their way to the retail store. Blake stood and told them to enjoy the rest of their day as he hurried to help Ellie with the rush of new customers.

They wandered back to the car and dropped off the wine and their cooler and then made their way to the old church. The door was open and they saw it was being decorated for a wedding.

"What a cool old building," said Mitch, peeking around the corner.

"Blake and Ellie have quite the enterprise going here. It's swamped during the summer with events and weddings. They've done a terrific job of sprucing it up and making it a must-see destination."

They looked around the restored space and scooted out of the way when they saw a delivery van pull to the front steps. Mitch took the long way home and detoured for a hike at Young Hill.

They rested on a boulder and looked out over the coastline. "A guy could get used to this view," said Mitch. He glanced at his mother. "I'm sorry I couldn't make it here for Mother's Day."

She gripped his hand. "You're here now and that's all that matters."

"Karen's birthday is always a hard day for me as well. I still miss her."

"Always," she said, swiping a finger under her sunglasses. "Always."

Chapter Twelve

For Kate's last full day with Mitch, Spence had arranged a boating excursion for the three of them and Roxy. Spence rented a boat at the marina and they set off for Lopez Island. They took their time, enjoying the coastal views of San Juan Island before turning to their destination. They kept an eye on Roxy for any signs of anxiety, but she enjoyed the ride and delighted in the wind blowing across her face. Spence docked the boat at Fisherman Bay and they walked to Lopez Village.

The waterfront area was much like Friday Harbor with shops and restaurants lining the streets. They found a bakery and sandwich shop and enjoyed lunch outdoors with a view of the bay. They did some wandering and poked their heads into several of the shops, taking turns staying outside with Roxy. None of them had ever spent time on Lopez Island, making it a fun adventure.

Spence spied an ice cream shop and insisted they stop for a treat. The village was buzzing with tourist activity but wasn't as populated as Friday Harbor. They finished their ice cream while walking to the beach. Spence and Mitch were wearing shorts, but Kate stopped to roll up her pants in order to wade into the water and treat her feet to the coolness of the bay. Roxy walked along the shoreline, fascinated by the water nipping at her legs.

As they walked back to the village they came upon a caricature artist. He asked to sketch them and within a few minutes presented a cute drawing of Kate in between the two men with Roxy at her feet. Mitch peeled off some money from his pocket and paid the man. "I love it. Could you do another one for my mom?"

The man obliged and with a quick hand produced an almost identical copy and handed it to Kate. She smiled and hugged Mitch. "What a great memory. Thanks, Mitch."

They did a bit more meandering through the town and decided to head for home. As soon as they reached Friday Harbor, Kate called Big Tony's and begged for a table. He didn't have anything until a bit later in the evening, so they spent some time in the backyard, enjoying a glass of wine before dinner.

Roxy ate her kibble and flaked out on her bed, tired from the outing. The sun was setting as they walked to town and claimed their table at the pizzeria. "I can't believe you have to leave tomorrow," said Kate, taking another slice.

"Vacation's almost over. I've got to be back to work on Tuesday and need a day or two to get organized and do laundry." He retrieved the last piece from the pan. "This has been a great time. I'll be here for Thanksgiving, but hope to make another trip before that."

"We'd love that. September is perfect here. Much less crowded and the weather is wonderful," said Kate.

"I'll do my best, provided work cooperates."

When they returned home, Spence apologized and retired to his office to get some work done on his consulting case. Kate and Mitch changed into pajamas and watched a movie. Kate didn't make it all the way through and when it ended was startled awake by a gentle tap on her shoulder. "Mom, it's over. Time to go to bed."

It took her a minute to get her bearings and she chuckled. "I guess I'll have to watch that one again." She hugged him and wished him happy dreams as she padded down the hall to her room.

* * *

Despite working late into the night, Spence was an early riser. He brewed coffee and took Roxy for a quick walk. Mitch and Kate slept late and when they emerged ready for the day, Mitch announced he wanted to take them to a late breakfast before the ferry left. He drove and they walked to the harbor and found the Front Street Café busy with a line waiting to be seated. They opted for Harbor Coffee where Kate secured a table on the deck. The men returned with coffees and a variety of pastries and slices of pie.

Kate laughed when she saw the heaping tray of food. "Oh, my. You guys are a bad influence."

"Whatever we can't eat, I'll take home. Sam's pie is the best I've ever had. Not to mention I'll need some snacks for my drive home." Mitch gave his mom a sheepish grin.

"You've always been a planner." Kate bit into her delicious croissant and watched the ferry approaching. "Looks like your ride is almost here."

Mitch turned and looked. "I'll need to get moving and get back to the car. I left it in line. I'm not far from the front."

They hurried and finished. Kate knew Sam kept containers and bags in the outdoor storage cabinet and she fetched them and packed the leftovers for Mitch. He took the bag and gave Spence a hug and a handshake and gripped his mom in a long and hearty squeeze before depositing a kiss on her cheek. "I love you."

Tears threatened her eyes and she hoped her sunglasses hid them. "Love you, Mitch. I'll miss you."

He let go and gave a wave as he hurried down the street to the ferry landing, toting his bag of provisions. "Do you want to go and watch him leave?" asked Spence.

Kate shook her head as tears leaked out from behind her glasses.

She gripped her cup and let the warm liquid soothe her throat. "It's never easy to say goodbye."

* * *

After a lazy stroll through the streets, Spence coaxed Kate into going to the theatre for a movie, hoping to distract her from Mitch's departure. The feature, nothing close to award-worthy, was action-packed and kept Kate's mind occupied for a couple of hours. They left the theatre and stopped by the market to get a few items.

Kate had suffered from separation anxiety after Karen's death and twenty years later the same panic set in whenever Mitch left. She loved his visits and spending time with him, but they were always bittersweet. Each time he visited she thought it would be better, but the old feelings of unease crept into her mind with every departure.

Spence was aware of the sadness and anxiety surrounding Kate after Mitch's visits and tried to keep her occupied and busy. He checked his watch, thinking soon Mitch would be calling to say he was home. They gathered groceries and carried the bags home, with Spence setting a slow pace.

Kate's phone buzzed and she fumbled with the groceries as she hurried to answer. "Oh, Mitch, are you home?"

She nodded and smiled. "Glad you made it. Thanks for visiting and I'll talk to you later." She poked the button on her phone to disconnect and let out a long breath. She glanced at Spence. "He's okay."

She picked up the wayward bag and looped her arm in his. "I wish I could turn off these horrible thoughts. I think I have it licked and tell myself I'm not going to worry this time and then what do I do?"

Spence trudged up the walkway and unlocked the door where Roxy stood to greet them. They made their way to the kitchen and unloaded the shopping bags. "I'm no expert in this stuff, but your mind is stuck in a rut. It's like a river. It follows the same old patterns. Maybe you need to see if there's a way to retrain it with new thoughts or something like that?"

She frowned and stood at the counter while he finished stowing the groceries. "That makes some sense. I'm not sure how to do it, but I understand what you're saying and you're right about the old thought patterns. I went to a counselor after Karen's death, maybe I need to talk to someone."

"Might be worth looking into," he said. "I need to do some work on the case. Are you going to be okay?"

"Yeah, I'm fine. I think I'll take Roxy on a walk. I might stop by Andi's if she's home and visit for a few minutes."

Roxy saw the leash in Kate's hand and jumped from her bed to stand by the door. Kate stuffed her cell phone in her pocket and took off down the sidewalk. They walked the few blocks, with Roxy sniffing at things along the way. Andi's car was in front of the house. She guided Roxy across the street and knocked on the door.

Andi answered in shorts and an oversized gray US Army t-shirt. "Hi, Kate."

"I should have called, I'm sorry. I was taking Roxy for a walk and thought we'd stop in."

"Oh, please, come in. Oscar would love to have a playmate. He's in the backyard." She led them through and Oscar greeted the guests and the two dogs ran together on the grass.

"How about some tea?" asked Andi, retrieving glasses from the cupboard.

"Sounds great." Kate took a seat at the kitchen table, keeping one eye on the dogs. "Are you feeling settled in?"

"I'm getting there. I'm still a little unorganized. I need to get rid of some things. This place is a lot smaller than our house. I discarded lots of stuff before I moved, but I underestimated how much less space I was going to have here."

"You could always get Jeff to build you a storage shed. He does a great job and is reasonable."

She placed the glasses on the table and offered Kate sugar. "I'll keep that in mind. That would probably be a good idea."

Kate's eyes drifted to a scattering of papers on the table. "I think we all could use more storage."

Andi swept the papers into a pile and Kate noticed the envelopes underneath. They were letters from Andi's husband. "I was reminiscing today," said Andi. "Sometimes it helps. Sometimes not."

"I know the feeling all too well. There's both comfort and pain in looking and touching old things. I have some of Karen's things in a dresser and drag them out occasionally. I wore a scarf of hers for years because I could still smell her."

Andi's eyes widened. "I still wear Chad's t-shirts for the same reason. I've slept in one since the day he died."

Kate glanced at a framed photo of a tree with a heart and initials carved in it. She pointed to it. "I like that."

Andi nodded. "That was the tree in our backyard. I almost didn't sell the house over losing that tree. Chad carved that on the day we moved in and it ripped my heart out to leave it behind. A friend of mine took the photo and framed it for me so I'd have it no matter where I went."

Kate told Andi about her rose garden tribute to Karen and the same feeling of loss she experienced leaving it behind. "I felt like I was betraying Karen or abandoning her when I left." Kate took a deep breath. "I had to leave for me. I knew I needed to move…to give myself permission to do something new and be happier. There's nothing easy about loss. I'm so much better now, but still have bouts of depression and overwhelming grief and guilt."

"I still think about Chad multiple times a day. At night, it's worse. He was deployed during much of our marriage, so I learned how to get along on my own. This is so much harder. Sometimes I try to trick myself into thinking he's just deployed and will be home again." She took a sip from her glass and gave a meek laugh. "It's pathetic, I know."

"You have to do what gets you through the day sometimes. I applaud you for embarking on this new adventure. It takes strength to move on and leave things behind. You have to be tough to take steps forward and make new memories and a new life without the one you lost. Believe me, I know how exhausting it is. There were many days I wanted to give up. I was lucky enough to have Spence helping me along."

Tears streamed down Andi's face as she watched the dogs play. "Some days are harder than others. I was reading some old letters today. I had miscarried once while Chad was away. I thought that was the worst I would ever feel. He tried to cheer me and told me we would try again and have a child, but it wasn't meant to be. I think if I had a child, I wouldn't feel so alone. I'd have a piece of Chad, something real, you know?"

Kate nodded and gave Andi a strong hug. "You're strong and smart and capable. I know you're going to make it through this."

Kate spent the next hour telling Andi about the collapse of her marriage after Karen's death, including Maggie's reaction and the end of their friendship. Andi's eyes widened as she came to understand the huge schism between the two old friends. "I had no idea you hadn't spoken to Maggie for so long."

"This whole ordeal is beyond belief. I'm trying to let go of the past anger and strong feelings of disloyalty I've felt about her for years because I do feel so sorry for her now. I would never wish the loss of a child on anyone. Now with her terminal illness, I can't imagine how she's even coping."

"It's the little girl. That's the reason she's upright, I'm sure. That's a lot of loss for one woman. I admire you for putting aside your past and stepping up to help her. That tells me so much about your character, Kate."

Kate dabbed at her wet cheeks. "That's nice of you to say. I'm not sure I could have been so forgiving if Maggie wasn't in such a horrible situation. I'm not proud of my past feelings for her, but I've never been able to fully absolve her of her behavior." She paused and looked outside. "I'm not sure I've done it now. I'm trying to do the right thing, but if I dig deep, I can't say I've totally forgiven her."

"Give yourself a bit more time. That's a huge wound you have and it may take more than a few weeks for you to forgive her. Even after a patient heals, there's always a scar. The wound may not be visible, but the scar serves as a reminder. Sometimes it's a warning—not to do it again.

Chapter Thirteen

Ellie left early after handling the wedding event in the barn, leaving Blake and Izzy to serve the last customers of the night. As soon as they finished their wine and said their goodbyes, Izzy flipped the lock on the door. "Another busy night in the books."

"Yeah, it's been great," he said, pushing buttons to ring out the register.

Izzy gathered glasses and began cleaning the counter. "You've done such a great job with making this the perfect spot for events. I'm proud of you."

He gave her a grin. "Thanks, Izz. I'm really happy here." He tore off the printout and bundled the cash. "So happy, in fact, I've been thinking about asking Ellie to marry me."

Izzy's eyes twinkled with excitement. "You're smarter than I thought." She gave him a wink and wrapped him in a hug. "I couldn't be happier for you. I think it would be wonderful."

"Do you think she'll say yes?"

Izzy nodded. "I'm sure she will. She'd be lucky to have you."

"I'm hatching a plan. I want to make it special when I ask her. I'm thinking of making her dinner in a romantic setting. Was toying with asking her out on the boat, but then thought maybe her backyard would be better. What do you think?"

"Hmm, that's a tough one. My first inclination would be the

backyard idea. It's so beautiful and private. I can imagine it with candles and twinkling lights." She finished cleaning and packed all the dirty dishes to the back. "I'd be happy to help you," she hollered over the sound of running water.

"I'll take you up on that," he said, taking the money into the office.

Izzy joined him and placed a tall glass of water with a slice of lemon on his desk. She plopped in Ellie's chair and put her feet up on the desk. "So when are you going to propose?"

"I don't have it all worked out, but soon. We've got one free Sunday later this summer that would work for a wedding here in the barn and I'm hoping she'll agree to it."

"Wow, that's fast. It might be too fast for her?"

He shrugged and took a long drink from his glass. "I'll be okay if she wants to wait, but I don't need time. I know she's the one for me. I know we're better together. We spend almost all of our time with each other now. It wouldn't be that big of a change. She's down to earth, so I think we could pull a wedding together."

"Well, she does do it for a living and always does a great job. With all her connections, it should work. It'll come down to her own feelings and choice. Not to mention the complications with her family."

Blake rolled his eyes. "That'll be the dilemma. I'm sure her dad would come and her aunt. I think her sister would make the trip, but her mom will be the issue."

"First things first. Start with the proposal and present the date as an option and see what she says. Even if you want the wedding this summer, let her control it and decide. She doesn't need any pressure."

"I'm just excited and see an opening that would work." He looked at the wall calendar. "But it would work after the busy season and the harvest. Like you say, I'll leave it all up to her."

"Let's figure out what we can do to make the proposal special," said Izzy, grabbing a pad of paper.

Blake talked and she jotted down ideas, interjecting a few of her own. It was well after midnight when they left the winery with a final plan.

* * *

The winery opened late on Mondays and closed earliest on Sundays. With that in mind, Blake's plan was shaping up for a Sunday night delivery of his all-important question. As soon as Ellie left for the winery on Sunday, Izzy and Linda used Blake's key and crept into Ellie's house. Linda's eye for detail and decorating proved indispensable. She had visited the winery early Saturday morning and with Blake's help, stashed all sorts of party furnishings in her van.

She and Izzy spent several hours draping lights in the tree branches and wrapping the trunks with tiny white lights. They hefted the patio table to the grass below the deck and nestled it below the biggest tree. They covered the pathway to the table with rose petals and lined the edges with glass luminarias. Izzy swathed the deck with twinkling lights while Linda added some potted plants borrowed from the nursery.

Sparkling china and crystal graced the white linen draped table. Linda used white flowers with touches of soft pink to create a tasteful centerpiece and spread small glass votive candles around the table and deck.

The two women stood back and admired the setting. "It looks gorgeous," said Izzy. "I couldn't have done it without you."

Linda smiled and picked up a box. "Ah, this is easy. I'm used to setting up large weddings."

"I think we've done all we can do. The rest is up to Blake. I better get moving and get out to the winery." Izzy gathered up the bags of wrappers from their decorating frenzy. "Thanks again for the help. Blake owes you a few cases of vino."

Linda tossed the empty boxes in her van. "Let me know how it goes," she said with a wave goodbye.

Izzy locked the door and drove to the winery, passing Blake his key when she found him outside sweeping. "You're up," she whispered with a wink.

The three waited on customers and helped them taste and select wines throughout the day. A couple of hours before closing, Blake received a call and told Ellie and Izzy he needed to run to town to take care of a problem with his boat.

"We'll be fine. We can close up when it's time if you're not back," said Ellie, as he hurried out the door. The next hours drew a scattering of customers, more than manageable for the two on their own.

* * *

While they were busy taking care of the winery, Blake was rushing to prepare a feast fit for his proposal. He had called Ellie right before closing and told her he'd wrap up at the marina and see her at her house within an hour. She had no inkling he was already at her house, ready for her arrival.

He had changed into a suit and tie after prepping the meal. All the candles were lit, champagne was chilling, soft music was playing, and Blake was pacing. He checked on the oven where he was keeping things warm.

He heard Ellie's garage door and hurried outside.

Ellie opened the door and Oreo bounced into the house and made a beeline for the patio. Ellie stopped and looked at the sticky note Blake had left her, directing her to change into her favorite outfit and meet him outside for a drink before dinner.

She frowned, breathing in the aroma of something delightful

cooking in her kitchen. She smiled and shook her head, taking the sticky note with her into her bedroom. She flipped through the hangers in her closet and found a sleeveless pink blouse she liked and paired it with a matching flyaway cardigan. She slipped on a pair of white pants and spritzed some perfume on her neck.

She stopped by the bathroom and checked her face, swiping shimmery gloss over her lips and brushing a bit of color on her cheeks. She fluffed her hair and headed for the patio. When she stepped outside she gasped. Although it wasn't yet dark, the twinkling lights and the candles flickering added to the magical setting. She felt the soft rose petals touch the tips of her toes as her sandals brushed over the path.

Her eyes widened as she arrived at the large tree and saw the gorgeous table below the thousands of lights wrapping the branches. Blake stepped out from behind the tree and presented her with a single red rose. "You look beautiful."

"Wow, what's all this?" she asked, sniffing the fragrant stem.

"Just a little something for my favorite lady." He pulled out her chair and poured them both a glass of champagne. "I'm happier than I've ever been, Ellie. And that's because of you."

She took in all the lights and flowers. "I can't believe you did all of this. It's so beautiful and elegant."

"You deserve it." He moved to a side table and retrieved a plate of Lou's crab cakes and two salads. He took his seat and bit into one of the flaky concoctions. "I wanted to make you a special meal, but had to enlist a bit of help for a couple of items."

She took another bite of hers. "These are the best. I've never even tried to make them because I know they'd never be this good." She reached for her water glass. "How's your boat?"

He gave her a grin. "She's fine. Actually, there was no problem. I needed time to get ready for tonight."

"I never knew you were so sneaky. I'm impressed." She gazed at the yard. "It's...like a fairy tale."

They continued talking as they finished their first course. She started to clear the dishes and he said, "No, you just sit and enjoy the view. I'll go get our entrees." He refilled their water glasses and hurried back to the kitchen.

She breathed in the evening air, infused with the fresh aroma of the variety of flowers on and around the table. Blake returned with a tray and placed a plate in front of Ellie. "Careful the plates are hot."

She looked at the filet mignon and lobster tail with potatoes and veggies. "Oh, my goodness. This looks delicious. Did you do all this?"

"I can handle steak and lobster. I had to subcontract the dessert."

She cut into the filet and took a bite. "Mmm, this is delicious. I feel so spoiled."

"I'm glad you like it. I know you're not supposed to eat much sugar, but I hope you'll make an exception for a bite of dessert tonight."

"I'm intrigued. What did you find?"

"You'll see soon enough." He cleared the plates as soon as they had finished and returned from the kitchen bearing dessert plates.

It was now dark and the candlelight flickered in Ellie's eyes as she craned her neck to get a look at the plates, but they were covered with linen napkins. "I commandeered Sam to help with this. I know you're the best baker on the island, but I think you'll like this."

He whisked the napkins away and revealed crystal plates with mini strawberry pies and a skewer of alternating strawberries and brownies, drizzled with chocolate. Each plate was garnished with chocolate covered strawberries dusted with silver glitter. "Wow, that looks yummy."

"I figured it was mostly fruit, so you could cheat a little." He passed her a plate and sat down in front of his own. His attention was focused on her as she admired the dessert before picking up her fork. He saw her eyebrows rise as she investigated her pie.

"Oh, my gosh." She plucked a brilliant diamond ring from the dollop of whipped cream.

Blake beamed and slipped from his chair to kneel in front of her. He took the ring and wiped if off with his napkin. "Ellie, I love you more than anything. Will you do me the honor of marrying me?"

Tears leaked from the corners of her eyes and she smiled and laughed as she slipped her arms around his neck. "Yes, I'll marry you. You make me so happy." Their lips met in a long kiss.

He rested his forehead against hers and slipped the ring on her finger. "I'm so glad you said yes."

"You're irresistible," she said, admiring the ring sparkling in the flicker of the candles.

Blake slipped back into his seat and took a bite of his pie. "So, when shall we get married?"

She laughed as she slid her fork into the pie. "I haven't even thought of it. Are you in a hurry?"

He wiggled his brows at her as he popped a strawberry in his mouth. "I say the sooner the better, but I'll leave it up to you."

"It'd be fun to do it at the winery, don't you think? I love our barn."

"I do too. I'd like to do it there." He ate another bite. "Also, I know the proper thing for me to do would be to talk to your dad before I asked you to marry me, but I didn't. I wasn't sure about that whole situation and didn't want to tell your family until you were ready."

She blew out a breath and her bangs fluttered. "That was just sinking in as I was thinking about a wedding. I don't even want my mother there. I'm sure Ceci and Dad will come and I know Aunt

Ginny will be there, but that's probably the extent of my family. If you're family comes, we'll definitely need the barn." She gave him a quick grin. "There has to be at least fifty of them."

He reached for her hand and brought it to his lips for a kiss. "We'll do whatever you want to do. Big or small. Barn or not. You decide. I want to marry you and I don't care where or who comes."

"Let's enjoy tonight and I'll work on it starting tomorrow and see what I can come up with. It depends on our bookings."

"I think you'll find a hole in the schedule in August. I'm not sure if that's enough time for planning." He carried the champagne in one hand, handed her the glasses, and took her other hand in his. "I like the idea of enjoying tonight."

Chapter Fourteen

Roxy seemed to know it was Monday morning and as soon as Kate's feet hit the floor, she was looking at her with expectant eyes. Kate threw on some clothes and they hit the trail for their walk around the harbor. Roxy was becoming well known to the small group of early morning walkers they encountered, earning pets and hellos along the way. Kate savored the scent of the blooms from the flowers that decorated the walkways and sitting areas throughout the blocks ringing the waterfront.

They spent time at their spot near the wall, taking in another impressive sunrise. No two were alike. The dominant colors changed from gold to pink and even violet and it was a treat to see what nature would provide each week. The display was always stunning, no matter the hue.

After their walk, Spence suggested they visit Harbor Coffee and Books. With their coffees, they indulged in one pastry to share and carried their breakfast outside to the sunny deck. They found Izzy with Linda and Max at a table and joined them.

Izzy filled them in on the latest news about Blake's proposal. As Izzy was telling them about Ellie accepting, Sam and Jeff strolled up to the table, dragging two more chairs into the circle.

"I'm so happy for Ellie," said Jeff. "She and Blake make a great couple and after what she's been through she deserves some happiness."

They sipped coffee and recollected the recent tragedies in Ellie's life, beginning with her birth daughter finding her because she needed a kidney transplant and dying shortly after they met, to Ellie's beloved uncle dying a few weeks later. Ellie's childhood had been difficult to the point of her parents dropping her off on the island as a teenager and never looking back. "I know we'll do everything we can to make sure Ellie has a wonderful wedding celebration," said Sam.

The group nodded in agreement. "If they pull it off this summer, we'll need to find space for my family. I know Ellie's family is relatively small, but ours is huge," said Izzy.

Sam and Linda both offered their homes. "My place is smaller, but I'm happy to have someone stay with us," said Kate. "Regi and Nate have lots of room and I'm sure they'd be happy to help."

"That would be wonderful. I could offer a couch and that's it. My place is the size of a walnut shell," said Izzy. "I know Blake is hoping they can do it this August. I'll call around and see if there's a chance of snagging any rooms in town."

Jeff said, "I'll check with my brother and see if any of the cabins happen to be available at the resort."

"We could pitch some tents in the yard for the kids if we have too," said Max. "We've got plenty of room for that. Kids like to sleep outside, right?"

They laughed and Jeff said, "They used to. Who knows nowadays?" He finished his mocha and added, "We could put somebody in the apartment above the coffee shop. These days Hayley is staying at Charlie's more than she's home."

Izzy ticked off her fingers, counting people. "We may squeak by, but Ellie's family will need places to stay too. I'll check around today."

"Do your parents know yet?" asked Kate.

"I haven't said anything. I told Blake I'd let him make all the announcements. He texted me last night and told me Ellie said yes and that I could share the news with all of you. He's close to our parents so I'm sure they'll be his first call."

Linda stood and said, "I need to run out to the nursery, so I better get moving." Max joined her and the others finished their drinks and went their separate ways.

* * *

Kate greeted Izzy with a hug and smile when she came to work Tuesday morning. "How was your day off?" asked Izzy, stashing her purse in the backroom.

"Lazy. We binged on a British series and lounged in the sunshine. Spence grilled burgers last night and we vegged out most of the evening."

"That sounds like a well-deserved day off to me. I spent the afternoon talking to my sisters about Blake's wedding. Everyone is so excited and can't wait for the big day."

"I bet your parents are over the moon. Ellie is such a sweetheart."

Izzy nodded and readied the counter for customers. "How's Maggie doing?"

Kate wrinkled her nose. "I feel so horrible and guilty. I should have gone to see her yesterday but was relishing my selfish day too much. I'll have to make a point to stop by one day this week. It's hard to explain, but I don't enjoy our visits."

"I can understand that. I'm sure you associate her with some brutal memories. Not something you want to relive."

Their conversation was cut short by a quartet of shoppers fresh off the ferry. They kept busy throughout the day, with only enough time for a quick bite of lunch between customers. Late in the afternoon, Kate turned from wrapping a purchase and gasped when she saw a man standing at the register. A man she never expected to see.

She fumbled with the package and said, "Jack? What are you doing here?"

"Nice to see you too," he said. "I need to talk to you."

"What's wrong? Is Mitch okay?"

He shook his head and raised his voice, "Mitch is fine, Kate. When are you going to get over your obsession?"

Kate's shoulders relaxed and she said, "Well, I'm working right now."

"I can wait. What time do you close?"

"Give me your number and I'll call you when I'm done."

He grabbed one of her business cards from the holder on the counter and scribbled on the back of it. "I leave tomorrow morning, so make sure and get in touch with me tonight."

Kate gritted her teeth and noticed a woman approach the counter. "I'll be in touch." She turned her attention to the customer and when she looked up her ex-husband was gone.

As soon as she handed the woman her bag and thanked her, she found Izzy showing a customer some antique doorknobs. "I've got to run up to the office. I'll be right back."

She hurried up the stairs and punched Spence's button on her cell phone. "Hey, I'm going to be late. Jack showed up here at the shop and told me he needs to talk."

"Do you want me to come with you?" he asked.

"No, I'll be fine. I'm going to have him come to the store when we close after Izzy leaves."

"You don't know what he wants?"

"No clue. He was being his charming self. I just know it's not about Mitch, so I don't really care what it is."

"Okay, if you need me, call and I'll be there in a couple of minutes."

She disconnected and slipped her phone into her pocket. As soon as they closed she had Izzy do the reports and asked her to drop the deposit at the bank. When she heard the back door close, she punched in Jack's number.

She told him to come by the store and knock on the front door. She left the lights on and kept watch behind the counter, her mind racing with ideas about what would bring her ex-husband to the island.

She knelt to straighten the bags and tissue under the counter and heard a loud rap on the door. She took a deep breath and walked to the door where he stood. She unlocked the deadbolt and waved him inside.

"Looks like you've got a good business here."

"It keeps me busy." She guided him to a round table in the corner and said, "Have a seat."

He pulled out a chair and noticed the top of the table. "That's neat. I like the checkerboard top."

She nodded and said, "What brings you to the island, Jack?"

"I'm here because of Maggie."

Kate's frowned. "What do you mean?"

"Mitch told me he had come to see you and Maggie was here. He explained she had terminal cancer and wasn't doing well." Kate nodded but said nothing. "Anyway, when he told me how bad she was I thought I better come, and you know, say goodbye."

"Oookay. That's thoughtful of you."

"There's more you need to know. Back after Karen died, we, uh, Maggie and I, we had a fling."

Kate's throat felt like she had swallowed a piece of gauze. She stared at Jack, who was looking anywhere but at her. Her mind struggled to grasp his words. "You what?"

"It wasn't that big of a deal. You were so depressed you didn't even know if I was there or not. Maggie, she…was there for me."

Kate's heart beat faster and her face reddened. She cleared her throat, trying to quell the shaking of her voice. "Let me get this straight. Our daughter killed herself. You and Maggie both suggested that it was my fault and I should have known. Then you and my friend decide the best thing to do is sleep with each other. Do I have it right, Jack?"

He slammed his hand on the table. "No, not exactly. You left out the part about you barely functioning. The only person you paid any attention to was Mitch. So while you were wallowing in your sorrows and could barely get out of bed, Maggie was someone who understood me." He stood and yelled, "What the hell difference does it make. You were screwing around with Spence."

"Wow, you haven't changed a bit over the last twenty years. I was never unfaithful in our marriage." She twirled her finger next to her head. "You told yourself lies for so long they became your reality. Apparently, the fabrications in your mind gave you a free pass to sleep with my best friend. You are both despicable."

"I'm not sure why I bothered to come here, Kate. It's the same old thing with us. Maggie thought you knew about us. When I told her I had never told you she became inconsolable. She was distraught and told me I had to tell you everything. That's the only reason I'm here."

"Good to know, Jack. All the vile things you said about Spence and you're the one having an affair. How long did this go on?"

"I don't know. I guess until after the divorce. Maggie assumed she caused the divorce."

"And you, being the gentleman you are, let her?"

He shrugged and paced, heading toward the door. "Whatever, Kate. Nothing's changed. I can see that. I knew I shouldn't have come."

Kate stood and turned to face him. "I haven't heard you say you regret any of this."

"I'm sorry about our daughter." He turned his back to her and then made a quick turn. "I'm sorry I bothered to come here."

"I feel sorry for you, Jack. I would have thought over these years you would have thought of more than yourself. Maggie's guilt drove you here, not your own. I have always regretted that we couldn't survive Karen's death. I know I was at my worst. I will always mourn the loss of our daughter and the end of our marriage, but I've done my best to move on with a new life. I'm happy here."

"Yes, I'm sure you are." He smirked. "Maggie told me Spence moved here with you. He was always the man you wanted, not me."

"That's not true, Jack. We had a happy marriage and a good life for many years. Spence and I have been friends forever. That was it. Friends. It changed recently, not twenty years ago. But, it's pointless talking to you. I'm done explaining. You've done what Maggie wanted, now you can go."

She strode to the door and opened it. He walked through the opening and then turned to her. He started to say something, then shook his head and plodded down the sidewalk.

Kate shut the door and leaned her back against it. The tears she had held back during Jack's visit now streamed down her face. A tap on the glass startled her and she turned to see Spence standing at the door with Roxy. She flung the door open and fell into his arms.

* * *

Spence and Roxy ushered Kate home where he had dinner waiting. She had no interest in food and instead changed into her pajamas. Spence ate while she paced around the kitchen ranting about her ex-husband. "I wish I had never married that lying scoundrel. The only good that came of it was Karen and Mitch." She continued to stomp out on the patio, muttering to herself.

It was well after midnight and Spence was still listening to Kate recount Jack's sudden visit. She was wrapped up in a blanket on the couch, resting her feet on Spence's lap, and petting Roxy.

She stroked the dog's fur as she went over Jack's revelations. "I shouldn't be surprised, but I can't believe this whole situation. It explains a bit more about what I thought was Maggie's sudden betrayal." She punched the throw pillow. "And I let those two make me think I was responsible for Karen's suicide. I never once blamed Jack for her death, but that's what he did to me."

Spence made another pot of tea and let her vent. His efforts to convince her to eat something proved futile. "I guess Maggie must think I'm a real idiot." She shrugged. "I guess I *am* a real idiot. I don't remember many details about those dark days. The thought of Maggie and Jack never entered my mind. I was clueless."

Spence patted her leg. "Don't be so hard on yourself. You're not the one who did anything wrong."

"I hate feeling stupid."

"You aren't stupid now and you weren't then. You were grieving and barely hanging on. Jack abandoned you in your time of need."

Her eyes widened. "Did you know about them?"

Spence's forehead furrowed. "No, I didn't know. I was focused on you and your well-being. And Mitch, of course. Jack was never around when I was there."

"I wonder if he told Mitch about all this?"

"I doubt it, hon. It's not something I would think he'd be proud to share with his son."

She nodded. "The only reason he told me was because Maggie asked him to." She sobbed and reached for a tissue.

"You should call Izzy and see if she can work tomorrow. I think you need a day to rest and recover. You're in no shape to work in the morning."

Kate glanced at the clock. "Oh, I had no idea it was so late. I'll text her and wait to hear in the morning. I hate to do that to her."

"I don't think she'll mind. You need your rest." He collected her cup. "You're better off without Jack. Try to think about all the good things you've got going and don't let his latest admission ruin your happiness."

"I'm trying," she gave him a small smile. "I know what you're saying. It burns me up that he and Maggie could stoop that low."

"Let's get to bed and try to get some sleep. Things always look better in the morning." He pulled on her hand to get her up and coaxed her to bed.

As she stared at the ceiling she said, "Were you waiting for Jack to leave tonight? You showed up right when he left."

Spence gripped her hand in his. "I was there the whole time. I was sitting on a bench across the street with Roxy."

She brought his hand to her lips. "You've always been my protector and my best friend. I love you."

Chapter Fifteen

Ellie had been in full wedding planning mode since the morning after Blake's proposal. She had contacted all her favorite vendors and was able to secure everything she wanted for the only day in August available at the winery. She had even tried on a few dresses they had in the small boutique she had helped set up as part of their full-service wedding planning. She dismissed most of them and decided she would have to take a trip to the city to visit Maureen and try on more gowns.

Blake's family had received the news with enthusiasm and his parents were working on travel plans to get the whole clan to the island. Izzy was working for Kate today, so Ellie was trying to finish her office work before the tasting room opened for business. Blake was out in the vineyards getting his chores done so he could help Ellie with the customers.

Ellie checked the clock and saw she had a few minutes. She hadn't yet talked with her dad or sister about the upcoming wedding. Aunt Ginny had been overjoyed when she called her early Monday morning. Her aunt cried with happiness when she told her how much Uncle Bob would have loved to see her married.

The long history of rejection by her family weighed on her as she considered telling them her news. She stared at her cell phone for several minutes, before picking it up and calling her dad. Relief flooded her thoughts when she heard his voicemail message. She asked him to call her back in the evening, telling him she had some news. She opted to send a short email to her sister, Ceci.

After she hit the send button, she dialed Maureen in Seattle to set up a time to try on gowns. In between Maureen's well wishes, she asked Ellie several questions about the gowns she had tried and what she liked and disliked about each of them. Within a few minutes, Maureen was convinced she had the ideal dress for Ellie and they set up a date.

As they were disconnecting she heard Blake come through the backdoor. He came into the office to change into a clean shirt. "Did you get in touch with your dad?" he asked, stripping off his work shirt.

"I left him a message and I emailed Ceci. We'll see what they say," she shrugged. "I'm trying not to worry about it." She stood and helped him button the last few buttons. "On a happier note, Maureen says she has the perfect dress for me. I'm going to go see it next week."

He gave her a quick kiss. "Take Izzy with you. She'd love it."

"I'll ask her. I think I'll stop and pick up Aunt Ginny on the way."

"You do whatever makes you happy," he said, grabbing her hand as they shut the office door and began their day in the tasting room.

* * *

Ellie's journey to Seattle started on Sunday when she and Izzy made the trip on the ferry and drove to Aunt Ginny's. After they arrived, Aunt Ginny treated them to a homemade dinner and dessert, including a sugar-free option for Ellie. The three women sat on the deck and visited as the sun went down.

"Dad called and said he'd come for the wedding and wants to

walk me down the aisle. He sounded happy and excited," said Ellie.

"Did he mention your mother?" asked her aunt.

Ellie chuckled. "She came up in our conversation. I told him I wasn't interested in having her attend the wedding since she had made it clear she didn't care about me or my life years ago." Ellie took a breath as she looked at the darkening sky. "He said she told him she wasn't going and would not allow my brother to go. She implied that my marriage would be a disaster and would fail and she wanted no part of it or me."

Aunt Ginny slapped her hands on her thighs. "That woman is awful. She should never have been blessed with children." She reached for Ellie's hand. "I'm so sorry, my dear."

Ellie shrugged. "It's what I expected. She's despised me forever. I'm not naïve enough to think she would have had a change of heart. Especially after Dad spent time with me. I'm sure she's miffed."

Aunt Ginny squeezed Ellie's hand. "It will be a wonderful celebration and you'll be a beautiful bride. You're going to embark on a fantastic journey with the man you love. That's all that matters."

Izzy nodded and said, "You'll be surrounded by way too many Griffins and will have so many of us fussing over you, you won't know what to do. Your mother is the one missing out on you, Ellie. Not the other way around. You're a lovely young woman and Blake, as much as I tease him, is one of the best men I know. I know he adores you and I'm positive you will have a wonderful life together. Everyone who loves and cherishes you will be there for you."

Ellie gave a slow nod. "I'm lucky to have so many wonderful people around me. I think there's still a tiny part of me that hoped my mom would someday change and come back in my life." She took a sip from her mug of tea. "Ceci and her family will be there. I'll miss Uncle Bob not being there more than I'll miss Mom."

"He would be thrilled to see you married and happy. I think he'll be there watching it all," said Aunt Ginny, the glint of tears reflected in her eyes.

Ellie turned to Izzy. "I have a request, but don't want you to feel obligated. I'd like you to be my maid of honor."

Izzy brought her palm to her heart. "Me? You want me?"

"I do. You've felt like a big sister to me since the day I met you. I want to keep the ceremony simple. A best man and a maid of honor. Blake is going to ask Jeff to be his best man."

"I'm touched, Ellie. I would love to be such a special part of your wedding day."

Aunt Ginny stood and said, "I better get to bed and get ready for our day tomorrow. You girls lock up when you're done." She hugged them both before heading to her bedroom.

* * *

The next morning they braved the heavy traffic and with the help of Izzy's navigation skills, Ellie pulled up in front of Rose's Bridal Boutique only thirty minutes late. Maureen greeted them and welcomed them to a sitting area where she offered them snacks and drinks. She whisked Ellie away to the back and she returned wearing a stunning gown.

Ellie was grinning as she stepped closer to the two women. Aunt Ginny gasped and Izzy clapped her hands together. "You look beautiful," said her aunt.

Ellie twirled around and looked in the mirror. "I think this is the one." She turned to face them. "I also think Maureen is the wedding dress whisperer."

Maureen beamed as she looked at the bride to be. "It's gorgeous on you." She turned her attention to Izzy and Aunt Ginny. "Now we need to find something fabulous for both of you." She took

Ginny's hand. "I understand you're the mother of the bride. I want to show you a few dresses to try and see what you think."

Ginny started to say something and looked back at Ellie, who was smiling and nodding her agreement. While Maureen helped Ginny, Izzy asked, "What colors are you going to use?"

"Of all the weddings we've done and seen, I'm always drawn to the purple and lavender ones. You choose anything you like in that color family. Will that work for you?"

"Oh, yes. I love those colors." She stood and wandered to a rack of dresses. Maureen tapped her shoulder and motioned her to a fitting room. "Here are some for you to try. I've selected some darker and a few lavender ones. We'll see what you and Ellie like best."

Ginny was standing next to Ellie, wearing a dark plum chiffon jacket dress with illusion sleeves and shimmery beading at the neckline and cuffs. She was smiling as she took a look in the mirror. "I like this knee length style and I love the color."

Izzy joined the women in a wisteria colored long A-line dress. It had a high bateau neckline with an illusion sweetheart bodice and a sheer overlay in the back. The dress was covered in beading and sequins with a long flowing skirt. Izzy glanced in the mirror and took in the threesome. "I love all of our dresses," she said. "What do you think, Ellie?"

Ellie's eyes glistened with tears as she smiled and hugged Aunt Ginny. "I think they're perfect."

The ladies enjoyed a few more moments admiring their gowns and each other before Maureen asked two seamstresses to inspect the dresses for any needed alterations. The two made quick work of pinning here and there and sent them to change back into their street clothes.

Ginny found Maureen busy at her desk writing up the orders. She handed her a credit card. "I want to pay for all three dresses."

Maureen nodded and took the card. "I'm giving Ellie a discount because of the boutique at the winery. I'll get it tallied and get you a total."

Izzy and Ellie were looking through shoes and Ellie found a style she liked and added them to the order. She started to hand Maureen her credit card when Ginny interrupted and pushed her hand away. "No, this is my treat to you. Uncle Bob would insist that we pay for your wedding party's dresses. You can do everything else, but let me have this as my contribution."

Ellie wrapped her aunt in a hug. "Thank you," she whispered.

The women wished Maureen well and she promised to ship the gowns within two weeks and said, "I'll see you at the ceremony. I wouldn't miss it."

It was well after lunch when they left the bridal shop. Ellie wasn't familiar with the restaurants in the area, but Izzy used her phone and found a French café and bakery not far from where they were.

Izzy treated them to a celebratory meal and a plate of mini cakes for the table. Ellie limited herself to a small sample bite of each. They even had a chocolate mousse cake, but they all agreed Ellie's was much better.

After a long lunch, they fought through the heavy traffic and dropped Aunt Ginny at her house on their way to the ferry landing. While they sat at a table inside, Ellie checked her email, hoping to see confirmation of her wedding invitations delivered.

"I think we should gather the ladies and get those invites out this week. I'll organize something if that's okay with you?" asked Izzy.

Ellie smiled and said, "I knew you'd make the best maid of honor."

* * *

Kate attended the group invitation stuffing party for Ellie that week at Linda's. Regi sought Kate out and found a private corner on the patio.

"I've been spending my days with Maggie's sweet granddaughter. She sure is a cutie."

"Has she adjusted to being at your house?" asked Kate.

"I think so. Maggie ordered duplicates of all her favorite toys and we keep a pile of her stuff at our house now. It makes it easier than carting everything back and forth. Murphy's been curious and gentle with her and Emma gets excited when she sees the dog."

"I'm glad it's working out for her. She's a sweet little girl."

"Maggie hinted that things are rocky between the two of you. She mentioned she'd like to talk to you."

Kate shook her head. "I'm not interested in talking to Maggie at the moment."

Regi placed her hand atop Kate's. "I don't want to upset you. It's between you and Maggie. It's none of my business."

With the invitations done, the rest of the women moved outside and arranged the chairs to watch the sun dip into the sea. "What are you two doing over here in the corner?" asked Sam. She took one look at Kate's pale face and the tears threatening her eyes and said, "Oh, Kate, what's wrong?"

Kate shook her head and pursed her lips. She took a deep breath and let Sam and Regi guide her to the table surrounded by her friends. They placed a glass of cool lemonade in front of Kate. "It's Maggie."

"Oh, no. Is she worse?" asked Linda.

"I'm not sure about her health." Kate glanced at Regi. "Regi and I were talking about little Emma. Regi mentioned Maggie wanted to talk to me and knew I was upset with her." Kate shook her head in sadness.

Regi shrugged and said, "Maggie told me there was a strain with Kate and she hoped to talk to her. I'm not sure why, but I can tell by Kate's reaction that it's serious."

Kate replaced her glass after she took a sip. "My ex-husband came to see me the other night when the store closed. He was on the island because Mitch told him Maggie was very ill. He came by the shop to tell me that he and Maggie had an affair after Karen died."

There was a collective gasp among the women. Sam put her arm around Kate's shoulders. "I'm so sorry, Kate. That's horrible news."

The others murmured kind words and nodded their agreement. "I cannot talk to her right now. I'm beyond angry. Jack said the only reason he told me now was because Maggie demanded it. She thought I knew all along and that's what led to our divorce. I can't believe I never saw it."

Sam sighed and said, "I'm the queen of not noticing, so trust me, I totally understand how you feel. My ex-husband had been unfaithful for years and I never knew. I hated myself for being so stupid. I've learned over time, to let go of those feelings. He's the one who cheated and he's the person I trusted with everything. I know you're better off without someone like him in your life now."

"I can't believe your best friend would do that," said Regi. "That's so hurtful."

Kate reached for a napkin. "They both deceived me and betrayed me at the most horrible time of my life. When Karen died I was a mess. My world stopped. I was at my most vulnerable and needed my best friend. Now I understand more about why she was so hateful to me, but it doesn't make it any easier."

"I admire you for doing all you've done to help Maggie. It's not easy to forgive someone," said Linda.

"I don't feel very forgiving at the moment. I'm not sure I ever want to see her again."

"I feel horrible now. I can't believe she would try to put me in the middle as the messenger to you. I'm so sorry, Kate," said Regi.

Kate patted her hand. "Not to worry. It's not your doing. You just keep taking care of Emma. It's not her fault either. She deserves to be a happy little girl."

"It makes me want to go and pop Maggie right in the nose," said Ellie. "But, smacking around a sick lady would be frowned upon." A smattering of muffled laughter followed Ellie's statement.

Kate gave a small smile and said, "I appreciate all your support. I'm sorry to bring the mood down. You would think after all this time I'd be less upset."

The women continued to console Kate and assure her they understood her feelings. They encouraged her to wait until she was ready and mentally prepared to have a conversation with Maggie.

As the glow of the sun plunged into the water, Izzy lifted her wine glass and said, "Here's to all the ex-husbands in the world. They serve as a constant reminder as to the power we have to create better lives for ourselves, despite our past pain. I know Kate's strength and resolve will get her past this latest revelation and she'll continue to build a happy life here with Spence, surrounded by her friends."

The rousing praise for Izzy's toast was interrupted when Spence walked through the door and entered the patio. He found his way to Kate and took her by the arm. "Katie, I need you to come with me. Mitch has been in an accident."

The conversation evaporated and Kate's body struggled to support her as she tried to comprehend Spence's words. "Is he...is he?"

"He's all right, Katie. He's going to be okay." He guided her to a chair and took both of her hands in his. "Listen, listen. Look at me." He focused on her and waited for her eyes to quit darting back and forth.

"We need to go to him," she jerked to her feet.

"We'll go, I promise." He put a gentle hand on her shoulder and steered her back into a sitting position. "He was leaving work and was hit by a car in the parking lot. He's conscious and alert. He told them to call me on his way to the hospital."

Kate's head bobbed up and down. "Okay, okay." Her whole body was shaking and she felt a blanket being wrapped around her.

"Max is talking to the doctors now. Let's get you inside and keep you warm." He lifted her out of the chair and guided her to the living area. The women fussed over her and made sure she had pillows behind her. Linda brewed tea and the ladies took seats on the couches awaiting Max's report.

A few minutes later he emerged from his home office. He carried a notepad and took a seat next to Kate. "First thing, Mitch is doing well. He's having some tests done now, but the doctor suspects a fractured leg and wrist. He did not hit his head in the fall, which is good news. He'll need surgery on his leg, which will happen as soon as they can get him prepped. He's in good shape and young, so all signs point to success." He tore off a sheet from the pad and gave it to Kate. "Here's the doctor's name and the room number Mitch has been assigned."

Kate looked at her watch. "The last ferry leaves at ten tonight. That gives us time to get there."

Spence had already talked to Max about keeping Roxy until they returned and had the car ready to go with an overnight bag. Kate ran to the car and Spence thanked Max and told him they'd call as soon as they could before speeding toward the ferry dock.

Chapter Sixteen

Kate felt like she was trapped underwater as Spence shepherded her from Friday Harbor to the ferry. The vehicle count was low and Kate didn't want to budge from her seat. They stayed in the car as the ferry churned its way to Anacortes. Her legs shook and her entire body felt cold. Spence reached into the backseat and did his best to turn Roxy's blanket inside out and drape it around Kate's shoulders, stuffing it around her like a cocoon.

He reached for her hand and rubbed it in an effort to keep it warm. "Take some deep breaths, Katie."

She complied and sucked in a long breath, letting it out slowly, picturing Mitch's smile as she tried to let her anxiety escape with the air in her lungs. She closed her eyes as the all too familiar fear of losing Mitch washed over her like a fast moving wave. The thing that terrified her more than anything was happening. After Karen's death, she had clung to Mitch like a life raft. She had struggled to let him out of her sight. She had made clandestine trips to his school and sat in her car watching. She knew in her mind she had to let him live his life, but her heart fluttered each time he left the house. These feelings of dread lessened over time, but all these years later she still struggled with worrying about losing Mitch. Now it could be happening and she was too far away.

She bowed her head and prayed that God would spare her son.

She knew she couldn't survive if she lost him.

She checked her watch. Only minutes had passed since she last looked at it. The ferry felt like it was barely moving and she took another deep breath. She envisioned the relaxing view from Sam's deck and Linda's patio. In the past, she had had some success picturing her worries as leaves traveling along the current of a clear creek. She watched the leaves float away with the movement of the water and let them disappear. She focused her mind on watching the leaves bob along the top of the water and vanish as the easy flow drifted by, taking her fears with it.

She continued to pray for Mitch, asking God to comfort him and heal him. She heard the announcement for their arrival and her eyes snapped open. She knew Spence would get them to Olympia as fast as he could. As he drove off the ferry and took to the streets, she stared ahead. The glow from oncoming cars blurred as her eyes filled. Once they were on the highway Spence ramped up his speed and flew by other cars. Traffic slowed as they neared Seattle and she heard Spence talking on the phone. She had a vague memory of him calling someone while they were waiting to disembark. She heard the other person over the Bluetooth connection in the car explaining about incidents on the road and giving Spence directions.

Her head throbbed and pulsed with every bump in the pavement. As they reached the outskirts of Olympia her heart began to race. She wanted to see Mitch and be close to him, but a cold stab of fear cut through her. She didn't want to face what might happen to Mitch and the feeling that he would slip away was overwhelming.

They reached the hospital in the wee hours of the morning, so parking was a breeze. After a hurried walk through the garage and navigating the elevators and hallways, they found Mitch's floor. Spence positioned himself at the nurse's station, ready for a challenge due to their late arrival, but instead was welcomed. A young nurse indicated Dr. Sullivan had been in contact with them since Mitch had been admitted and the attending physician had requested they be taken to his room no matter what time they arrived.

Kate's heart hammered and her body hummed with anxiety as they followed the nurse down the hallway. Her cold fingers wrapped around Spence's hand. The nurse led them into the darkened room, lit by a soft light over the counter. "He's fresh from the recovery room. He'll be sleeping for a bit. I'll tell the doctor you're here."

Kate's pale face was filled with dread as she crept to the side of the bed, steeling herself for what was to come. She saw Mitch's eyes were closed and he looked relaxed. His left arm was in a cast and his right leg was covered with bandages and a plastic contraption.

She slipped into the chair and rested her hand atop his. He didn't stir as Spence moved closer to Kate. He rubbed the back of her neck and shoulders as she curled her fingers around Mitch's hand.

She sat that way, keeping watch for a couple of hours. As the first light of the day crept through the window, a doctor came through the door. "Ms. Alexander?" he asked.

Kate's eyes moved from her son to the man standing at the end of his bed. "Yes, yes. I'm Mitch's mother."

"I'm Dr. Jamison. I did the surgery on your son."

Spence extended his hand, "I'm Spence Chandler, Kate's significant other. "What's the prognosis?"

"The wrist break was a clean break, so it's been set and will need to heal. The leg was more complicated. It was a compound fracture involving both of the bones in the lower leg. The tibia is the larger bone and bears all the weight of the leg, so we inserted a rod and screws in it. The fibula was left alone and will heal on its own."

Kate brought her hand to her mouth as she inhaled a sharp wince.

Dr. Jamison caught her eyes. "I know it sounds horrible, but I do surgeries like this daily and have excellent results. Mitch is in great shape. He's going to need therapy, but I expect a full recovery." He pointed to the plastic encasing Mitch's leg. "I've applied this in lieu of a plaster cast. He can't put any weight on it at all for six weeks. We've had greater success with this method and it will allow him to do more therapy, which will make for quicker healing and improved functionality."

"We live on San Juan Island. Will Mitch be able to make the trip there and stay with us to recuperate? We've got a wonderful hospital and physical therapy there," said Spence.

The doctor nodded. "I heard from your friends, Dr. Sullivan and Dr. Doyle last night and I'm more than confident in the facilities you have available. Dr. Sullivan suggested Mitch go to Seattle for follow-ups at UW, but he can do his therapy on the island. I've got him lined up with a colleague of mine in Seattle if that's more convenient than coming all the way here. It's up to Mitch. It may be possible to do some telemedicine for some of the appointments, as long as I have access to Mitch's x-rays. Having your help will be essential for the first few weeks. I've seen patients like Mitch playing golf within a couple of months. It all depends on the healing process, but he'll be back to normal this time next year."

Kate let out the breath she had been holding and squeezed Spence's hand. "How long will he be here?" she asked.

"Not long. We want to monitor him a bit and then we'll give him a crash course in some exercises, do's and don'ts, and some tools to help him get around. With the wrist, crutches are going to be difficult at first. I'd suggest a wheelchair or scooter. If he's looking good, I think he'll be able to leave in a couple days. We want to make sure the wounds heal on his leg and there's no infection. I'd also like him to use a bone stimulator to speed the healing."

Kate and Spence nodded as the doctor handed Spence his card. "We'll get Mitch set up with some follow-up appointments when he decides which location he prefers and I'll prescribe the therapy. You can have the doctors on the island get in touch with me for any questions."

Kate stood and shook the doctor's hand. "Thank you so much. We appreciate all you've done for Mitch. We'll take good care of him as he recovers." Her voice began to falter and she grabbed a handful of tissues.

"I'm going to check him out and expect he'll be more alert when I'm done. I'll be a few minutes if you two want to step out and get some coffee or something."

Kate retrieved her purse and Spence wrapped his arm around her as they left Mitch with the doctor. "Coffee sounds like a grand idea," he said.

They followed the signs and found a coffee cart outside the main cafeteria. Spence brought muffins and coffees to the table Kate had found near a window. The adrenaline was long gone and she was exhausted. The lack of sleep coupled with the unrelenting stress over the past ten hours had taken their toll. Spence yawned as he pulled out a chair.

She reached across the table and held his hand. "Thank you for being here. I couldn't have done this alone."

He gave her a wink. "You could have. You're a tough one. It's just better to have a partner."

She took a sip of the warm drink. "Nothing like Sam's, but it hits the spot." She brought the cup to her lips and gazed outside. "I've got a key to Mitch's, so I thought we could stay in his guest room."

"Suits me. Once he's fully awake we can talk to him more about coming to the island and figure out what he needs. I'll call Max and have him organize it on his end."

She nodded and took a bite of the streusel topped muffin on her plate. "I don't think we'll bother with his car. He's not going to be driving it for several weeks."

"It's not good to let it sit that long."

Kate grinned. "It couldn't be an excuse to drive the sporty thing, right?"

He smiled back at her. "It crossed my mind."

They finished what passed for breakfast and made their way back through the corridors. Kate saw a sign for the chapel and told Spence she'd meet him back at Mitch's room. She took the short walk and opened the doors to a small sanctuary lined with a few empty pews. She slid into one and gazed at the cross on the wall. Tasteful flowers were displayed at the front of the room and instrumental music played in the background, accompanied by the faint trickle of a small fountain.

She bowed her head and prayed, thanking God for saving Mitch. She'd had a complicated relationship with God after Karen's death. Last night on the trip from the island she had prayed more than she had in her life. As she whispered, tears flowed down her cheeks. She murmured her thanks and for the first time since she heard about the accident felt herself relax. The relief of seeing Mitch and hearing he would recover coupled with the tranquility of the space eased her mind.

She spent a few more minutes consuming the peace she felt in the chapel. She concentrated on the faint sound of the water babbling over the smooth rocks and closed her eyes. She left feeling revived and rested. She saw Spence waiting outside of Mitch's door for her.

They found him awake with a cup in his hand staring at the television. He glanced at them, "Hey, Mom. Spence. Thanks for coming."

Kate reached the bed and gave him a kiss on the forehead. "You gave us quite the scare. How are you feeling?"

"Loopy and thirsty. The doc told me the deal. He said you offered to have me come to the island to recuperate."

They discussed logistics and he asked them to pick up his car from work and contact his boss to explain what was happening. "Could you also call Dad and let him know?"

Kate's shoulders tightened thinking of having a conversation with Jack. She nodded and said, "Sure, you get some rest." After he assured Kate he was fine and wanted to sleep, she agreed to leave.

As they walked through the hallways and to the parking area Kate's legs faltered. She gripped Spence's arm tighter and turned to him. "I hate to ask you this, but would you please call Jack and tell him about Mitch? I don't want to talk to him right now. He'll bring up the whole Maggie thing and I don't have the strength to deal with it."

He wrapped her in an embrace. "Sure, I'll call him from Mitch's when we get there." They took a few steps and he added, "We need to get his car and then get you some rest."

She and Spence drove to the Washington State Legislature, where they parked and entered the Legislative Building. They checked in with a receptionist and were shown into the office of Director Hill.

Kate had met Mr. Hill a few times in passing when she had visited Mitch at work. As soon as they walked into the lobby area of the office, a woman came up to them. "Hi, your Mitch's mom, right? I'm Michelle, Mitch's assistant. I know Rich will be right out. We're all so worried about Mitch. Is he okay?"

Kate nodded, her hand still held tight by Michelle. "Yes, we just came from the hospital. He asked us to come by and talk with Mr. Hill and pick up his car."

Michelle let her hand go and shook her head. "I can't believe it. People drive too fast through here. You let Mitch know we're all thinking of him."

Kate nodded and before she could respond, Mr. Hill stepped from his office and hurried to them. "Hi, Ms. Alexander. Please come in." He led them to his large office suite.

She introduced Spence and then said, "We just left Mitch. We need to retrieve his car and he asked that I bring you up to date on his situation." She explained the injury and that Mitch would be staying with them on the island for at least six or eight weeks. "It depends on how it goes and when he can drive and put weight on his leg."

Mr. Hill nodded and listened with a creased forehead as Kate talked. "You tell Mitch not to worry one bit about work. We'll take care of things while he recovers. It's technically a workplace injury, so he has nothing to worry about with regard to costs or time off. I've already got HR on top of it. Whatever he needs, he gets. If he gets bored and wants to work from home on something, we can make that happen. I've already talked to our legal team and we have the flexibility to work that out."

Kate smiled and said, "That's a huge relief. He enjoys work, so he may take you up on that as he progresses. We're so thankful they expect a full recovery."

"We're all devastated this happened. The person who hit him is also upset. He's a young aide to a legislator, driving the legislator's car no less. He was in a hurry and not paying attention. The legislator, Senator Wellson, is beside herself. She wants to visit Mitch if it's okay."

"I'm sure that would be fine. Mitch loves his work here. He didn't know who hit him. Just said it was somebody driving like a dumbass."

Mr. Hill smiled. "Sounds like the Mitch we all know and love. He's got my cell and home number, so you tell him to call day or night if he needs anything." He stood and shook both their hands. "Let's get you in contact with the police so they can get you access to the secure parking area where Mitch parks." He walked them through the corridors and arranged for an escort.

Spence drove the car out of the garage and dropped Kate at his own car and they set out to Mitch's house. He lived less than ten miles from work near Cooper Point Estates. Spence put Mitch's car in the garage and used the key on the ring to open the house.

Once inside, Spence called Mitch's dad and explained about the accident and his condition, along with giving him his room number. Kate was in the guest room organizing their things but could hear Spence's side of the conversation. In his all-business detective voice he said, "No, Jack, he's going to be released soon. Kate will be taking care of him on the island." There was a bit of a pause and he said, "I'll let Mitch know. It'll be up to him, but I can tell you now, you're not welcome at Kate's home or at her store. She hasn't told Mitch about your visit or your revelation and would like to spare him those details."

She didn't hear more than a stern farewell and Spence disconnected. He joined her in the guest room and enveloped her in a long hug. "That's done," he said. They both collapsed on the bed and slept until mid-afternoon.

Kate bolted upright, startling Spence. "I just remembered I didn't have anyone put a closed sign at the shop. I didn't arrange for anything." She rummaged in her purse for her cell phone and put in a call to Izzy.

Spence continued to stay in bed as he listened to Kate's conversation. He gathered that Izzy and Andi had already handled the shop and were keeping it open in Kate's absence. She disconnected with tears streaming down her face.

"What's wrong, it sounds like they handled it?" he asked.

She nodded as she dabbed at her cheeks. "They did. I'm just so...so lucky. We have wonderful friends." She flopped back down and Spence wrapped his arms around her. She let herself relax hoping for a few more minutes of sleep.

After a long overdue rest and showers, they foraged in Mitch's cupboards and found the makings for a late lunch before returning to the hospital.

They peered into his room and saw Mitch surrounded by bouquets of flowers, flipping through channels. "Wow, this place looks like the display case at Buds and Blooms," said Kate, sitting in the chair next to him.

"They're from work. Senator Wellson already came by. Hers is that giant bouquet," said Mitch. He pointed to a monster arrangement of white flowers that had to be three feet tall. "She told me about her idiotic aide."

"Mr. Hill told us when we saw him today. Everyone wishes you a speedy recovery." She relayed the good wishes and information from Mitch's boss. "We got some rest, hopefully, you did the same?"

"I slept for several hours." He sighed and added, "I'm already bored. I'm not sure how I'm going to handle two months of this." He adjusted himself and winced. "I don't want to take a lot of medication, but this is starting to hurt."

"You've had a traumatic surgery. I understand the fear of pain meds, but I think you'll have to use them for a few days," said Spence. "We'll make sure you don't overuse them."

"Spence thought we might want to take your car to the island so it doesn't sit for months without being driven." She gave him a sly smile, "I think it's his transparent scheme to drive it."

Mitch gave him a lopsided grin. "It is fun to drive. I agree. We need to take it. Can you guys empty the fridge and pack up my stuff to take to the island? I figure once they spring me, we can drive to the ferry from here. It's going to be a long enough day without having to stop and do that on the way."

Kate nodded in agreement. "Sure, we'll get your things ready."

Mitch rested his head against the mound of pillows behind him. "Summer on the island always sounded great, but not like this."

"I know what you mean, but we'll get through this. Max is already lining up the best physical therapist. We'll take good care of you and you can sit outside and enjoy the scenery."

"When you figure out how to maneuver, we can visit Jeff and Nate, maybe even take you out in the boat," said Spence. "Your doc said golf may even be in your near future."

Mitch's eyes began to close as he gave a low chuckle. "Okay, I'll try to think of it as a long vacation. Just be warned, I'm not an easy patient."

* * *

Over the next couple of days, Mitch developed a new routine of exercises and mastered using an electric scooter, with the help of several nurses and the physical therapist. Kate spent most of her day at the hospital while Spence readied Mitch's house for an extended vacancy and explained the situation to his neighbors, who were happy to help out and keep an eye on the place. He took care of all the practicalities in getting Mitch's mail forwarded and making sure the grass would be mowed. Spence put several lights on timers, so the house would appear occupied.

Jeff called Spence to let him know he had arranged for Steve to pick up Mitch at the marina in Seattle. "I know what it's like to travel when you're recovering. I thought he could use the speed and convenience. Andi offered to go with him so she could tend to Mitch on the trip. I know you and Kate are each driving a vehicle and didn't want her to worry about him."

"Wow, that would be fantastic. I know Kate will appreciate that. We've been dreading the long trip and the wait for the ferry. It would have been a long day. Seattle isn't much more than an hour, so that's doable. I'll keep you posted on our release plans, so Steve knows when to leave."

Spence finished packing Mitch's laptop and everything in the office he thought Mitch might need and then went to pick up Kate for the evening. He found her doing a crossword with Mitch.

Spence shared Jeff's news about the transport for Mitch and saw the relief in both of their faces. "That is so nice of them. The doctor said I can get out of here tomorrow morning, but I was worried about the drive and the whole day," said Mitch.

Kate disbursed all the bouquets to other patients and nurses while Spence sat with Mitch. She had a clean set of clothes ready for him and a slip on shoe for his good foot. She checked the room and gathered all of his belongings. "I think we're ready for take-off in the morning."

"You two go ahead and get some dinner and relax. I'm going to try to get to sleep early tonight so I'm ready for tomorrow. I made them promise to get me out first thing because of the long trip, so don't tell them I've got a quick ride." He gave his mom a grin, reminding her of the mischievous young boy he had been.

"Mum's the word," she said, kissing his cheek. "Rest easy, my sweet boy."

Chapter Seventeen

Even with Steve's transportation, it had been a long day. Mitch beat Kate and Spence home. When they pulled up, the first thing they noticed was the wooden ramp that had been installed over the steps to the front door. They looked at each other as they jostled bags up the walk and both of them said, "Jeff."

They found Mitch propped up in the guest room sleeping. Andi and Roxy were keeping watch. Spence dumped their belongings and delivered all of Mitch's things outside the guest room. "I'm going to take Roxy on a walk. Be right back," he said, attaching her leash and heading out the front door.

The aroma of something wonderful led Kate to the kitchen. She noticed another wooden ramp at the patio door and smiled. She found a slow cooker full of soup, along with a salad and some fresh bread from Linda. Inside Linda's card was a meal schedule. She marveled at the list showing their needs were covered for the next two weeks. Tears formed in her eyes as she studied the names of her friends.

Max left a packet with Mitch's appointments set up as telemedicine calls with Dr. Jamison and had arranged for a home care physical therapist to evaluate him. Dr. Jamison had agreed to the plan, provided there were no complications. Mitch wanted to stick with Dr. Jamison and would see him in-person in six weeks.

Kate fixed a pot of tea and she and Andi sat on the patio to enjoy the sunshine. Andi went over the medications with Kate and provided answers and suggestions to questions Kate hadn't even considered. Andi outlined things Kate should watch for and how best to help Mitch maneuver, showing her the shower chair she had installed in the guest bathroom.

"I helped him take a shower when he got home. We covered his leg and forearm with plastic to keep them dry. He was happy and felt good, but worn out after the trip and the activity."

"I can't thank you enough for accompanying Mitch on the boat. He would have been miserable on our trip. You and Izzy have been so wonderful to take care of the store. I truly appreciate it and all that everyone has done to help us."

"It was nothing. I've found I always feel better when I'm helping someone else. I enjoy it and I know your friends are happy to help," said Andi. She stood and added, "I'm going to get home. I'm sure he'll sleep for a few hours. He had a snack when he got here." Kate walked her to the door and thanked her again. Andi gave her a hug and said, "If you need anything, I'm a phone call away. I'll see you at the store, if not before."

Kate made a shopping list and as soon as Spence returned from his walk, he did the marketing. Kate tossed some laundry in the washer and caught up on chores while Mitch napped. She and Spence let him sleep while they made a meal featuring Linda's delicious soup.

When they were done she cracked Mitch's door open wider and saw he was awake. "Hey, how are you feeling?"

"Better. I can't believe I slept so long."

"Linda made us some wonderful soup. Are you hungry?"

He nodded and said, "Andi gave me some yogurt and fruit, but soup sounds great."

The sleep had done Mitch wonders. His eyes were brighter and he wasn't near as pale as when he had been in the hospital. Kate fixed him a tray and chatted as he ate a whole bowl of soup. Spence enticed him to join them in the living room for a movie and a scoop of raspberry sorbet before bedtime.

Once they helped Mitch and had him settled for the night, they crawled into their own bed. "I'm so glad to be home," said Kate, taking his hand.

* * *

Kate left Spence with a hug and a whisper in his ear to urge Mitch to spend time outside when she left for work. Spence had mastered helping Mitch in and out of bed and to the bathroom. She felt guilty as she walked to town, but knew Mitch was comfortable with Spence and that he would take excellent care of her son.

Kate spent the first hour of work holed up in her office catching up on the reports from the days she had missed. Business had been brisk. She opened her mail and did the payroll, adding a small bonus to the meager paychecks in an attempt to thank Izzy and Andie for their extra work.

She heard the door chime several times and wrapped up her work so she could get downstairs and give Andi a hand with the customers. In between sales, they chatted about Andi's adjustment to life on the island and Mitch. Andi stressed the importance of using the bone stimulator on the wrist and the leg. "It would be great if we could get his wrist healed so he could use crutches. I think he feels like an invalid in the scooter," said Andi.

"I know. I could tell it bothered him. We keep stressing it's temporary, but I understand. I wouldn't like it either."

Kate glanced out the window late in the afternoon and said, "Wow, look who's out and about." She saw Spence walking alongside the scooter, with Mitch in sunglasses and a ball cap, looking more like himself. She made for the door and met them on the sidewalk.

Spence stood behind Mitch and gave Kate a thumbs up signal. She said, "What a pleasant surprise. What are you two up to?"

Mitch smiled. "Spence convinced me to go for a walk. Or should I say a scoot?" He laughed and added, "We went to the park and watched the boats in the harbor and have been roaming the sidewalks."

"Can you take a break and join us at Sam's for a drink?" asked Spence.

"Sure, let me tell Andi." She popped back inside and Andi gave a wave as the threesome set out to the coffee shop.

Spence pointed out the ramp at the back of the deck and got Kate and Mitch situated at a table with a perfect view. Before he could go inside to order, Sam appeared with a small plate of brownies. "Hey, Mitch. Great to see you," she said, bending down to give him a hug. She took orders for frozen drinks and promised to join them for a quick visit.

Jeff wandered across the street from Cooper Hardware and dragged another chair to their table. "How are you doing, Mitch?" he asked.

"Hanging in there. It feels good to be outside. I'm not sure how you handled being in the hospital for so long."

"It wasn't fun, but you do what you have to do. I can tell you there's no better place to heal than this island. It'll do wonders for you."

"Thanks for the ramps, by the way. I'm hoping to get out of this thing soon, but the ramps make it easy for me to get outside in the meantime."

Jeff waved away his thanks. "Ah, it's some scrap I had at the store. Nothing to it."

Sam returned with drinks for everyone and took a seat next to

Jeff. "I wanted to invite you all to my birthday bash this year. We're having a barbecue and hanging out until it's time for the fireworks. Nothing fancy, just a day of visiting and eating."

"Bring Roxy, she'll have fun playing with the others," added Jeff.

"I can't believe it's already the Fourth of July in a few days," said Kate. "I'm sure we'll be there. Thanks for including us."

"We're asking everyone to bring a side dish. We've got the rest of it covered," said Sam.

Mitch contemplated the activity along the street and the harbor. "This is a great spot to watch all the action."

Sam stood and said, "You're welcome to hang out here anytime you get bored at home. We've got Wi-Fi so you could sit out here and enjoy this glorious weather and video chat or do email. I've got to get back inside." She gave Jeff a quick peck on the cheek.

Kate glanced at her watch. "I need to get moving. I'll see you two at home for dinner. Ellie and Blake are bringing it and I invited them to stay and eat with us," said Kate.

"We'll finish up here and get home to make sure the patio's ready," said Spence.

She gave Mitch's shoulder a squeeze and retrieved another drink to take to Andi. When she came through the door of the shop Andi was finishing with a customer at the counter. When the woman left, Kate handed Andi the fruity drink and said, "You go ahead and go home. I'll wrap up here and see you tomorrow."

Andi was reluctant to leave, but Kate persisted. There were only a handful of browsers before she closed for the day. Alerted by the chime of the door, she looked up, scolding herself for not locking it sooner. Maggie stood before her.

"Kate, I'm sorry to show up unannounced, but I wanted to talk to you. Regi told me Mitch was hit by a car. I'm so sorry and hope he's doing well."

Kate felt her pulse throb in her neck and heat rise in her cheeks. She hadn't given Maggie a thought since the night Spence told her Mitch had been hurt. She was weary and frazzled from the ordeal and in no mood for Maggie and her apologies.

Kate put up her hand. "Maggie, I'm closed for the day and heading out. I have neither the time nor inclination to speak with you about Mitch or anything else right now. I thought I was impervious to any more wounds dispensed by your hands, but Jack delivered the fatal blow and I'd like that to be the last one. I'm done."

Tears flowed down Maggie's face and she struggled for words. "I'm sorry, Kate. I didn't want to upset you. I understand you not wanting to see me. I need to talk to you, but I'll wait until you're ready. Just don't wait too long." She turned and disappeared down the sidewalk.

* * *

Kate stomped all the way home, griping to herself as she thought of Maggie. *How dare she show up like that. She has some nerve asking about Mitch. I wish I'd never seen her again. I could have lived out my life just fine not knowing what happened to Maggie. Except for poor little Emma. She's the innocent in all of this. And then there's that miserable Jack. Ass.* She chuckled at her pun.

She turned the corner for her house and saw Ellie and Blake had arrived. She took a deep breath and stood taller. She hoped she looked calm. Mitch didn't need to know about his father, not now. Maybe not ever.

She crossed the threshold and heard chatter coming from the patio. She stashed her things and joined the party. Mitch was laughing as Blake told stories about his sisters. They turned when they heard her come through the doorway.

"Sorry, I'm a bit late," she said, reaching for Spence's hand. He stood and pulled out a chair for her. "I let Andi go home early today."

"Well, we brought lasagna for you. It's heating in the oven. Sorry, it's nothing special, but there's plenty for leftovers and we have salad and bread."

"Sounds wonderful, Ellie. I appreciate you guys doing this."

"Don't give it a thought," she said. "I'll go check on it."

Blake followed and returned with a huge pan of bubbling cheesy pasta goodness. He joined Kate and Spence in a glass of wine and regaled the group with a few more anecdotes from his family. "I haven't seen Lauren's baby in person yet. She's bringing her to the wedding. They named her Sabina and call her Beanie."

They chuckled at the cute nickname. "That's going to be here before you know it," said Kate, popping a morsel of Ellie's homemade garlic bread in her mouth.

"I'm sure I'll still be here for it," said Mitch, commenting on how much he liked Ellie's bread. "I'm hoping to be more mobile by then."

They chatted throughout the meal. After dinner, Blake and Spence offered to clean up while Ellie shared photos of her dress shopping excursion with Kate. As she scrolled through the photos, Kate oohed and aahed at the shots of the dresses. "I love your selections. It's going to be beautiful."

"I think so. I showed it to Linda and left it up to her to choose the flowers. She's a pro and I know it will be wonderful. I'm working on the cake with the Flaky Baker, talking directly to Milt. I don't want Connie touching my cake."

"She's still a pill, isn't she?" said Kate.

Ellie nodded. "I think Milt's trying to give her the benefit of the doubt, but I got the feeling he's going to replace her. She's too cranky with the customers."

They noticed Mitch struggling to stay awake. "I made cupcakes for dessert, but you look like you need to get to bed," said Ellie.

He nodded. "I think you're right. I'll eat one tomorrow."

"I'm leaving all of them, so eat as many as you like. I hope you heal quickly. When you feel up to it, have Spence bring you out to the winery one day."

He promised to do that and motored up the ramp and into the house. Blake offered to help him with his new nightly rituals and got him into bed. Roxy watched the whole operation from the doorway and followed Blake down the hall to rejoin the others in the kitchen.

"He's tuckered out. I'm sure he was asleep before his head hit the pillow," he said, plucking a cupcake from the tray.

"It was good to see him laughing and smiling," said Kate. "Andi said to watch for signs of depression. It's common in patients who are suddenly immobile and have to rely on others."

"I think getting outside was good for him. We'll have to do more of that," said Spence. He took orders for hot drinks and selected several pods from the variety pack he had purchased to go with Kate's new fancy single server brewer he had bought her for Mother's Day.

They sipped and sampled Ellie's cupcake flavors. Blake promised a fishing expedition as soon as Mitch was feeling up to it. It was after eight o'clock when Ellie said, "We better get going. Gosh, we didn't mean to stay so late. I know you guys must be tired."

Kate wrapped her in a long embrace. "This night was what I needed. I hate the reason you guys are here, but I love visiting. We need to do this more often, when there's no trouble."

Blake wrapped his arm around Kate and kissed her forehead. "I agree. We've been so busy, I've missed our get-togethers. I think the next one is Sam's birthday, right?"

"That's right. The Fourth of July here is magnificent. It's one of the highlights of the summer for me. I'm looking forward to it," said Kate.

Spence and Kate stood on the front steps, thanking them again and waving as Ellie headed to her house and Blake took the route to the harbor. "They're sweet kids," said Kate.

"And she makes the best cupcakes," said Spence, with a wink, hurrying into the house for one more.

Kate changed into her pajamas, debating whether to tell Spence about Maggie's stop by the shop or let the evening end without interruption. She snuggled with him on the couch in front of the television.

She waited for a commercial and shared Maggie's visit with him, telling him what she said to Maggie. He patted her leg. "You talk to her when you're ready. Don't let her guilt you into anything. Mitch is your priority right now, as he should be."

She rested her head against his chest, at ease and sheltered by the man who had always been her champion. She let her eyes close and the stress of the day evaporated as she felt the thud of his heart close to her.

Chapter Eighteen

Kate woke up the next day with a horrible sore throat. She lifted her head off the pillow and it pounded. As she flopped back down, a coughing fit ensued. Spence came through the door, having awoken early. "Hey, you sound horrible."

She croaked out something between a whisper and a growl, "I feel like I got run over by a truck."

"You stay here. I'll fix you some tea and honey."

She didn't have the strength to resist and shut her eyes, hoping more sleep would help. He returned with a steaming mug of tea, with a heavy dose of lemon and honey. She let the steam infiltrate her sinuses and took a gulp.

Spence gave her a concerned look and she nodded. "I can't work," she whispered.

He made sure she was situated with extra pillows, added her soft throw blanket, and tried to shoo Roxy out of the room. She stayed rooted to the end of the bed, watching over Kate. "You rest, I'll call Andi."

This had happened before. Kate powered through a stressful event and then got hit with a horrific cold. After her mother died and the funeral was over, she woke up with similar symptoms and tried to work through it. It worsened and turned into a severe case of strep throat and then scarlet fever. She knew whatever this was, it was from the stress of Mitch's accident and vowed to rest and do her best to heal.

She drank down the tea and curled into her pillows. She woke a couple of hours later to the whisper of her name. Through her half-opened eyes, she saw Max. "Hey there, sorry to wake you. Spence said you're under the weather and wanted me to check on you."

"It's just a bad cold, I think," she whispered.

He went about examining her. "Spence said you've had this happen a few times. We'll do a test and make sure."

He took a swab from her throat and said, "I don't think it's strep, but I'll drop this by the lab and double check." He gathered his bag. "You need to rest for a couple of days and drink lots of fluids. If the lab tells me anything more, I'll call." He gave her shoulder a squeeze. "If you need anything, let us know."

She gave him a weak smile. "Thanks, Max. Linda's got our meals lined up already, so I think we'll be okay." She murmured her thanks as Spence appeared with another mug of tea and a tall glass of water.

She heard Max talking to Mitch as Spence handed her a couple of pills to help with her headache. She swallowed hard and then followed the cold water with a long sip of hot tea.

He turned on the television and tuned it to one of Kate's favorite channels before placing the remote near her hand. "How about some soup?" he asked.

She wrinkled her nose but nodded. "Yeah, that might help my throat."

He made a quick exit and returned with a tray. The soup was delicious and soothed her throat. She finished off the bowl and then hunkered back under the blankets to watch a favorite old movie.

When she woke again it was dark outside and it took her a few minutes to realize she had slept most of the day. She padded down the hall and found Mitch and Spence watching television.

"Hey, Mom. How are you?"

She gave a thumbs up and in a soft voice said, "I'm a little better."

Spence offered to fix her something to eat and she agreed, waiting at the counter for more soup and tea. He coaxed her into a dish of sorbet before she headed back to bed.

She knew from experience she had to stay in bed and let her body rest. She also didn't want to expose Mitch and get him sick. She confined herself to the bedroom and over the next couple of days ventured out only a few times. By Sunday night she was beginning to feel human again.

* * *

Monday Roxy and Kate set out on their usual jaunt to town. Kate's stamina was waning. She felt the impact of the last few days. After the first block, she turned and guided Roxy home. She didn't want to expend all her energy too early in the day.

Instead, she brewed one of her new flavored coffees and took to the patio. The day was ushered in with an impressive sunrise. Although not as breathtaking without the water backdrop, it was still a stunner. Kate swallowed several more sips of coffee, relieved that the pain in her throat was gone. It was the Fourth of July and Sam's party and she was thankful she was feeling better. The shop was closed and she was looking forward to the annual pancake breakfast downtown and the fireworks tonight.

Roxy ate her breakfast and perched on a cushion watching the birds flutter among the flowers. "We've got a party today and you'll get to play with all your friends. What do you think of that?" Roxy's ears twitched and she turned her brown eyes to face Kate.

As the sun continued to rise it illuminated a peaceful blue sky, the color of well-worn jeans, embroidered with a scattering of plump clouds. Kate took a few deep breaths and caught a whiff of rose. Her eyes traveled to Karen's garden and she saw a few new buds among the already bloomed roses. Sam's birthday would be celebrated with the gift of a flawless summer day.

Kate had texted Sam yesterday and asked her to reserve a table on the deck so Mitch could sit and enjoy the view during the morning's festivities. She knew he felt self-conscious being in the scooter and the shelter of the umbrella tables at the deck helped him feel more normal.

She finished her coffee and went about disinfecting everything she had touched over the past few days, changed the sheets, and took a hot shower. Spence helped Mitch get ready and the threesome, joined by Roxy, walked into town. Kate got Mitch situated on the deck and Spence retrieved his pancakes for him. Kate saw Izzy pass by on the sidewalk and waved her over to their table.

She gave a wide smile from under her large hat and joined them. "How are you feeling, Kate?"

"Much better, thanks. I was stuck indoors for a few days, so it feels great to be outside."

Izzy smiled and said, "Oh, good. I was hoping you would rest and take care of yourself." She looked at their plates piled high with breakfast and said, "Oh, that looks great. I decided to venture out on my own this morning, counting on running into someone who knew me."

Kate motioned to a chair. "Join us. Leave your things and go get a plate. We've got a perfect spot for watching the parade."

Izzy pulled her sunglasses down to reveal her eyes. "Are you sure? I don't want to intrude on your time together."

"Of course, we'd love to have you," Kate said, making room at the table.

Izzy took some money from her purse and hurried across the street to the park, where breakfast was being prepared. She returned with her own huge stack of pancakes, bacon, eggs, and fruit. She laughed as she set it on the table. "I can't possibly eat all of this. I told them I wanted small portions."

"I don't think they understand the concept of small. They make a ton of money in extra donations since almost everyone gives more than they charge. I think they're generous with their helpings as a thank you," said Kate.

Mitch finished his plate. "I had no problem finishing mine." He gave Izzy a smile. "I'm going to need to cut back though." He tapped the arms of his scooter. "This contraption doesn't give me any exercise. I used to walk several miles a day at work."

"You'll be back at it before you know it," Spence said, giving Mitch's arm a pat. "Pretty soon you'll be walking Roxy." Hearing her name the dog raised her head and gave Spence a sweet look.

They finished breakfast and visited while they waited for the parade. As the band music began a young woman wearing oversized sunglasses came up behind Izzy and put her mouth close to her ear. Izzy jerked at the surprise and turned to look at the woman. "Mia? What are you doing here?"

The young woman laughed and wrapped her arm around Izzy's shoulders. "I knew I'd surprise you, Mom."

Spence stood and retrieved another chair and scooted around the table, making room. "Have a seat," he gestured to Mia.

"Thank you." She extended her hand before sitting, "I'm Mia, as you probably guessed."

Spence shook her hand. "Spence," he said and motioned to the others. "This is Kate and her son, Mitch."

Izzy's eyes fluttered as she stared at Mia. "I'm sorry. These are my wonderful friends, Mia. I'm surprised you're here."

"Grandma told me where you were and I just arrived this morning on the ferry. I was grabbing a coffee, planning to give you a call when I saw you sitting here."

"It's a big day today. The parade is about to start," said Kate. "If you're hungry they're serving breakfast in the park."

Mia smiled and shook her head. "No, I'm fine, but thanks. I need a coffee." She stood and Izzy followed her inside to the counter.

"Izzy never says much about her daughter. I never even knew her name," said Kate.

Spence nodded, looking at the band approaching. They watched the musicians and clapped along with others as floats went by the crowd. Mia and Izzy returned to the table and took in the rest of the parade.

Kate and Spence stood and whistled at Jeff when the firemen went by. He gave them a huge wave and threw some candy their way. They piled it on the table and offered some to Mia and Izzy.

"This place is busy. I can't believe all the people along the harbor and in the street," said Mia.

"Wait until tonight. The fireworks are spectacular. Jeff, the man on the fire truck, lets us watch from his family's resort a few miles away. They have fireworks right over the water and it's beautiful."

"Sounds cool. Are you going, Mom?"

Izzy nodded. "Oh, yes. Uncle Blake will be there and you can meet his fiancé, Ellie."

The last vehicle in the stream of classic cars passed them by, signaling the end of the parade. The throngs of people along the street began to disperse, making for the local eateries. The crowded tables on the deck emptied and were refilled with new customers toting treats and drinks from Sam's shop.

"I think we'll get home and rest up for Sam's party. I've still got to make a dish," said Kate, standing from her chair and placing a hand on Mitch's shoulder. "Are you ready to head home?"

He gave her a nod. "Sounds good, Mom."

"Lovely to meet you, Mia. I'm sure we'll see you tonight at Sam's party."

They left Izzy explaining who Sam was and that she owned the coffee shop and was married to the volunteer fireman who threw the candy.

When they returned home, Mitch opted for a nap while Kate decided to pick up something from the store, rather than risk any germs in the dish for the party. When she arrived back home she found Spence napping in his recliner with Roxy asleep at his feet.

She smiled at the pair, poured a glass of tea, grabbed a novel she had been reading, and headed out to the patio to enjoy the afternoon.

* * *

Sam's birthday bash consisted of a selection of barbecued food, tons of salads, delicious fresh fruit, and two beautiful birthday cakes baked by Ellie. Despite her career change from baker to event planner at the winery, she hadn't lost her touch. Sam gasped when Ellie unveiled a decadent cheesecake topped with chunky strawberries in a sweet sauce and a four-layer white cake filled with zesty lemon curd and covered in whipped cream.

"These are gorgeous, Ellie," she said, admiring the cakes with the sizzling sparkler candles on top. "I can't wait to taste them."

Ellie cut each of the cakes while Linda and Jen helped pass out plates. While they enjoyed dessert, Sam opened her cards and a few gifts. Kate sat next to Izzy and noticed her glance never wandered far from Mia.

"You seemed quite surprised by Mia today," she said.

Izzy let out a sigh. "She never fails to surprise me." She turned to look at Kate. "We haven't had the best relationship. She took her dad's side in the divorce and I've been persona non grata ever since.

Her being here means she needs something."

"Oh, that's too bad. I'm sorry I've never asked about her. I knew you had a grown daughter, but not much else."

"It's nothing to apologize for." She touched a napkin to her eye. "It's actually difficult for me to discuss. Being a mom is the hardest job I've ever done."

"How about lunch tomorrow? Just the two of us."

Izzy gave Kate a faint smile. "That sounds perfect."

As the sky grew darker, Jeff made the rounds and organized a caravan of vehicles to transport everyone to the Harbor Resort. His brother, Jeremy, was expecting them all on the deck of his cabin for the fireworks.

Getting Mitch to the upper deck wasn't feasible, so Spence and Kate stayed below with him and watched the burst of fireworks from the ground level. The brilliant lights stood out in the night sky, illuminating the beauty of the islands. Mitch grinned with delight as he took in the explosions in the sky reflected in the water below.

The evening culminated in a monstrous display of pyrotechnics that lit up the heavens and caused everyone at the resort to erupt with shouts and applause. Mitch looked up at his mom and said, "All I can say is wow. I hate why I'm here, but I loved being here tonight."

* * *

The following Monday brought with it Mitch's initial visit from a home care specialist. Lydia introduced herself to all three of them and went about assessing her new patient and checking his wrist and leg. Kate offered her iced tea while she tapped notes into her laptop.

She told them she had moved to the island only about a month ago, having worked in Colorado previously. "I worked for the same company and was ready for a change, so when I saw the ad for a therapist here, I jumped on it. I get bored easily, so I like the idea of a new adventure."

She worked with Mitch on some exercises, explaining how much the muscles atrophy when they aren't worked and that when he could start putting weight on his leg, they would do more.

Kate worked in the kitchen and listened to Lydia's happy chatter as she used humor to help Mitch work through the exercises. She heard her tell Mitch goodbye and promised to return to check on him later in the week.

When Spence returned from taking Roxy on her second walk of the morning, Kate gave him a peck on the cheek as she headed out the door. "I made you two some lunch. It's in the fridge. I'll be back later."

She opted to walk to town and secured a table in the back of Soup D'Jour. As she perused the menu, which she knew by heart, her phone buzzed. She read a text from Izzy asking if she would mind getting lunch to go and meeting at Izzy's cottage.

She texted a quick reply and ordered their lunch. While they prepared it she hurried back to the house to pick up the car. Kate's waitress, who was one of her favorites, was kind enough to run the order out to the car since parking was impossible.

Kate secured their lunch and headed for Izzy's new place. She drove through the yard and parked next to Izzy's car. Izzy waved from the deck and helped Kate with the bags. "I'm so sorry to put you to all this trouble." Izzy's eyes were red and ringed with mascara. "It's been a difficult night and morning."

"What's wrong?" Kate moved to the table on the deck.

"Mia. I guess really it's John, my ex-husband."

Kate unboxed their lunches and put them on plates. Izzy poured iced teas and slid into a chair. "Where's Mia now?"

"She's at the winery with Blake."

"So what's going on with your ex-husband?"

Between spoonfuls of soup and bites of sandwiches, Izzy filled Kate in on the latest drama. "I had Mia when I was in my early twenties. It wasn't planned and John and I had to get married because of the pregnancy. Not a good start, as it turns out. We hung together for longer than I thought. Longer than we should have. We divorced when Mia was almost out of high school. She was a daddy's girl all the way."

Kate nodded. "Daughters and their dads have a special bond."

"So I was the bad guy when we got divorced and Mia elected to live with John. He spoiled her and gave into her every whim. She went to college and changed majors dozens of times. She came to see me from time to time, but her visits always seemed to end in heated arguments." Izzy brought her hand to her chest. "I take full responsibility. I should have been softer, but I was trying to prepare her to be independent. I suggested she get a job and earn some money instead of living off her dad and basically partying at his expense."

Kate gritted her teeth. "I'm sure that didn't sit well."

"No, she resented my interference. I told her she could work for my parents, but she didn't want anything to do with that." Izzy shook her head. "She still has no direction or clue. She's here because dear old Daddy has a serious girlfriend now."

"Uh, oh. So now Mia is not the center of his universe, right?"

Izzy nodded. "Not to mention his new bride-to-be is only a year older than Mia. I'm sure Mia feels as if she's been replaced. His new love interest is demanding his attention and his money."

"Ah, not a good situation."

"I called John this morning. From what he is, and isn't, saying, I can tell he's focused only on Barbie." She rolled her eyes. "Yes, her name is Barbie. Anyway, John thinks it high time Mia grows up and is responsible. He's cutting off her endless supply of money."

"What is Mia going to do?"

"Besides run to her mother? I don't think she has a clue. She's talking to Blake about working at the winery, but I'm not sure that's a great idea."

"What do you think Mia should do?"

Izzy sighed, her spoon in mid-air. "I think she needs to finish a degree, get a job, and grow up. She's just shy of thirty years old and still relying on her parents to support her. John pays all her expenses. Her apartment. Her schooling."

"Has she ever had a job?"

"She was a barista on campus. For about two minutes. It interfered with her free time, so she quit. Sometimes I'm embarrassed to say I raised her. She's so far from being independent, it's sad."

"You're disappointed in her?"

Tears fell from Izzy's eyes. She nodded. "You're the last person I should be complaining to about my daughter." She reached across the table for Kate's hand. "I know how much you miss your daughter and would give anything to have her back. This is all petty and stupid. Mia just needs to get her life together."

Kate squeezed her hand. "Because I lost Karen doesn't mean I think everything she did or everything Mia does is right. I agree with you. Mia needs to be self-reliant. You want your daughter to have a better life than you had. You don't want her to ever feel stuck. You want her to succeed and be responsible. You want her to be happy."

Izzy dabbed at her face with a paper napkin as her head bobbed in agreement. "John indulged her too much and didn't make her stand on her own. I was the bad guy for trying to make her be more responsible. Our conversations always end up in a quarrel, so I just withdrew from her life. Mia and I talk occasionally, but not about anything important. Over time, I've learned to steer clear of anything that could result in a conflict."

They nibbled on a few more bites of lunch and took in the scenery. Izzy started to take another spoonful of soup and then put the spoon down. "I'm sure I haven't made it easy for Mia. I've overcompensated for John's lackadaisical style. I've tried to show her by example. I've worked hard, got my law degree, had a successful career, have always been there for my family and helped my parents, but nothing seems to resonate with her."

"Maybe she knows she can't live up to your expectations," said Kate.

Izzy's forehead wrinkled. "What do you mean?"

Kate shrugged. "I don't mean it as a criticism. I'm wondering if perhaps you have shown her too much success and strength? She believes she can't do it so she doesn't try. I'm sure it was easier for her to let John take care of everything. She may have seen you struggle for your independence and took the effortless road and now she doesn't think she can do it."

Izzy's eyebrows rose in thought. "Maybe. She's beyond logic or reasoning right now. I tried to tell her that it's time she grew up regardless of John's situation. She suddenly wants to stay here with me. She hasn't wanted to be around me for more than a few days since the divorce."

"She needs a soft place right now. You're it. You're her security. She knows she's safe with you. Those are good things." Kate's eyes sparkled in the sunlight.

"I suppose. When you say it like that it sounds better." She shook her head and took a sip of her tea. "It's so frustrating. I can see a clear path for her and know what she needs to do."

"It's that age-old problem of knowing what's best for them, but figuring out a way to make it their own idea."

Kate's comments sparked a slow smile. "Blake always says I'm a bit too bossy. I think I'm just an excellent problem solver."

Kate grinned. "What did Mia go to school to do?"

Izzy rolled her eyes. "What didn't she go to school to do? She studied liberal arts, of course. Business, then journalism, then psychology, then marketing." She continued to tick off items on her fingers. "There was some sort of medical assistant or x-ray technician, computer something, you name it. She's been to school at UW when John was living in Seattle and she's studied at UCLA since he's been living down there."

Kate's eyes were wide in disbelief. "Wow, you weren't kidding. She's definitely been exposed to options. I agree she needs to buckle down and choose something."

"She's plenty bright. She's lazy or unfocused or whatever it's called nowadays."

"Maybe Blake will have some luck talking to her."

"I hope so. Something has got to change. Her free ride with John is over and she knows I'm not going to support her without work and school requirements. She's about to figure out the party is definitely over."

"I'm sorry this is so stressful for you. Mitch was my perfect child and Karen had always taken more of my time. Looking back, she was struggling and troubled before she took her life. I didn't realize it in time."

"I'm sorry to even make you think of such things, Kate. I know this is a bump in the road and nothing compared to what you had to go through."

Kate shook her head. "No, don't be sorry. I remember I never had to worry much with Mitch. He's always been responsible and done the right thing. Got a job while he was going to school. Finished school early followed by a lucrative job he likes. I wish he had a girlfriend, but that's about my only complaint. He's a terrific son and man. Karen was much less focused. I didn't realize the extent of her troubles until it was too late."

"I'm afraid Mia's troubles stem from over-indulgent parenting and the lack of her having to be responsible. She's had it much too easy, in my opinion."

"Keep in mind, she's in pain right now. She needs you and your guidance, but from what you said, she'll resist direction from you and probably resent it. Maybe she should stay here for the summer and between you and Blake she'll have a plan in place for finishing school in the fall. If she senses pressure she may withdraw further."

Izzy gathered their dishes and shrugged. "I'm not sure I could take an entire summer with her." She whispered, "I know how that sounds. I'm sorry." She turned around, "I'm not good with drama and right now that's all I'm getting." She moved inside and returned with a bottle of wine and two glasses. "How about we spend the rest of the afternoon enjoying a glass or two?"

Chapter Nineteen

The afternoon spent at Izzy's had been a welcome respite for Kate. She hadn't realized, until she sat and did nothing for several hours, how long it had been since she'd done that—nothing. It felt good to listen to Izzy talk about Mia and her worries. Izzy's situation served as a mental diversion for the thoughts of Maggie that plagued her mind whenever it was idle.

Now that Mitch was on the mend and doing well, her anxiety shifted to the ordeal she had to resolve with Maggie. The thought of another encounter exhausted her. She couldn't bear the idea of listening to Maggie prattle on about how sorry she was for betraying Kate. Not to mention how stupid she felt for not knowing Jack and Maggie had been carrying on with each other.

She had spent the whole day at Izzy's and enjoyed a movie with Mitch and Spence after dinner. Now the house was quiet. Spence had gone to bed early and Mitch was fast asleep in the guest room. Soft snores came from Roxy's bed. Minutes slipped away with each gentle tick of her antique clock. Her mind was reeling with ideas about how to handle Maggie. She had rehearsed conversations in her mind for hours.

She poured the last cup of tea from her stainless steel pot and held the warm cup in her hands. She hadn't heard from Maggie since her last attempted ambush at the store a couple of weeks ago. Kate knew she had to figure out how to forgive Maggie, for her own well-being, but she also knew she couldn't trust her.

She wasn't interested in hearing more about the affair or anything else Maggie had done. Kate made up her mind that her focus would be on moving forward, not revisiting the past. She decided to stop by Maggie's this week and surprise her with a visit of her own.

* * *

Tuesday was Izzy's day at the store and when she arrived Kate descended from her office. "How's it going? How's Mia?"

Izzy rolled her eyes. "Time will tell. Blake convinced her to help out at the winery for the summer." She readied the cash register and counter while she continued to chat. "She's staying with Ellie for the time being. Honestly, that will probably work out better than Mia staying with me. The cottage is too small and she'll have fun with Ellie."

"Oh, Ellie probably enjoys having the company. Mia might be some help to her with the wedding."

"Mia is all over that idea. She's fully immersed in bridal magazines and websites. I warned Ellie that Mia has no concept of what things cost, so she needs to rein her in if she gets out of control. I know Blake and Ellie are trying to keep the costs down."

"It might be a good learning experience for Mia. I don't think Blake will let it get out of hand." They were interrupted by the first of many customers and kept busy straight through the lunch hour.

Regi hollered out a greeting when she came through the door with Emma in a stroller. Izzy was finishing with a customer and Kate was straightening some items in the window. She turned from her work and said, "I'll be a quick minute."

Regi made her way to a settee in the corner and sat down, making sure Emma had a toy in her chubby hand. Kate and Izzy both joined

Regi and perched on nearby chairs. "What brings you two by?" asked Kate, smiling at Emma.

"I needed to run to the store and took a walk around the harbor. Emma likes looking at the activity and watching the boats. I told Maggie I'd keep her overnight tonight. She had her all day yesterday and is worn out."

"She looks like an easy going little gal," said Izzy, letting Emma wrap her fingers around one of hers.

"She's happy most of the time. She can be cranky when she's tired, but she's a good napper."

Kate took a deep breath. "I decided last night I'm going to visit Maggie this week and clear the air."

Regi's eyes widened. "That's terrific. She's been down lately. I think she's depressed."

"I can understand that," said Izzy. "She's in a hopeless situation and has to worry about Emma. Not to mention she's dug herself into a huge hole with you, Kate."

Kate nodded. Regi took out a sippy cup of juice for Emma and said, "She's distraught. And I know she should be and deserves to be after all she's done to you. I know she wants to mend your relationship. She's gone downhill the last few weeks and I think it's her mental state more than anything." Regi kept an eye on Emma and the cup, making sure she hung onto it. "The thing is, I don't know how or if I could forgive her. I'm hoping you're a better person than I am and will find a way."

Tears burned Kate's throat. She swallowed hard and whispered, "Nobody deserves what's happened to her." She grabbed a tissue and said, "I know I can't trust her. I can't believe I was dumb enough to open the door a crack and let her back in my life, only to have her trample on my heart again." She sighed and shook her head. "Actually, Jack is the one who gave the knife a final twist."

"He's got my vote for moron of the century," said Izzy.

"I could think of a few other adjectives for the imbecile," said Regi with a snicker.

Kate laughed and smiled. "I could too." She picked up a tiny stuffed animal Emma dropped. "I've made up my mind I'm done with the past as it relates to Maggie and Jack. When I lost Karen, I learned the hard way that I can't continue to dwell in the past. I have to look at the happiness in my life and the good things, like Spence and Mitch. And all of you here on the island. I have to forgive her for my own sake."

Kate dabbed at her eyes. "But, I don't have to have the same bond with her. I can forgive her and move forward in a different relationship. It can never be like it was. She's suffered more sorrow than I could ever inflict. Not that I want to cause more grief, but I'm not the one who gets to judge her or punish her. That's between her and God."

Regi reached for Kate's hand. "I told you a long time ago, I wished you were my mother. I wish it even more today."

Izzy gave Kate a smile and a wink. "You, my friend, are a wise woman. It takes a lot more strength and courage to forgive someone than to harbor animosity. It's also easier to forget someone than forgive them. I admire your resolve."

"It's actually a bit selfish on my part. I'm not going to waste my energy or happiness on any hatred for Maggie. I'm going to do what I can to help her without being too involved. I'm not sure how it's going to work, but I know in my heart I can't get too close again."

"I know she'll be happy to see you. I think she's given up," said Regi.

"If you want to go over this afternoon, I can handle the shop," offered Izzy. "You can get it over with and enjoy the rest of your week. This hanging over your head only adds to your stress. What you've told us makes perfect sense. I think you're on a roll and need to address her while all your good lines are fresh in your mind."

"That's a good idea. How about we have a bite of lunch and then I'll head over there?"

Regi packed up Emma's things and gave Kate a long hug. "You'll do fine. I hope I'm half the woman you are when I grow up," she said, releasing Kate and wiping her own eyes.

* * *

Kate stood in front of Maggie's door and adjusted her blouse before knocking. She waited several minutes and knocked again, louder. She put her ear to the door and heard footfalls. Maggie opened the door and brought her hand to her mouth. "Katie, oh, please come in."

"How are you doing, Maggie?" She made her way to the living room.

Maggie ran her hands through her short hair and looked down at her baggie sweatpants and wrinkled shirt. "I'm a mess. I've been in bed all day."

"I probably should have called. I'm finally ready to talk."

"It's not a problem. I'm happy you're here, just embarrassed." She motioned Kate to a chair. "Let me change and I'll be right back." She disappeared down the hall before Kate could respond.

Kate took in the décor, which was sparse and consisted of Emma's toys and her playpen for the most part. She was sure Maggie didn't have the energy or inclination to decorate.

Kate was lost in thought when Maggie returned. "I should have offered you something to drink. I'm sorry."

"I'm fine, thanks. I wanted to clear the air, in a sense."

"I've been so upset about Jack's visit with you. You have to know how sorry—"

Kate held up her hand. "Let me stop you right there. I know you're sorry and I'm done rehashing what happened. You and Jack made some really rotten choices. Let's leave it at that. I came to tell you I'm done with all of it. I don't want to hear about our life back in the city when we were neighbors and best friends. I don't want to relive what happened to my daughter. I don't want to listen to you apologize or feel you have to make amends. It was done long ago."

Silent tears streamed down Maggie's face as she nodded. "I understand," she murmured.

"It can't be the same. We can't go back and be best friends. It saddens me to see you ill and I know your sense of loss is immense. I'm focused on moving forward, not backward." Kate smacked her hands on her knees. "So, I'm willing to help you or help with Emma, but it has to be on my terms."

Maggie continued to nod her head. "What does that mean, Katie?"

"I'm not quite sure, but I mostly know what it doesn't mean." She sighed and said, "It means I'll run your errands, make calls for you, go shopping, bring you meals, and babysit if you're in a pinch. It also means I'm not going to let you back into my life. We had lots of fun in the past and many happy memories. When that all shattered into a million pieces you were gone. But you were still in my life." Kate pointed to her head, "You were here for years, even though I didn't realize it. When you came to the island and told me about Kaitlin and your granddaughter and apologized, I was starting to let you back in, but I know I can't."

Kate cleared her throat. "So, that's it. I'm not interested in reminiscing or talking about Jack. I've found happiness again. I'll miss Karen forever and the hole her death left in my heart will always be there, but I have to go on. I'm thankful for Spence and Mitch and the life I have here and you can't become part of that. Not again. Those are my terms."

Maggie stared at Kate. "I'm not sure what to say. I hoped we could go back like we were." She shrugged her shoulders. "I think part of me knew it couldn't ever be the same." She let out a breath and stared out the window. "I accept your terms and thank you for being kind enough to help me."

Kate stood. "That's settled then. Do you need me to do anything? Shopping or errands?"

Maggie shook her head. "No, nothing like that. I need your help with Emma."

"Okay, what can I do?"

"I need to arrange for her adoption now. Before I die."

Chapter Twenty

Blake saw Izzy walk through the door of Harbor Coffee and waved her over to a table. He had pastries and coffee waiting. Izzy slid into the chair and said, "Thanks for meeting me." She took a sip of her latte from the warm cup. "Mmm, that hits the spot."

She gave him a quizzical look. "So, what did you learn from Mia?"

"She's pretty broken up about John's upcoming wedding. She feels like he sort of dumped her for Barbie." He chuckled. "That sounded creepy, but you know what I mean. His attention."

"And money," said Izzy.

"There's that." He ripped off a chunk of his cinnamon roll. "He didn't do her any favors by footing the bill all these years."

"Tell me about it. Is she working hard at the winery?"

He grimaced. "I wouldn't say hard."

"You've got to stay on her. Izzy shook her head. "She needs to learn how to work and budget her money. Not to mention finish her damn degree."

"I know. She's not as mature as she should be. Right now she seems lost. John yanked away his support without any warning. I hate to say it, but she doesn't have the skills to support herself."

"I don't want you supporting her. You don't need to give her work unless you need the help. You're trying to get established yourself."

"I can use her a little, but not full-time. I was thinking Linda always hires people to work at the nursery in the summer. Sam usually has a need for extra help at the coffee shop. Maybe one of them could give her a shot."

"Those are some options. I don't want anyone to feel like they have to hire her." Izzy took another swallow from her cup. "I think she should look for something on her own and see what she lands. If she can't find anything, I'll mention Linda and Sam as options." She took a sip and added, "My vote would be the nursery. Manual labor would do her good."

"You're right. I can keep her busy on the weekend shifts. I'll let her know when I get back, so she can look for more work. She went in with Ellie today."

"Speaking of Ellie. Is she okay with Mia being there?"

"I think Mia's a good distraction for her. Mia is feeling sorry for herself because of her dad's current situation. Ellie faced the brutal rejection by both her parents as a teenager and can offer Mia a unique perspective." He took another bite. "Ellie's happy her dad is coming for the wedding, but she's still disappointed that he hasn't cut the cord to her mom. I'm moving into Ellie's after we're married, so if Mia is going to stay, she'll need to figure out something."

"You two need to concentrate on your wedding plans and building your life. Don't get too wrapped up in Mia's drama. She can be manipulative." She raised her brows over the edge of her cup. "If she'll go back to school we could probably handle living together at my place for a few weeks."

"I'll keep an eye on her," he said.

"Try to nudge her to buckle down and finish school."

He drained his cup and gave her a wink. "Give her a little space, Izzy. Sometimes your advice can feel like a shove." He stood and put his hand on her shoulder, giving it a firm squeeze. "I know you want what's best for her. Let her come to you and seek out your guidance."

Izzy felt her shoulders tighten in defense but then took a long breath. She saw the sincerity and kindness in Blake's eyes and bent her cheek to touch his hand. "I'll do my best, little brother."

He gave her a kiss on top of her head. "That's all any of us can do. Our best. I'll see you later. Ellie wants you to come for dinner one night. She'll call you." He made his way through the crowd forming in front of the counter and gave her a wave.

* * *

Mitch had gotten in the habit of spending a good portion of his afternoons stationed on the deck of Sam's coffee shop with his laptop. He had a couple of video meetings each week with the staff in Olympia. Most days Kate took a break and joined him for coffee or tea. She noticed he took a small delight in listening to his coworkers blather about how pretty the island looked. He even held up the camera to the harbor and let them envy his view.

She watched him from the side of the deck and didn't approach until he had disconnected the call. She slid a frozen smoothie drink in front of him and plopped into the chair. "How's work?"

He chuckled. "I hate to admit this, but I sort of enjoy my new office space."

"There are worse places to recuperate." She let out a sigh.

"What about you? You sound tired."

"Not really tired, concerned, I guess." She had been processing Maggie's latest request and hadn't spoken about it to anyone. Not even Spence.

He patted her hand. "I'm doing okay. Honest. You don't need to worry about me."

She gave him a slow smile. "I'm your mother, so I'll always worry, but it's not you at the moment." She told him about Maggie's quest to find parents for Emma.

"Does she really think you can adopt her?"

Kate shook her head. "No, thank goodness. I'm too old to raise a baby. She's hoping I can help her convince Regi and Nate to adopt Emma."

"Wow. That's a whopper."

She nodded. "I know. I told her I'd ask Izzy to stop in and discuss the legalities of the whole thing. Maggie wants all her money to go to supporting Emma. She's looking for someone who will care for and love her. A family."

"Regi seems like she does that," said Mitch.

Kate took a sip from her smoothie and nodded. "Yes, she's wonderful with her, but adopting Emma would be a lifelong commitment. It's an important decision. Not to mention very personal."

"They hold you in such high regard. I'm sure you could approach them in a way that doesn't make them feel pressured. You're the middle-man, not trying to sway them one way or the other, right?"

Kate wiped a napkin across her lips. "Right. If it would make Regi and Nate happy to have Emma, I would be all for it, but I don't want them to feel browbeaten."

"If they don't adopt her, what will happen?"

"She'll have to go into the system. Nobody in the family will step forward. Maggie's the youngest of her siblings, so they aren't feasible. There are some nieces, nephews, and cousins, but none of them have any interest or even know Emma."

"She seems happy when she's with Regi. I can see why Maggie would think it might work."

Kate gritted her teeth. "Yeah, but like you said, it's a big ask." She took the last sip of her drink. "I don't want to jeopardize my relationship with Regi and Nate. I don't want this to be awkward for us no matter what they decide."

She stood and tossed her cup into the trash. "I better get going. See you tonight at dinner." She squeezed his shoulder and left him to finish his drink.

Kate returned to work and after helping Andi with a few customers slipped upstairs to her office. She was scribbling ideas for the conversation with Regi and Nate on a notepad when Spence and Roxy surprised her.

"You look lost in thought," he said, taking a seat on the sofa.

She removed her reading glasses and sat back in her chair. "I've got something on my mind." She relayed Maggie's request that she facilitate a conversation with Regi and Nate concerning the adoption of Emma.

She rambled on for several minutes, voicing all her concerns, as she had with Mitch. Spence listened without comment and let her enumerate her worries. Andi hollered out that she had closed the register and would lock the door on her way out.

"I understand your apprehension about getting involved, but it might not be as risky as you think. I don't think they'll be totally surprised. They know Maggie is terminal and they've been spending a lot of time with Emma, so it's not out of the blue."

"Hmm. I guess I never thought of that." She sat in contemplation for a few moments. "I'm happy here now. I didn't think I would ever feel this way again. I'm being selfish because I'm worried Maggie could jeopardize my relationship with Regi and Nate. My happiness. My world. She was a significant part of the wrecking ball that destroyed me before, so I'm hesitant to give her another opportunity."

"You, my dear, are not the same person you were. She doesn't have that much power. You're giving her way too much credit. Regi and Nate are not going to hold you responsible for her request. They may actually want to adopt Emma."

"I think I'm afraid they might."

His forehead crinkled in disbelief.

"I know that sounds horrible. Part of me wants Maggie gone." She gasped. "I don't mean dead. Just gone from my life. If Emma is here, she'll be a constant reminder for me."

"Ah, I see." He hesitated and then said, "Somehow you have to reframe how you see Emma. Maybe she could be a reminder of all that was good. I know you enjoyed the years when the kids were young and growing up together. Those were happy moments and they can't be erased because of Maggie, or Jack, or even Karen."

She felt the burn in her eyes and her throat tightened. He gave her his signature grin. "You're amazing and strong, Katie. I've always supported your focus on looking forward. I can see you physically flinch when you dare to let your mind drift into those not so happy memories. You seem to do better not concentrating on the past, but maybe we were wrong. Sometimes you have to go back to move forward. Did you follow up and look into talking with a therapist?"

She gave him a sheepish look. "No, I've been too busy."

He approached her desk and sat on the edge of it, taking her hand in his. "How about I call someone in Seattle and see if we can find a therapist who could do video meetings with you from the city? It might do you some good."

"I hate the idea of it. It makes me feel weak."

"I know you wouldn't judge someone else for seeking help. I've even heard you recommend it."

Her brow furrowed. "I don't think less of anyone for getting help. It's silly, I know."

"What could it hurt, Katie? I can't stand to see you miserable and filled with worry. This thing you have going on when it comes to Mitch is something you've got to solve."

She inhaled. "I know you're right. I'm scared. And embarrassed."

"Let me do some checking and find someone in the city. Nobody will know. You can do it here after hours or at home, whatever works." He stood and called Roxy. "You think about it. I'll have dinner ready when you get home."

She saw the affection in his eyes. Spence always had her welfare in mind. He was her real life white knight. She knew he was right. She would say the same to him, but the fear of delving into the past clung to her like dog hair on her antique velvet settee. It was relentless and never disappeared. She had pushed it away, ignored it, relegated it to the back of her mind, but it was always there.

She walked along the harbor and rested against the stone wall. She swung her legs over and faced the water. She'd begun to think of this refuge as her spot. And Roxy's, of course. Not only did she and Roxy visit on Monday mornings, but she stopped at this point often, listening to the sound of the water against the rocks below. The slow movement of the gentle waves washing up on the shore was hypnotic. She concentrated on the sloshing sound and relaxed. She kicked off her sandals and stretched to dip her toes into the cool water.

She recounted the times she had felt out of control with worry about Mitch. She immersed herself in work or projects to avoid the anxiety that hounded her when she thought too much. She had trained herself to push Karen's suicide deeper inside and confined wallowing to the time near Karen's birthday. She did her best to surround herself with pleasant memories and photos. She avoided reminiscing about Karen in her college years and concentrated on happier childhood days. All the tricks and ploys she employed were exhausting. She was terrified of falling back into the dark abyss that had swallowed her for so many years after Karen's suicide.

Maggie's reappearance and Jack's confession had brought the past bubbling closer to the surface. It was harder to deny. Harder to ignore. Harder to pretend. The thought of seeing Emma or avoiding Regi and Nate because of Emma was generating more anxiety. She hated to admit it, but was happy Mitch was here. Not that he had been hurt, but that he was with her. Having Mitch on the island had relieved the senseless worry she always felt for his safety.

She couldn't begin to count the number of times her heart lurched when he didn't answer his phone or return a text. She didn't worry much when he was at work, but if he was away for the weekend or traveling and didn't respond, her thoughts went to worst case scenarios. She recognized how unhealthy this was, but couldn't seem to control the worry.

She pondered what Spence had said. She knew Spence would give her all the space and time she needed. His patience was legendary. He knew her well enough to know she had to think things through. She didn't like to rush or make snap decisions. What he said today was the most pressure he had ever applied when it came to her anxiety.

She knew if Mitch hadn't been nearby where she knew he was safe, she would have gone over the edge already. The insomnia she experienced near Mother's Day had returned with a vengeance as she struggled with thoughts of Maggie and Emma. If she approached it with logic, she knew she couldn't continue coping as she had been. If Regi and Nate adopted Emma, she would see her often and couldn't live with the constant torment of negative thoughts.

The problem was more profound than Emma. The little girl wasn't the issue. It was far deeper. The sun was getting closer to the horizon and the light had softened. She moved and placed her feet on the flat stone, knees bent, as she let the sun-soaked wall dry her toes. She made up her mind to let Spence make the call and focus on dealing with the past and all it meant.

Chapter Twenty-one

True to his word, Spence connected Kate with a therapist in the city, who came highly recommended. She agreed to video meetings and was willing to work with Kate on a convenient schedule. Her first meeting was scheduled for Monday when the store was closed. Kate elected to use her office, knowing she wouldn't be disturbed.

She tested the software and looked at the view window on her screen, adjusting her hair and shirt. She disconnected and waited for the call, glancing at the clock. She took a sip from the coffee drink she had picked up from Sam's and drummed her fingers on the desktop.

She fiddled with the papers on her desk, straightened them, dusted the picture frames and made sure her cell phone was on vibrate. She heard the telltale sound announcing an incoming video and clicked to connect the call. Dr. Westman introduced herself and came across as organized and caring.

The apprehension Kate had felt all morning began to disappear as she listened and answered questions. Today's initial meeting was a two-hour block and included many questions and a couple of tests she completed online. The doctor was a good listener and after spending time with Kate and evaluating her needs recommended they meet twice a week. She also provided her cell phone number should Kate need to get in touch with her in an emergency.

Dr. Westman explained she would use cognitive therapy as her primary method for Kate's treatment. She outlined the basic principles and promised exercises and tools Kate could use to alter her negative thoughts and behaviors. She agreed that Karen's suicide was something Kate had never fully dealt with or reconciled and it was at the root of her issue. They also discussed Jack and Maggie and Kate's obsession with worry over Mitch. She explained the current predicament with Emma.

The doctor gave Kate some suggestions on her approach with Regi and Nate and they discussed the potential outcomes, likelihoods, and Kate's reactions to those possibilities. Kate's natural tendency to focus on the negative was exposed and through questions and logic, the doctor helped her adjust her thinking.

Dr. Westman recommended some books for Kate to read and they set up a schedule for Mondays and Thursdays. They signed off and Kate was amazed at how fast two hours had passed. She knew it was too soon to credit the therapy, but felt more positive after talking with the doctor.

She hurried down the street to meet Spence for lunch at Big Tony's. She found him at a table in the back of the restaurant. He stood and gave her a quick kiss before she slid into the booth.

Over salads and pizza, she shared the highlights of her first session. Spence smiled and said, "I'm glad you like her and it went well. I didn't expect you to be this enthusiastic."

"I surprised myself." She said, taking a second piece of pizza. "She wants me to consider talking to Regi and Nate about the adoption and explaining my own issues. She thinks they deserve to know the whole story."

"Sounds like wise advice. I thought it might help if Mitch and I joined you and we talked to them together."

Her eyes sparkled with delight. "I would be grateful. I was going to ask you to help me. Dr. Westman said I need to do more of that...asking for help. Mitch would also be a good idea."

They finished lunch and ran into Mitch perched at his usual table on Sam's deck. He was getting ready for a staff call, so they waved hello on their way to the market to shop for dinner groceries.

Spence and Kate spent the afternoon playing with Roxy, taking a walk around the neighborhood, and watching a few episodes of a British detective series. Spence started the grill as soon as Mitch arrived and Kate put together the rest of their dinner.

While they ate, Kate explained about her new adventure in therapy. She didn't disclose her constant worry about Mitch but told him about the idea to talk with Regi and Nate to explain things while asking them to consider adopting Emma.

Mitch agreed to the plan without reservation and Kate put in call to Regi to invite them to a weekend dinner. She also invited Izzy so she could be on hand to explain the legal issues involved with Emma's adoption. That night, for the first time in several weeks, she slept.

* * *

Thursday's appointment was scheduled after the store closed and Dr. Westman discussed Posttraumatic Stress Disorder with Kate. The doctor suspected Kate had been suffering from the disorder since Karen's suicide. Kate had never connected her symptoms to the condition she associated with war veterans. As they dug into the issues Kate realized she had gotten rid of several things associated with Karen's death. Dishes, furniture, and the like. After the call about Karen's death, the sound of her phone ringing had been unbearable. She had insisted all the ringers be turned off. She sold the car she had driven when Karen died, tossed the clothes she had worn when she had to go to the morgue, had never eaten beef stroganoff since the night Karen died, and ditched the perfume she had worn that day. The scent of it all these years later still makes her gag.

Her insomnia, the recurrent memories especially around anniversary dates, the avoidance of items and memories were all hallmarks of the disorder. Kate was shocked when the doctor put all these pieces together.

They discussed strategies with the goal of getting Kate to stop these behaviors. The doctor warned her part of the therapy could be painful because she would be required to retell the story of Karen's suicide several times in an effort to stem her reactions. It was called exposure therapy and sounded horrible to Kate. The doctor said there were other avenues to explore, but she wanted to start with exposure.

After the session ended, Kate was thankful the doctor had recommended scheduling their appointments after hours, so she would not be expected to perform work when she was done. She felt like a dishrag that had been wrung out one too many times.

She grabbed her tote and stopped at the wall along the beach for a few minutes, letting the view soothe her heart and quiet her mind. The next sessions would be hard, but as the doctor explained, necessary to end this cycle of despair she'd embarked on for decades.

She took several deep breaths and shut her eyes, listening to the soft lap of the water against the shore. A soft breeze ruffled her hair and she could hear the call of the birds. She concentrated on what she sensed. The trace of salt in the air, the soft spray of the sea when it hit the rocks below, the distant rumble of a boat engine, the cool stone of the wall, and the hint of warmth from the sun on her arms. She felt her shoulders relax and the tension in her neck eased.

She sat that way for a few minutes, allowing her mind to concentrate only on her surroundings and the calming impact of the space. She took her time getting home, once again focusing on nature. The color of the flowers, the shape of the petals, the many shades of green in the plants that grew along her path. Despite the apprehension and emotions associated with therapy, the tools worked. She was relaxed when she came through the front door. She was greeted with an eager wag of a tail and the delicious aroma of dinner waiting for her on the patio.

* * *

Mitch had been making steady progress with his therapy and was becoming more independent each week. He checked in with a local orthopedic specialist who was in contact with his doctor in Olympia. He thought the wrist was healing quicker than expected and after conferring with Dr. Jamison scheduled the removal of Mitch's cast almost two weeks early.

Mitch was upbeat about the prospect of ditching the scooter and using crutches, as he still could not put weight on the leg. He was scheduled for a checkup in Olympia the week after Blake and Ellie's wedding. Kate was happy to see him healing and doing well but felt a gnaw of dread in the pit of her stomach, knowing he would be leaving soon.

She did her best to focus on the positive, knowing she would be further along in her therapy and perhaps stronger and able to let him go without the usual panic attack that accompanied his departure. For now, she chose to focus on the present and Mitch's excitement in getting his cast removed.

Spence suggested a mini-celebration with dinner at the Jade Garden. Kate met her two favorite guys after work on Saturday. They discussed the menu for tomorrow's dinner party and conversation with Regi and Nate. Spence wanted to grill steaks and Mitch talked Kate into twice baked potatoes.

Spence had already ordered a pie for dessert from Sam and had picked up some bread at the bakery and fresh produce at the farmer's market. The restaurant was busy and as they waited for the waitress to take their order they saw Jeff and Sam come through the door.

Spence waved them over and they made room for the two of them at their table. "You'll be waiting forever. It's a madhouse tonight."

"Are you sure you don't mind us horning in on your evening?" asked Sam.

"Of course not. We're celebrating the news that Mitch gets his wrist cast off next week."

Mitch smiled and said, "Any excuse to eat out, right?"

The harried waitress arrived and took their orders. Sam and Jeff knew the menu by heart so didn't need any time to study and decide. They ordered some appetizers since the kitchen was overloaded and the entrees would take some time.

Jeff engaged Mitch in conversations about Olympia, where he had worked as a firefighter before retiring and moving home to Friday Harbor. They yacked about politics and the best restaurants, with Jeff smiling and reminiscing about his youth and his firemen friends.

"I haven't been back for a visit in several years. I have a lot of good memories from my time there," said Jeff.

"You should come when I have my checkup in a couple of weeks. I'm going to spend the night, maybe two, but will come back here for the rest of my therapy and rehab."

Kate breathed a sigh of relief. She had been hesitant to ask Mitch about his plans but was glad he would be staying. "Spence and I were planning to take him to the appointment, but I'd be happy to stay home if you three boys want to make the trip."

Jeff looked at Sam. "You should go. You'll have fun."

"I've got plenty of room for you guys to stay at my house. The only thing I need to do is stop by work one day, but outside of that, no plans."

Jeff nodded and said, "Okay, I'm in. I'll call a couple of the guys and see if we can arrange to meet."

They spent the rest of the evening laughing and visiting. Kate toyed with the idea of telling Sam and Jeff about the upcoming conversation with Regi and Nate but thought better of it. She knew Sam and Jeff would never say a word, but she felt she owed it to Regi and Nate to let them decide if and when they would discuss the situation.

She had been obsessed with her own fears about the possible adoption, but over the last week had begun to soften to the idea. She knew it would be a significant and tough decision for Regi and Nate. It was a choice that would impact their lives forever.

* * *

Early Sunday morning in the tranquil time before the new light of day dawned, Kate whispered to Spence. "Are you awake?"

He grumbled and mumbled before turning over. "Sort of. What's wrong?"

"I need to tell Mitch about Jack and Maggie. I don't want him to find out some other way. Regi knows so it could slip out in our discussions and I don't want him blindsided."

"Are you sure?"

"Yeah. I talked to the doctor about it and she thought it best to be honest. Mitch isn't a kid and deserves to know the truth. I'm not going to berate the point. I'll tell him I found out and how. He can talk to Jack if he wants more information. I don't want him to think I'm keeping things from him."

He gave her hand a squeeze. "I think that's the right choice. I'll take Roxy for a walk this morning and let you and Mitch hang out here. You can text me when it's okay for me to come home."

She pulled his hand to her lips and kissed it. "Have I told you how much I love you?"

He grinned and slipped his arm around her. "Not nearly enough."

He got ready and ran to town to pick up some breakfast treats from the bakery and when he returned helped Mitch shower. As soon as that chore was over he announced he'd be taking Roxy for a walk and left Kate with a long kiss.

Kate enticed Mitch outside for some fresh squeezed juice and pastries. The morning was postcard worthy. A perfect sky awaited with a few puffy clouds scattered across a cerulean canvas. A gentle breeze carried the perfume of the nearby roses and the faint ring of wind chimes from next door.

She put a plate in front of Mitch and said, "I need to tell you something I found out right before your accident. It's something I've wrestled with sharing, but have concluded you have a right to know."

She took a breath as she placed a croissant on her own plate. "Your dad came to the island and surprised me at the shop."

"Wow, that is news. What was he doing here?"

"He came to see Maggie. He mentioned you had told him how ill she was and he came to say his goodbyes."

He nodded as he chewed on his cinnamon roll. "Yeah, yeah, I did tell him."

"Anyway, while he was here he came to tell me that he and Maggie had an affair after Karen's suicide."

Mitch's forehead creased and he set his fork down. "Oh, Mom. I'm so sorry. I didn't know."

"Me either. He said Maggie thought I knew all along and became distraught when he told her I was essentially clueless about it. She made him promise to tell me. She thought that's why we divorced."

"He's a real piece of work. I know you've gone out of your way to never say anything bad about him. I think I blamed the divorce on Karen, in a way. I thought you guys couldn't deal with her suicide and staying together was too hard. Now that you say it, I do remember Maggie being at the house a lot and talking to Dad when you were in your room."

"I was pretty much out of it after Karen died. I was oblivious to everything. It hit me hard. Not so much your dad, but Maggie. I felt betrayed by her and how she treated me when Karen died. We drifted apart, as you know, and I wrote her off as someone who was out of my life. When she reappeared here on the island and I found out she was sick I started to let her back in."

"Then you found out about the affair?"

She nodded. "Right. And it made it even worse." She fingered her glass. "That's part of what prompted me to start seeing a therapist."

"That's good, Mom. I'm sorry Dad was such a bastard."

She smirked. "Me too."

"It's hard to think of Maggie, your best friend, doing that to you." Tears formed in his mother's eyes. "I'm sorry, Mom. I shouldn't have said that."

"It's okay. It's true. That's the struggle." She used a napkin to wipe her eyes. "I told Regi about the affair and with them being here tonight to discuss the adoption, I thought something might be said about it and didn't want you caught off-guard."

"I'm sorry you've had to go through all this. Losing Karen. The divorce. Maggie. Now the affair. It's a lot to handle and I think you're amazing. You're a wonderful mother and person."

She sniffed and wiped her eyes again. "Aw, you might be giving me too much credit. I struggle a lot. I'm hoping therapy will help me move on and have less anxiety."

He nodded and looked across the yard. "You deserve to be happy. Spence is a good guy, Mom. I'm glad you have him in your life. More than ever now."

She smiled. "I agree."

* * *

Late Sunday afternoon, Regi and Nate arrived with a bottle of wine. They greeted Kate and Spence with hugs. "It's been too long since we've gotten together," said Regi. "I can't believe summer will be over next month. Time flies."

"I know. The older I get, the quicker it seems to go," said Kate, leading them to the patio. "We're grilling steaks tonight."

"Sounds perfect to me," said Nate. He gave Mitch a shoulder squeeze. "How's the leg coming? Can we set up a fishing weekend soon?"

Mitch laughed and Spence tuned into the conversation. "We should pencil a trip in for the end of August. I think Mitch will be able to put some weight on his leg after his visit to Olympia in a couple of weeks."

"We've got the wedding, then Mitch's checkup, so yeah, I think the end of August makes sense," said Nate. "I'll see what we can set up and get in touch with Max and Jeff."

"Blake might not be able to get away until later when the vineyard slows down. I think he's feeling the pressure just to organize a few days away for a honeymoon," said Spence.

"I'll ask him anyway, but he'll probably have to skip this one," said Nate, taking the cold beer Spence offered.

The doorbell rang, announcing Izzy, who also brought wine. Kate embraced her in a hug. "It looks like we'll be well stocked with vino for the evening." She took the bottle and whispered in Izzy's ear, "We may need more depending on how the evening goes."

Izzy gave her a smile and squeezed her hand. "Don't worry. It'll be good to get it out in the open and have the conversation."

Izzy helped Kate in the kitchen while the others made their way outside. Kate placed platters of veggies and crackers and cheese and fruit on the table. Spence poured wine and iced teas and they gathered to snack and visit.

After sipping half a glass of wine, Kate cleared her throat. "Regi and Nate, I actually have something important to discuss with you."

They both gave her wide-eyed looks and then glanced at Spence. "Sounds serious, are you okay?"

Kate released a nervous laugh. "Oh, yes, we're fine. It has to do with Maggie. Emma, actually."

"I know Maggie's declining. I can see it. She's weaker and thinner each day," said Regi.

"I know. Her situation is dire, to say the least. She talked with me a couple of weeks ago and asked me to help her find Emma a home. Maggie knows she's dying and doesn't know how much longer she has, but wants to make sure Emma is adopted and has a family." She paused and looked around the table. "She would like you to consider adopting her."

Nate and Regi looked at each other. "We've become pretty attached to little Emma. She's a sweet child in a tough situation," said Nate.

"We wondered what was going to happen to her when Maggie did pass away but were afraid to broach the subject. We didn't want to cause Maggie any undue stress," said Regi.

Izzy gave Kate a questioning look and she nodded in return. Izzy turned to the couple and said, "I met with Maggie and discussed the financial and legal implications to see if we could figure out the best approach. She's given me permission to share those facts with all of you if you have even the slightest interest in adopting Emma."

Nate gripped Regi's hand. She nodded. "We're listening," he said.

Over the next hour, Izzy outlined the provisions Maggie was making for Emma and her adoptive parents. While she discussed the legalities of adoption, Spence started the grill and Kate and Mitch worked on filling the potatoes and putting them in the oven. They didn't want to eavesdrop or insert themselves into the process, so made sure they kept busy in the house until it looked like the conversation was ending.

Kate added the side dishes to the table and Spence plated the steaks. They sat down to the meal and Kate said, "I need to be honest with both of you. I've been struggling with the reappearance of Maggie in my life. I stored a load of bad memories in a deep dark cupboard and now it's open and stuff is falling out all over the counter. When she asked me to talk to you, it got worse. Maggie is associated with Karen's suicide and lots of other horrible memories, so I was crazy with worry that if you guys adopted Emma I would have a constant reminder. One that I've been trying to bury for twenty years." She took a long drink of water from her glass.

"On the other hand, I didn't want you to feel any obligation to adopt Emma because of my past relationship with Maggie. I don't want to sway your decision either way. I will tell you I'm seeing a therapist to work through these issues and after talking with her, I'm confident I can overcome my anxiety and other issues. In time. I know it will take time. I want you two to do what works for you. Emma is a sweetheart and deserves a bright future. Either with you or someone else."

They passed dishes around the table and Regi said, "We admire you so much, Kate. We would never want to do anything to cause you grief. We know some of the history and how hard this has been on you. I'm sure you're torn. I know how devastated you were to learn about Maggie's affair with Jack. It makes me mad at her too, but I've tried to separate Emma from that."

Kate nodded. "Exactly. I'm trying to do the same."

"We want to talk it over and talk to Molly, of course. This is a big step. We talked about having kids, but at our age, it's not exactly a given. Regi didn't want to go through any extensive medical procedures to have kids, so we discussed adoption as an option, but hadn't decided on anything," said Nate.

"This opportunity sort of fell in our laps," said Regi.

"Sometimes when you don't have a plan, things have a way of working out," said Spence, giving Kate a smile.

Chapter Twenty-two

On the morning of her brother's wedding, Izzy woke to the soft patter of rain. Her eyes fluttered open against the pale glow of dawn and she moaned in disgust. "Oh, rats. Poor Ellie." As soon as she lifted her head from the pillow she plopped it back down again. She should have passed on the last glass of wine at Ellie's bachelorette party last night. She burrowed back into her blankets for more sleep in her quest to dull the nagging ache in her head.

When she woke again the rain had stopped. With slow movements, she rose and smiled. The fogginess was gone and the ache had dissolved into a niggle. As she readied herself for breakfast at Sam's before her salon appointment, she glanced at the couch in the tiny living space. She brewed some coffee and sipped it contemplating her last morning alone. Mia would be joining her tonight and staying until she left for school.

She let out a breath. She loved Mia but knew the next few weeks would test her patience. At least her daughter was saving some money. She was working at the nursery, which was a huge adjustment. The best part of the job was it made her too tired to do anything when she got off work.

Mia had wavered all summer on her decision to finish college. Max had finally been the one to get through to her and used his connections to get her enrolled in the imaging technician program at UW. Her time in school would be short and if she did well she could work at the medical center. At this point, Izzy had little faith and could only hope Mia would follow through this time.

Izzy had been prepared to foot the bill with Mia repaying her when she starting working, but Mia had called her dad and he agreed to indulge her one more time. After prodding from Izzy, he conceded to a work requirement for their daughter. She knew John would cave on it at the first sign of complaint from Mia, but she had scored a minor victory.

She gathered the items she needed in a tote and took one last look at her cozy refuge. She and Mia hadn't lived under the same roof for a long time and when they had the roof had been much bigger than this one.

* * *

All the Griffins had invaded Sam's by the time Izzy arrived. She found Sam in the kitchen manning the oven. "This was so kind of you to host a breakfast for us." Izzy looked around at the groupings on the deck and in the living room. "We would have never fit in a restaurant."

"It's my pleasure," said Sam, taking a gooey cinnamon and nut concoction from the oven. The doorbell rang. "That should be Ellie."

"I'll get it," said Izzy, hurrying to the door.

Ellie introduced her sister, Ceci, and her family along with her dad and Aunt Ginny. No mention was made of her mother or her brother. Sam set up the meal buffet style and marshaled Ellie and Izzy to start the line since they had salon appointments.

Jeff made sure Tim Jr. and Cyndi, Ceci's children, were introduced to Bailey and Zoe. They joined a lawn full of Griffin children to eat their breakfast and play with the dogs.

Blake's family was extensive and loud, so there was no problem with conversation. They did their best to draw Ellie's dad and her sister into the exchange. Blake's sisters harassed him with endless stories from his youth. After Blake's dad finished a story involving a late night covert party Blake hosted at the winery, Shannon asked Ellie's dad if he had an embarrassing story to share.

Ted fiddled with his fork as panic blanketed his face. During the awkward silence, Blake shot Shannon an annoyed look. He had asked his parents to try to keep things light since the situation with Ellie's family was fragile. Shannon lived in her own little world and although she was fanatical about causes like global warming, capitalism, carnivores, the homeless, and anything else she could protest for or against, she was clueless when it came to the feelings of others.

Everyone went out of their way to accept or at least ignore her strange garb. Like today, it included combat boots, bright colored long skirts, some sort of t-shirt emblazoned with a left-wing slogan, or an oversized ratty sweater. Her hair was either a frizzy swarm of braids or wrapped in a haphazard scarf. The contrast with the rest of the family was stark.

Blake's parents were hard-working and had amassed a fair amount of wealth throughout their lives. His other sisters were all dressed in appropriate celebratory attire, fitting for the occasion. Shannon stood out like a weed in an otherwise groomed flowerbed.

Blake cradled Lauren's new baby, Beanie, in his arms and stared at Shannon, willing her to stop yammering on about teenage memories. The color rose in Ellie's cheeks as she eyed her father. He looked down at the table for what seemed like an eternity and then looked across at Shannon.

"I'm ashamed to say I was an awful father to Ellie. She probably doesn't have any happy memories of her time in our household." He turned to look at Aunt Ginny. "My brother and Ginny gave Ellie the only happiness she ever received. She's a wonderful young woman and I'm thankful for their influence. I'll never be able to repay their kindness." He looked down and shook his head. "I don't have one funny story or memory of Ellie as a teen. I missed out on all of that."

He cleared his throat and looked around the table. "I'm so happy Ellie found Blake and all of you. She'll finally have the family she deserves. I can tell by listening to all of you how much you love and care for each other. Ellie didn't get much of that from me or my wife. I'm grateful she'll have it now."

He stood and placed a hand on Ellie's shoulders before bending and kissing the top of her head. "Be happy, sweet girl." He excused himself and went inside the house.

Blake's mom stood. "I'm so sorry, Ellie. I'm sure Shannon didn't mean to bring up bad memories for you or your dad." She looked at Shannon through slanted eyes. "Isn't that right?"

"Oh, yeah. Sorry if I said something wrong." Shannon shrugged and went back to nibbling on a celery stick.

"Mom, Shannon is a forty-year-old woman. You don't need to apologize for her at this point in her life. It would be nice if she would grow up and quit acting like she's some self-absorbed college student." He handed Beanie to Lauren. "Oh, wait, I guess she's not acting."

He turned to Mia and pointed at Shannon, "Pay attention, Mia. This is what happens when you let your parents take care of you and don't stand on your own two feet. You turn into this." He stormed into the house. Ellie scooted out of her chair and followed.

Sam and Jeff gave each other a terrified look. "Can I get anyone some dessert or coffee?" she asked, hoping to smooth over the outburst.

Helen's face went slack and she attempted a quick smile. "I think the wedding has Blake a bit out of sorts. He's been working too hard."

Lauren engaged Ceci in a discussion about her children and chattered about Beanie and how hard it was to be a mother. The rest of the clan followed her lead and peppered Ceci and her husband with questions in a group attempt to distract them from the uncomfortable exchange.

Shannon looked bewildered and stared at the door Blake had gone through before turning to look at her mother. Helen returned her gaze with a disgusted shake of her head.

Blake found Ted sitting in the living room and said, "I'm so sorry. I apologize for my sister. She doesn't think before she speaks."

Ted held up his hand. "Not her fault. It's a normal question. If we had a normal family." He turned his head to Ellie. "I meant what I said. I wasn't a good father. Your mother was…and still is out of control. I didn't have the guts to stand up to her. I took what I thought was the easy road."

He swiped his finger under his eye. "I have no excuse, Ellie. I'm thrilled that you have a happy life now and are marrying someone who loves you so much. I'm sorry your mother isn't a part of all this."

Ellie placed a gentle hand on her dad's shoulder. "What matters is that you're here. It took me a long time to realize Mom will never be a part of my life. She didn't want me and now I don't need her. I won't say it hasn't impacted me." She glanced at Blake. "I'm also not naïve enough to think it won't creep up on me from time to time. Her rejection was devastating. Your failure to come to my rescue almost destroyed me."

Her voice cracked as she continued. "But, I finally understand that I can't let my past define my future. I'd love to have a relationship with you. I'd like you in my world. More than anything. But, I'm not going to be a part of the dysfunction. I can't comprehend your devotion to Mom, but I'm done trying to tell you what you should do. I've told you I think you would be better off moving away, close to Ceci and the kids. You could come visit us here as often as you like. Your life could be happier. You could have friends. Think about it, all your friends avoid you because of Mom."

She moved and sat down. "But, it's your life. You get to choose. I'm done holding onto the hatred I had for her. I'm done blaming you. I'm happy I had Uncle Bob and Aunt Ginny. They showed me nothing but love and taught me how to work hard and be successful. That should have been you and Mom. You missed out. Now you have a choice to make. I'll always love you, Dad, but I'm done with the roller coaster. I'm going to make a life here with Blake. Someday we'll probably have kids of our own and I'd like you to be part of their lives. I'd like you to spend time with us, but it's up to you."

Tears stained her dad's cheeks. He reached out and patted her hand. "You're a good girl, Ellie. I'm not sure why I put up with your Mom. I felt sorry for her and always tried to make her happy. She convinced me getting you out of the house would solve all our problems. I have no excuse, but that's as close as I can get to an explanation. I think she became a duty and obligation for me. I should have never given in to her. Ceci hasn't said much. She hates to do anything against your mom. Tim and I have been talking. He found a small place for me close to them and said he could use me as a volunteer at his school." He let out a long breath. "I'm ashamed to say this, but I'm afraid. Afraid of change and your mother's reaction."

"That's her superpower. She's a master manipulator and controls you knowing you fear her outbursts or threats of suicide or whatever crazy antics she comes up with. She probably needs professional help, but I'm sure she won't get it."

He nodded. "And what she's done to Teddy is horrible. He's totally dependent upon her and nothing I've tried has worked to get him to be productive."

"It's not a healthy way to live. For any of you," she said. Blake sat beside Ellie and put his arm around her shoulder. "I'm living proof change can be a good thing." She smiled and took his hand in hers. "I've got to get going to my appointment."

Sorrow still lingered in Ted's eyes, but he smiled at his daughter. "You have a good time. I'll see you at the church." He squeezed her hand.

She gave Blake a quick kiss and hurried to collect Izzy and get to Jen's for their makeovers.

Blake stood when he saw Izzy. He sauntered over to her as she was gathering her things. "Sorry, Izz. I shouldn't have said what I said out there. How are they?"

Izzy laughed and said, "They'll survive. I didn't know you had it in you. Mia looked like the proverbial deer in the headlights after you stormed off. I don't think Shannon noticed the insult. Mom and Dad are mortified and Jeff and Sam are busy trying to pretend nothing happened."

He shook his head. "Shannon just ticks me off. She's a giant mooch and does nothing to contribute. She spouts off constantly how business is evil but has no problem letting Mom and Dad support her. All she does is wander through life, from cause to cause, protest to protest. How does that happen? We all work hard and she's oblivious."

She put up her hand. "I know. I've had the same conversation with Mom and Dad." She gave him a wink. "Not exactly the same words you used, but trying to make the same points. I've used Mia as an example. They're too easy on Shannon. They never had to do much to encourage the rest of us to work. We followed in their footsteps, but my baby sister…marches to her own beat."

"I'll apologize," he said, looking down at the floor.

"Mom wrote it off to wedding stress." She gave him a hug. "Don't be too hard on yourself. This should be the happiest day of your life. Take a breath and relax. We'll see you at the winery."

He gave Ellie a kiss goodbye and went back to the living room. "I'm going to go back out there and face the music," he said to Ellie's dad. "Wanna join me?"

Ted gave him a slow grin and followed him outside to the deck.

* * *

By the time the wedding preparations began, all hints of strife within the family had disappeared. Blake had apologized and the whole conversation was forgotten. He put it out of his mind and went about getting ready for the ceremony. Linda had been working all morning readying the chapel and the barn. Blake poked his head into the barn and saw she had transformed it into a wonderland of twinkling lights, candles, and flowers.

She used wine barrels stuffed with casual flowers throughout the venue. The tabletops held rustic arrangements in simple glass jars. Hints of plum and lavender accented the otherwise mostly white décor.

The casual tiered cake complimented the wedding colors and featured an ombre ruffled frosting in shades of plum. There were also trays of wedding cupcakes and brownies scattered throughout the barn for easy snacking. Lou was setting up a buffet of heavy appetizers and side dishes for the guests and Jeff's favorite band members were arranging themselves on the small stage area.

Blake knew Ellie would be pleased and hopped in the golf cart to check the chapel before returning to change into his tux. He found Linda loading her van. "Hey, the barn looks terrific," he hollered.

"Thanks, I think Ellie will like it. I just finished up here and am heading home to change."

He helped her load the last of her totes and waved goodbye before he stepped inside. The space was small, so there wasn't room for elaborate decorations, but Linda had managed to turn it into a romantic setting. With a few simple ribbons and flowers, it created the perfect backdrop for the ceremony. The scent of fresh lavender mingled with the soft scent of roses. Blake took one more look and locked the doors.

He knew Linda would do a great job, but had promised Ellie he would check on things, so she wouldn't have to worry. He checked his watch and eased his foot off the pedal. He had strict orders to stay away from the barn until after Ellie was due to arrive and would be hidden in the bride's room.

He detoured to the vineyard and gazed over the acreage. He had worked nonstop over the last couple of months to make sure everything was in order and done so they could squeeze in a quick honeymoon. The morning showers had given way to a lovely sunny day. He was looking forward to seeing Ellie in her gown and dancing with her for the first time as her husband.

He breathed in the fresh air, sensing the earthy dampness from the earlier rain and shut his eyes. He had finally found everything he had been searching for—a woman he loved, a business he enjoyed, on an island he hoped he'd never leave.

* * *

The ceremony went off without a hitch. Ellie watched as Izzy walked down the aisle in her shimmering elegant dress the color of the dark lilacs accenting her bouquet. Ellie felt her heart hammering in her chest as she listened to the soft notes from the pianist and cellist playing "A Thousand Years" and watched Izzy kiss Blake on his cheek before taking her place.

Ellie focused on Blake and saw his eyes widen when he caught his first glimpse of her on her dad's arm. She waited for the right note in the song and took her first step down the aisle. Ellie's new healthy eating regime had shaved off the pounds and her gown showcased her trim waist. The beaded and embroidered slip gown featured a dramatic V-neck in the front and back and shimmered in the soft lights of the chapel. She carried a gorgeous bouquet of white and soft purples dominated by peonies and, hydrangeas. The fresh scent of lily of the valley wafted behind her as she passed Aunt Ginny and gave her a grin.

Before she knew it the vows had been said, rings exchanged, and Ellie felt Blake's lips upon hers for the first of what she knew would be many kisses as husband and wife. They exited the chapel to the applause of their guests and circled around the building.

After photos in the chapel, Blake whisked Ellie away to the barn in a golf cart adorned with ribbons and flowers. Ellie gasped when Blake led her through the doors. The twinkle in her eyes conveyed her happiness as he led her to their first dance as husband and wife.

They visited, nibbled on plates of goodies from Lou, danced, and laughed into the evening. With only a few guests left, Ellie joined Ceci and her dad at their table. Ceci reached for Ellie's hand. "This was so wonderful. You have a fabulous group of friends and Blake is perfect. I'm so glad you included us in your special day."

"I'm happy you and Tim came. It means a lot to me." Ellie surveyed the room, sparkling with lights and the glow of candles. "It was the best day."

Ted cleared his throat and held onto his glass. "I've been talking to Ceci and Tim and have decided to move. I've been thinking about what you've said. I don't want to spend the years I have left in misery. I've felt so much better these last few days away from your mom and with all of you."

Ellie's eyes blinked to stem the threat of tears and she gripped his hand in hers. "That makes this day perfect."

Chapter Twenty-three

Kate worked the next few days so Izzy could cover the winery while Ellie and Blake took a short honeymoon on Vancouver Island. Everyone had pitched in and treated them to a getaway at the fabulous Gatsby Mansion in Victoria. Linda and Max had given them plenty of must-see spots and advice from their trip to the area.

Mitch had his follow-up appointment this week, so Kate would be on her own for a few days. Regi had invited her to dinner Friday night and she kept busy at the store and running errands for Maggie.

She hadn't been by Maggie's for several days and was shocked when she arrived Thursday night after her appointment, with groceries and dinner. Maggie was in bed, bundled in blankets, despite the warm weather. She looked small and fragile. Her skin was almost gray and when Kate helped her sit up in bed to eat, she noticed how thin she had become. Her arms looked like little more than a skeleton and she was beyond weak.

Regi and Nate were keeping Emma for the night, as Maggie wasn't up to caring for her. Megan would be coming to spend the day at the house tomorrow. She was good about doing housework while she took care of Emma and it gave Maggie an opportunity to play with her granddaughter without having to worry if she got tired and needed to rest.

Kate couldn't bear to watch Maggie's shaky hands try to guide the spoon into her mouth. "Let me do that for you," she offered.

Maggie rested her head on the stack of pillows behind her as tears streamed down her face. "Thank you, Katie."

"It's okay. I know it's hard for you to do."

She nodded and took a spoonful of her favorite soup. "I meant for everything. Regi said they're seriously considering adopting Emma. I'm so grateful."

Kate continued to deliver spoonfuls of soup. "I didn't do much. They're quite taken with little Emma."

Maggie wrapped her thin fingers around Kate's wrist. "I don't deserve your kindness, but I'm so thankful for it."

Kate's throat burned with grief. "You don't deserve what's happening to you, Maggie."

"If they do decide to take her, I hope you'll always be a part of her life. Maybe you could tell her stories about me when we were younger. The good stuff. Before I messed it up."

Kate nodded through her tears. "I will."

"You could do fun things with her and spoil her for me."

"I could do that," she said with a smile.

"Regi tells me her mother is not a part of her life, but I understand Nate's mother was the woman who was working at your shop, Lulu.

"That's right. She's a wonderful woman. She'd be a terrific grandma to Emma."

"She'll need another one. A girl can never have too many grandmas. I'd be honored if you stood in for me."

Kate smiled and gave Maggie's hand a gentle squeeze. "It would be my privilege."

* * *

Kate started Friday with a quick stop at Linda's and picked up some fresh cut flowers. She used her key and let herself into Maggie's and put the flowers in a vase and brewed Maggie a cup of green tea.

She carried it into the bedroom and found Maggie sitting up watching television. "You look better this morning," said Kate, placing the tea in her hands and depositing the flowers on her nightstand.

"I feel pretty good today. I think that soup is magic." She took a slow sip from the cup. "Mmm, that's perfect."

"I wanted to check on you and thought you would enjoy the flowers." She glanced at her watch. "Megan should be here in a few minutes and I've got to get to work."

Maggie admired the vase and the variety of pink and white flowers. "Thanks, they're lovely."

"Do you need anything else?"

She shook her head. "No, I'll probably have a snack with Emma. Thanks again, Katie."

"See you this weekend." She waved and headed for work.

She knew Andi would be at work and open the shop, so she stopped to pick up coffees for both of them. She found Andi ringing up a sale when she arrived. It was a sign of things to come.

The day was a flurry of activity and sales. She locked up the shop and headed home to pick up Roxy. They had been invited to a dinner party at Regi and Nate's. She fed Roxy and was thankful she didn't have to worry about cooking a meal after her long day.

They arrived and found the gang stationed on the patio, visiting and snacking. Blake and Ellie passed around a photo book from their time on Vancouver Island. It had been a short trip, but they had captured the beauty of the area. When dinner was ready everyone gathered around the table. Once they were seated, Nate gave a loud whistle and the chatter stopped.

"We asked you here tonight to tell you some exciting news. As you know we've been asked to adopt Emma and have been working through that decision over the past week. Molly is still in Italy with her dad and we've video chatted with her this past week. Regi and I wanted to make sure she'd be okay with the idea of a new baby sister. She assured us she was more than okay. We told her Emma's story and she agreed Emma would make a great addition to our household. My parents are over the moon with the idea of a grandchild they can spoil right here on the island. Regi and I are nervous, but we've come to love little Emma."

Regi gripped Nate's hand and smiled at him before she spoke. "Nate and I know there will be challenges. We had considered adopting before, in a casual conversation. Now that we've become attached to Emma and know her situation, we feel we've been put together for a reason. We couldn't be happier and Molly can't wait to meet her. She'll be here for Thanksgiving. So, with all of our love, including yours, we've decided to welcome Emma as our daughter."

Loud shouts and hoots erupted from the group of friends. Regi added, "We want to acknowledge Kate in all of this. We all know she's been through more than any of us can imagine and admire her strength. We especially thank her for introducing us to this sweet baby girl. The circumstances around this are so sad, but like Kate told us, Emma deserves a bright future and a happy life and we know we can deliver. We're counting on all of you to help us fill Emma's world with love."

Now everyone was near tears. Max stood and delivered one of his signature toasts, congratulating the newlyweds, celebrating the new addition in Nate and Regi's life, and committing the group to helping them as they navigate their new parental responsibilities.

Kate dabbed at her eyes as she was sandwiched between Nate and Regi with kisses planted on both cheeks. "I'm so happy for you," she said. "I've got to call Spence and let him know."

Nate grinned. "We put in a call to him right before you all arrived tonight. We wanted him and Jeff to know, along with Mitch."

"We swore them to secrecy," said Regi.

Izzy was sitting next to Kate and as they passed platters of food around the table, she leaned over and whispered, "Are you okay?"

Kate smiled through the last of her lingering tears. "I'm fine. Just a bit emotional."

Izzy gave her hand a squeeze. "You did the right thing. It's going to be okay."

Kate looked at Nate and Regi basking in the congratulatory hugs and said, "They are going to be wonderful parents."

* * *

Saturday after work Kate put in a dinner order and made her way to the harbor wall. She used the time to reflect on her week. Thursday's therapy appointment had been grueling. She had been retelling the story of Karen's suicide over and over. So many things she had stuffed away had been resurfacing as she related the narrative.

They had been eating dinner—beef stroganoff— when she got the call. The university called and said there had been an incident and Karen had been taken to the hospital. When they got to the hospital, the police were there and informed her Karen had died as a result of hanging herself in her dorm room. One of her suitemates had discovered her and reported it to the university.

When Kate retold the story, she felt the same fear she experienced standing in the hallway of the hospital wick up her body. She answered countless questions about Karen, her state of mind, when she had last spoken with her, what medications she took, and on and on. It was all a blur for the most part, but Dr. Westman made her dig deep and recount the hours and days after Karen's death.

Karen had talked to Kate several days before her death and told her mother she was thinking about dropping out of school. Kate had encouraged Karen to stay with it and suggested her feelings were due to the high-pressure time with finals coming up and lots of deadlines. She had written off her daughter's distress to the tension of school.

Karen had never threatened to harm herself. After her death, they found out she had been seeing someone and he had broken off the relationship. She never mentioned she had even been dating. When they learned more they discovered he was someone who might not have gained their approval. He was what Kate would have called a stoner. From talking to Karen's suitemates they learned she had been smoking marijuana with this guy and ditching classes to spend time with him. Karen had a secret life she never shared with her parents.

When the toxicology results came back months later, they showed drugs in Karen's system and a history of marijuana use. She also had alcohol in her system. The police said it was common for suicide victims to bolster themselves with drugs or alcohol before taking their life.

Jack, and then Maggie, suggested Kate should have known something was wrong with Karen when she said she wanted to drop out of school. That had thrown Kate into an even deeper depression. She had trudged through the funeral and the questions and then hidden in her bedroom for as many hours a day as possible.

When she wasn't weeping, she slept, getting up only long enough to make sure Mitch was ready for school and fed. The guilt and doubt nagged at her every waking hour. She began to think she was responsible for Karen's death.

Karen had not left a note, so there was no way to know what she had been thinking. The only thing Kate knew was that her baby girl had thought there was no solution. No better way. No help for her. It tortured her to think Karen didn't reach out to her for help.

Karen tended to be rebellious. She tested rules and always

pushed. Mitch had always been more obedient and after Karen's death was downright angelic. After watching his mother fall apart before his eyes, she guessed he didn't want to be responsible for her total implosion if something bad happened to him. He was right.

Spence had been the one constant visitor in her life after Karen's suicide. He stopped by often and brought her treats or things to eat in an effort to lure her from the dark hole in which she was living. He talked to the detectives on Karen's case and shared all the information with her. He never gave up and was the first person to elicit a smile from Kate in the months that followed that horrible night.

Despite the warm temperature, she shivered as she recalled the night her life changed forever. She let her eyes close and her mind focus on the gentle slap of the water against the beach. She took deep breaths and timed them to the slow rhythm of the tide sloshing in and then out again to the sea.

She focused on the sounds and smells around her. Her stomach rumbled when she caught a hint of dinner being served in the restaurants behind her. She opened her eyes and let the sight of the sun, tonight aglow with crimson and violet bands, distract her. Nature's presentations at the end of the day never disappointed and tonight's was magnificent.

She maneuvered from her seat and stood, taking one more deep breath before making her way back to the street to retrieve her order. Roxy met her at the door with an enthusiastic waggle and they ate their dinner together.

With the thoughts of Karen fresh in her mind, she didn't expect to slide into sleep, but she did. Maybe the therapy was working.

* * *

Mitch's appointment had gone well and the doctor gave him the go-ahead to start putting weight on his leg. He was outfitted with a cane, which he preferred to the crutches and greeted Kate with a huge smile when he returned on Sunday.

She had made some of his favorites for dinner and they sat down to roasted chicken, mashed potatoes and gravy, fruit salad, and fresh made rolls from the bakery. Spence and Mitch entertained her with stories from their visit with Jeff's firemen friends.

Mitch took another roll and said, "I'm going to ramp up my physical therapy now. The doctor said I should see a lot of progress in the next two or three weeks. He thinks I can be back to work by Octoberish."

She saw the excitement in his eyes and the panic she always felt when she contemplated him leaving wasn't near as strong. "That's wonderful news. I know you're anxious to get back to work."

"It hasn't been as bad as I thought. You guys have made it almost easy. Rich has been great about work. All in all, it could have been much worse."

Spence took another helping of potatoes and said, "Have you talked to Maggie since Regi and Nate's announcement?"

"No, I'll probably stop by tomorrow. I know Izzy is already working with a social worker to do the required home inspection and study report. She, of course, sees no barriers to getting Regi and Nate approved. I didn't realize that had to occur in a private adoption."

"If she uses a private social worker, it will be quick. The state system is overloaded and takes forever," said Mitch.

"That's what Izzy said. She's got everything ready, as far as paperwork. Maggie is relinquishing her rights. There's no known birth father. That research was done when Frank and Maggie adopted Emma."

Spence reached for another roll. "From what I overheard when they were here with us, Maggie has quite a bit of money set aside for

Emma and then the balance of her estate will go to the trust for Emma. Emma will have all she needs, from the sound of it."

Kate nodded. "Izzy said the financial part of the legal work is done. When Maggie dies, her estate will pass to Emma's trust. She said Maggie would like me to be the trustee. Izzy said it's best to have someone other than the adoptive parents, to keep the court happy."

"How do you feel about that?" asked Spence. "It means you'll be involved in Emma's life for as long you live."

Kate gave him a slight smile and nodded. "I think that's some of why Maggie asked that I do it. She and I talked and she asked me to be a stand-in for her in Emma's life. I told her I would. I know how much she loves the little girl."

Mitch reached for his mother's hand. "I think that will be good. For both of you."

She gripped his hand in hers. "And when I pass on, if it's before Emma is twenty-one, the job will go to you."

Mitch gulped on his sip of water. "Uh, okay. I can live with that. I think you'll still be around though." He gave her a grin.

"Izzy structured it so that I can relinquish the duties to you at any time I don't feel I can manage it. I'll be eighty, you know?"

"I'm not worried."

Chapter Twenty-four

After her therapy appointment in the morning, Kate decompressed by taking Roxy for a walk. The retelling of Karen's suicide felt like punishment, but she had to admit it was getting less daunting. She didn't have as harsh a reaction as she had the first time. The uncontrollable sobbing and exhaustion had stopped. There were still a few tears, but not the visceral response of the past.

Dr. Westman was pleased with her progress and always asked her questions about her habits, sleep, and thoughts since the last session. She had been sleeping better and felt more rested. When she reflected on her thought patterns, she noticed a change. The negative ideas had eased. She was still sad at the loss of Karen. She knew she always would be and Dr. Westman reminded her of the goal. It wasn't for Kate to forget Karen or the pain of her death, but to react in a different and healthier way.

The real test would come when Mitch left. She wasn't feeling as strong in that regard but was working to create positive thoughts and images in her mind, rather than negative and scary ones. They touched on Maggie and Jack during today's session. Kate had resigned herself to Jack's betrayal and his actions when he came to the island sealed the deal for her. He wasn't worth her time or energy. Her opinion of him hadn't changed and she felt almost nothing when she discussed him.

Maggie, on the other hand, was more problematic. Dr. Westman explained that the affair was a new betrayal. A fresh discovery. Kate would need time to process it, not to mention the sympathy Maggie evoked. Kate used a bit of humor at the end of their appointment and told Dr. Westman she was a therapist's dream with an unlimited supply of neuroses and issues.

After returning Roxy to the house, she picked up lunch and went to Maggie's. She was the most upbeat Kate had seen her since she'd arrived on the island. She was relieved and overjoyed at the idea of Regi and Nate adopting Emma.

Maggie explained she had decided it was best for Emma to stay with Regi and Nate full-time. They would bring her over for visits, but Maggie wanted to make the transition as easy as possible for her granddaughter. She wanted to help cement the bond between the three of them, knowing Emma would suffer less if she was secure when Maggie died.

Kate guided her outside for tea and a stint in the fresh air and sunshine. "I don't have the words to convey my thanks to you, Katie. I can't explain the comfort it brings me."

"You don't need to keep thanking me. I'm sure you would do the same for me."

"I can't get over how much you've helped me. I'm amazed you've been able to put aside the past. I'm not sure I would be so generous."

"It's okay. I told you I would help and Emma is worthy of my efforts. Regi and Nate are thrilled with the idea. It was a wonderful solution for them and for sweet Emma."

A tear plopped onto Maggie's shirt. "I'm going to miss her more than ever." She took a breath. "I'm trying to convince myself it will be okay and I'll get to see Kaitlin. I'm looking forward to that. But that idea is a tad murky to me, while Emma is right here and I can't bear the thought of leaving her."

"I'm not sure I have any advice for you, except to tell you I know you've done all you can to provide for Emma. I'm sure she'll miss you and as she gets older she'll have questions about you and her mother. I'm certain she will have a wonderful childhood and life with Regi and Nate. They're going to give her enough love to make up for the loss of you and Kaitlin. It could be so much worse if you were unsure about her future."

Maggie nodded with enthusiasm. "Oh, believe me, I know. I tell myself that and it helps calm my fears. I'm not worried about Emma. I know she'll be loved and have everything she needs. I'm being selfish now. It's me that will miss her." She used a tissue to wipe her eyes. "Goodbyes aren't easy."

"I'm not sure which is harder, saying goodbye or not getting the opportunity. I've always thought it would have been easier if I could have told Karen goodbye instead of her just disappearing."

"I felt that way when Kaitlin died. My whole world stopped in an instant. She was there and then she wasn't. I felt cheated."

Kate nodded. "Exactly. My world stopped spinning. I remember thinking how can everything just keep going. People told me they were sorry, and I know they were, but they kept going and moving. I was stuck."

Maggie reached for Kate's hand and said, "It's a club nobody should have to join."

They sat for a few minutes and finished their tea, absorbed in their own thoughts. Kate gathered the glasses and then helped Maggie inside and got her settled in the recliner. Maggie asked her to go through some old photos and scrapbooks. She wanted to make sure they were saved for Emma.

Kate sat on the floor and pawed through stacks of photos and school memories and passed them to Maggie. They laughed and cried over photos, depicting them through the years, as new neighbors, young mothers, and then with teenagers. It was like a time capsule, preserving the memories and showcasing the transformation of Karen, Mitch, and Kaitlin from babies to high school graduates. The most recent photos showed Karen and Kaitlin heading off to college. Kate picked up a photo from the bottom of the box.

"Oh, I love this one of the girls." Kate held up the picture of Kaitlin and Karen, all smiles, their arms wrapped around each other. "What cuties."

Maggie caressed the photo and smiled. "I remember that day like it was yesterday. They were playing in the backyard and begged me to take their picture." She looked at her old friend. "I would never have dreamed we'd be sitting here and they'd both be gone."

Kate didn't trust her voice and whispered, "Me either."

Kate straightened the piles they had been viewing and stacked them on the table. She made sure the dishes were done and things were tidied. She noticed Maggie fading as the day wore on and helped her into the bed for a nap, promising to return later in the week to help her with other projects in the house.

As soon as Maggie was asleep, Kate left her a note for reheating the leftovers for dinner and slipped from the house.

* * *

Mitch's increase in therapy was causing him some discomfort, which led to irritability. He was working with the therapist three times a week and after her visits, his crankiness increased. He refused to take prescription pain pills and opted to work through it, using ice or over the counter pain relievers. He was determined to get his leg in shape.

Max distracted him with a golfing excursion and Roxy was the recipient of several walks each day as Mitch worked to increase his stamina. On one such trip, he stopped by the store and Mitch handed Kate a large wrapped parcel.

She gave him a wide grin and said, "What's this?"

"A little surprise. I know I've been a bear lately and wanted to give you a peace offering. I'm also treating you and Spence to dinner tonight at Lou's."

"Wow," she said, removing the ribbon from the gift. She tore open the paper and saw it was the caricature Mitch had bought on Lopez Island. He had it matted and framed for her.

"Ah, I love this. I intended to get it framed myself. That was a great day." She gave him a hug.

"I had them frame mine at the same time."

"Well, I love it."

"Do you feel like getting a drink at Sam's?"

She gestured to Andi, who was helping a woman at the counter and they made their way to the deck of the coffee shop, where Spence was already seated. She treated them to frozen drinks and sat down to enjoy the view.

"Anything new at work?" Spence asked.

"I visited with Izzy today. She and Mia are surviving without too many issues. I could tell Izzy will be glad when Mia heads to the university. It's only a couple of weeks away."

"Mia seems like a sweet girl. A bit naïve and spoiled," he said.

"Izzy thinks, and I agree, she needs to apply herself, get serious, and grow up. She is so hopeful that this career path will work for Mia. Max seems to think Mia is serious about this and Izzy thinks she might stick with it because of Max's efforts. She keeps telling Mia how Max has put his reputation on the line to get her in and used his connections to secure her a position upon graduation. He insists it isn't as dire as all that since many times students don't finish and it's not the fault of their sponsor."

"A little extra pressure might do the trick," said Spence.

"That's the idea. Izzy is trying to decide if she should go with her when she leaves for college."

"Does Mia want her to go?"

Kate wrinkled her forehead. "I don't think so. I told Izzy to let her know she's happy to help her but to let Mia decide. She's almost thirty, I think she can handle it. Izzy wants her to grow up, so she might as well start with this."

"Did she seem receptive?"

Kate nodded, "I think so. She also doesn't want to leave me or Blake in a bind by leaving. They've got a lot of work to do at the winery to get ready for the harvest and I think the honeymoon put them behind."

"If she's worried, tell her I'll travel over with her and make sure she gets to where she's going. I can always use the excuse of checking on a case, so it wouldn't look like I was a chaperone."

"That's a good idea. That would ease Izzy's mind. I think part of her is afraid she won't actually go."

"Izzy did report that the home study for Regi and Nate is done and approved. They passed with flying colors and now the court needs to approve the adoption and then it'll be a done deal."

"I'm sure Maggie will be relieved," said Mitch.

"Yeah, she's getting weaker each time I see her. I think she's going to need a caregiver full-time before long. She doesn't want to go into the hospital or any type of care center."

"It's sad to see her like this. She's so different from when we were growing up."

"I know. As angry as I've been with her in the past, watching her decline and fade away sort of puts all of that in perspective."

"Is anyone in her family coming to see her?"

Kate shook her head. "She's got two brothers still alive, but they're in their seventies. She's never been especially close to them. They both live across the country. She's talked to them, but they have no plans to come."

"So, she's all alone?"

"Pretty much. I think she alienated all of her friends after Kaitlin passed away. Her whole focus has been Emma and with Frank gone, there's nobody. After they divorced his family didn't have anything more to do with her."

"Wow, that's harsh."

"I know. It makes me truly appreciate you." She glanced at her oldest friend and the man she adored. "And Spence."

"Not to mention all your friends here. I think you have more friends here than you ever did back in the city."

"Oh, yeah. I've never had the close relationships I've been lucky enough to find here. It's a huge comfort to know I can count on them and they can count on me. We've helped each other through all sorts of things, from moving furniture to holding the hand of a friend who lost someone."

"That's interesting. I have friends, mostly work related. We do things together, but when I think of who would be there for me in a tough situation, it's scary. I'm not sure I've done my best to cultivate a group of people like you have here. I'm always working."

"Maggie is a good cautionary tale. A reminder of what's important. Life is easier when you're not alone. As you get older, work will become less significant. Many times our identities are wrapped up in *what* we do for a living, rather than *who* we are. It doesn't take much to alter that view. An illness, a loss, a move, even a job change." She took a sip from her drink and savored the slushy blend. "What matters most isn't a job, money, a house, a car. It's the people in your life. The relationships you build. Those you would miss most when they're gone because they're irreplaceable."

"I hear you, Mom."

She smiled and took another drink. "I've been lucky to have a friend like Spence in my life since I was a teenager. You need to find your Spence." She smiled and gave the man she considered her soul mate a quick kiss.

* * *

As the days turned into weeks, Maggie's health declined. She gave in to the idea of around the clock care when she fell getting out of bed one night. Max was able to convince her she couldn't continue on her own.

The caregiver model morphed into hospice care within a short period of time. Regi stopped by with Emma during the day, which was the only time there was a hint of the old sparkle in Maggie's eyes.

The hospice workers indicated Maggie didn't have much time. Max stopped by Alexander's one afternoon and confirmed their predictions. Maggie still refused to go to the hospital and only allowed Max to check on her after Kate insisted.

With Maggie deteriorating, Kate made a habit of visiting her in the evenings after dinner. She always tried to persuade her to eat something, but she seemed to exist on only a few spoonfuls of soup each day and a couple of sips from a protein drink. Kate tried to keep her spirits up with flowers and cards and stories from town. Maggie always thanked her but spent most of her time asleep.

Kate noticed Maggie breathed easier and moaned less when she talked to her, but had a hard time coming up with things to say. She couldn't stand sitting there in silence so took to reading books aloud. She would spend a couple hours each night reading and visiting.

When Kate arrived the Sunday before Labor Day, Maggie was a bit more alert than usual. They talked about the upcoming celebration that would take place down by the harbor. "It's always a great day. Not that I don't appreciate the income from the tourist season, but come Labor Day it's nice to get back to a slower pace. Not to mention the parking. Once they leave, we get our sleepy little island back."

Maggie chuckled. "You sound like an old-timer." Kate held a spoon to her mouth full of ice chips and urged her to take a sip of water. "Remember when we thought thirty-five was old."

Kate smiled and said, "Yeah, those were the days."

Maggie's eyes closed. "I'm so tired."

"You can rest. I'll read to you."

She felt Maggie's papery finger on the back of her hand. "Thank you, Katie. You've been so good to me. I'm sorry we had to waste the last twenty years. I missed you and it's my fault."

Kate held her thin hand, so fragile she was afraid to grip it. "It's okay, Maggie. I forgive you. Just rest easy."

She saw a tear slide from Maggie's face onto her pillow. She inched her hand from Maggie's and tidied her bedside, removing dishes and glasses and taking them to the kitchen. The nighttime caregiver was in the living room watching television.

"I'll be a few more minutes," said Kate.

She did the dishes, collected a fresh glass of water and a straw and went back to the bedroom. She heard Maggie mumbling and stepped closer to the bed.

"Are you okay?" she asked.

Maggie's eyes were shut, but she heard her say Kaitlin's name. "I'm coming. I've missed you so much," she said. "I'll see you soon. Wait there for me."

Kate tried to wake Maggie with a gentle touch on her shoulder, but her eyes remained shut. She touched the top of her head with her hand. "It won't be long now, my friend."

* * *

The next morning the threesome and Roxy walked to the harbor and met the rest of the group at the Front Street Café. They timed breakfast to watch the start of the wooden boat race from the big table they reserved on the deck. Most of the tourists had left the island, but a few remained who were either watching or entered in the race. The course was slated to take three hours, with a finish line near the marina. The entire island was invited to a huge salmon barbecue in the park after the race, followed by a concert in the evening.

Most businesses, including the winery, were closed for Labor Day. Sam's coffee shop was open, but she was off, so the entire group, including Emma, was gathered for the last hoorah of summer. They whooped and hollered as the boats took off from the starting line. No motors were allowed, only sailing vessels.

Nate and Regi doted on Emma, making sure she had things to keep her busy and food on the tray of her high chair. She was babbling and saying more words each day. Kate hadn't seen her for several weeks, but she laughed when she heard her squeal and say "cookie" over and over, clear as day.

Regi laughed and handed her a cheese cracker. "I'm so glad the adoption was approved and filed with the court so quickly," said Regi. "It's a load off our minds."

Izzy nodded as she finished her swallow of coffee. "This place is much friendlier with regard to the court docket. Small towns are the best."

Nate added, "Izzy was kind enough to do all that work for nothing. We really appreciate her skills and the gift of her time."

Blake shoulder bumped his sister and said, "She's a keeper."

Izzy laughed and said, "It was my pleasure. It didn't take much time and was relatively straightforward. I'm glad it was settled while Maggie is still here."

Kate nodded. "She's in such a fragile state, but the news of the adoption being finalized brought a smile to her face."

The conversation shifted to happier topics, including the concert in the park and the upcoming Harvest Festival at the winery. It was the last sizeable event of the season and Izzy was staying through the end of the month to help.

Ellie's eyes danced with excitement when she described the plans. "We've had a ton of interest from artists and crafters in the area. We're going to have booths set up outside in the grassy area around the pavilion. Of course, we're doing wine tastings from our winery and the Griffin vineyard in Yakima. We're doing a fun run or walk, in my case, and a grape stomp contest. We've got a bunch of food caterers, including Sam, lined up so folks can purchase whatever they like from breakfast to dinner, and a live band is playing at the end of the night. I'm working on a dog event right now. I'm thinking Wags for Wine."

"Wow, you've outdone yourselves," said Sam. "That should be terrific."

Blake wiggled his brows at his wife. "She left out the part about hoping all of you can come and help out. Free food, free wine, a winery shirt to wear, and we'll treat you to a celebratory dinner after it's over."

There was agreement all around the table amid peals of laughter at Jeff's idea to let the dogs into the grape stomp. Mitch said, "I'm glad I'll still be here for the fun. I should be wrapping up my therapy by then, but this sounds like a can't-miss event."

Max wiggled his finger at him. "No grape stomping for you though." That caused more rowdiness.

The antics and good-natured jabs continued and Kate laughed

harder than she had in months. As she took in the group, she was reminded of what she loved and how this tiny island and the people around the table made her feel at home.

After breakfast, Jeff volunteered to take all the dogs to their house so they could play together. He pulled away with a truck running over with furry friends and promised to be back in time to watch the finish at the marina. The rest of the group took their time strolling along the waterfront.

They arrived as a rowing competition was getting underway. It got the crowd primed for the main event. The friends rooted for the first boats as they maneuvered to the finish and then spent some time wandering the docks to inspect the vessels. Many of them were in pristine condition with their lacquered hulls gleaming in the sun.

Jeff, Nate, and Blake were the most interested in all things nautical or wooden and struck up conversations with several of the owners from out of town. After spending time at the marina, they made their way to the park for the annual salmon barbecue. Nate and Regi opted to take Emma home for a nap but promised to meet up with everyone at the concert.

The fundraiser barbecue was a popular event put on by a local service club, but well worth the wait in line. As they chowed down on their grilled salmon, baked potatoes, and salad, Kate heard her cell phone ring. As she dug for it in her purse, Max brought his phone to his ear.

Kate tapped the button to answer, her heart pounding when she saw the caller was one of Maggie's hospice workers. She listened and nodded before saying, "Thanks for calling. I understand. I'll be there in a few minutes."

She disconnected and met Max's eyes. He gave her a sad shake of his head. Spence looked at Kate and said, "Maggie?"

She nodded and gestured to Max. He stood and said, "That was the hospice nurse. Maggie just passed away. I'm going to run over there." He looked at Kate. "You don't have to come right now, I can take care of things."

She pushed her plate away and gathered her purse. "No, I want to see her."

Spence and Mitch both offered to come with her, but she shook her head. "No, it's okay. I need to do this by myself. I'll be back."

She and Max walked to his car he had left at the flower shop and after dodging several pedestrians made it to Maggie's house. Kate let Max enter Maggie's room first and waited in the living room.

One of the hospice workers offered her tea, but she refused and eyed the pile of scrapbooks and photos she had helped Maggie sort. Emma's playpen and toys were still in the living room. The house was quiet and still.

Maggie had introduced her landlord to Kate, letting him know she would be handling things after her death. There wasn't much to do. The rental was furnished, so Kate had to deal with the personal belongings, but not much else.

Max returned with the hospice nurse and put his hand on Kate's shoulder. "You can go in now. I've notified the sheriff and the funeral home."

She gave his hand a gentle squeeze and went down the hall to the darkened bedroom. Maggie had shrunk to less than ninety pounds and her tiny body made an insignificant lump in the bed. Her eyes were closed and her face was slack. The sheets were neat and folded to cover her shoulders, her arms and hands resting atop the crisp whiteness.

Kate slipped into the chair she always sat in next to Maggie's bed. The book she had been reading to her last night was still on the table. She took Maggie's hand in hers. "Rest easy, my sweet friend. Give Kaitlin a hug from me."

Tears flooded her face as she continued to hold her cool hand. "When you see Karen, tell her I love her. Don't worry about Emma, we'll take good care of her."

She stayed that way until Max came to check on her and ushered her out so the attendants could collect Maggie. He guided her to the backyard where Spence and Mitch were waiting, sparing her the sight of Maggie being wheeled out of the house.

"Can we do anything to help, Mom?"

"Maggie arranged for everything before. I'll need to clear out some of her personal things and get the place cleaned before turning the keys over to the landlord."

"We can help you do that," said Spence. "She didn't want a service, right?"

Kate nodded. "She's going to be cremated and wanted me to hang onto her ashes until Emma was old enough to get them."

"Mitch and I can come over tomorrow and load up whatever we need to while you're at work," said Spence. "You can tell us which items need to go."

"All the baby items need to go to Regi. She can use them or take them to Lulu's for spares when they visit, whatever she wants to do. Maggie's clothes and stuff like that will be donated. Box them and take them to the church. She's only got a couple of pieces of cookware. Most of the stuff in the kitchen stays with the rental. We'll need to toss the food in the fridge and get rid of her leftover medications."

Spence was scribbling on the notepad he always kept in his pocket. A hangover from his days as a detective. "Okay, got it. She'll have sheets and towels, right? We can donate those."

"Yeah, donate all of it. That's what she wanted. I think hospice will take care of returning the hospital bed. I'll call the cleaning service once we have it emptied."

Spence looked at Mitch. "I don't think it will take us more than a day or two."

"There's a stack of boxes in the living room with scrapbooks and photos. Those are mine, so bring them home."

"Will do. What about her car?"

"Oh, yeah. Her will dictates that the car be donated. So, we'll need to get it to the church. They can sell it or keep it."

Max came outside and said, "They're taking her to the ferry now and said they had the order to return the ashes to you. They'll be ready next week and they'll call you so you can pick them up at the funeral home here on the island."

Kate stood. "Thanks, Max. I appreciate your help."

"I'll call her brothers and let them know. She had asked me to take care of that when the time came. You guys going to be okay?"

Kate clenched her jaw. "I knew it was going to happen, so I'm not shocked. It's just so…final." She inhaled a quick breath. "Oh, I need to tell Regi and Nate."

Spence said, "Already done. We stopped by on our way here."

"How were they?" she asked.

"They seemed okay, sad, but not surprised."

"Even though you're prepared and almost resigned to the idea, it's always a blow," said Max, putting his arm around her. "If it's any consolation, she thought the world of you and she was ready to go. She was in anguish with such pain the last few weeks."

Kate agreed with a rapid succession of nods. "I know she was suffering. It was almost unbearable to see her like that."

"You were a wonderful friend to her and gave her so much comfort. More than you know." He walked to the door. "I'm going to head back. Are you guys coming to the concert?"

Spence and Mitch looked at Kate for guidance. "Yeah, I think a concert sounds like a fine idea."

Kate doused the lights and locked the door. She let Mitch have the front seat and Spence held the rear door for her. She climbed in and gazed at the now empty and somber house.

Chapter Twenty-five

With the help of Spence and Mitch, Kate was able to get the cleaning arranged and would be able to return the keys to the landlord by the end of the week. Nate helped transport the entire collection of baby items back to their house and then used his delivery truck to haul all the boxes of donations to the church.

Spence and Mitch made sure the house was emptied of personal items and deposited the photo memorabilia in a corner of Kate's home office. Kate had agreed to be the executor of the estate in addition to the trustee for Emma. As she and Spence took a last look around the house, she shrugged. "I should have given Maggie more credit. She was smart to sell everything and spend her last days in a beautiful spot. She made it simple since she didn't own anything, except the basics. All the proceeds were placed into the trust for Emma."

"Yeah, I thought it sounded like a frenzied decision, but I see the logic to what she did. She didn't want to leave someone with a bunch of stuff to handle."

"She was planning to make Janette the executor because she didn't have anyone in her life. That all changed when she showed up here."

They left the keys on the counter, as the landlord asked, and made their way to the sidewalk.

He slipped his arm around her shoulders. "It turned out to be a good thing, right?"

"Yeah, surprising, but it was. I was able to tell her I forgave her Sunday night. The last time I saw her alive she was dreaming and talking to Kaitlin. At least I think she was dreaming."

"It's not the first time I've heard of people on the brink of death seeing or talking to loved ones that had passed on before. I find that comforting."

"Max said she basically went into a coma and died, so I think it was as peaceful as possible. At least at the end. Getting there was the nightmare."

"I'm sure some of that peace and letting go came when you told her you forgave her." He gave her hand a squeeze and she returned it and nodded.

They turned the corner at Kate's street. Mitch was cooking dinner for them. He had been doing well and was able to be more productive, which buoyed his spirits. He had grilled burgers and they sat down to a casual, but delicious meal.

After watching television and having a bowl of ice cream for dessert, Kate excused herself for the evening. The grief of the last few days washed over her. She changed into pajamas and found herself in the office opening the boxes from Maggie.

She saw a large shallow box with an envelope taped to the front. She took a closer look and saw it had her name scrawled on the envelope and a sticky note from Mitch saying it had been delivered earlier in the day. She took the envelope to her desk and opened it. It was dated over a month ago.

Dear Katie,

Gwen, my favorite nurse, is writing this for me. I'm too shaky to do a good job so she agreed to be my scribe. I never expected to be here like this. So many things have happened in my life I didn't anticipate. Finding you here on the island was a big surprise. I was scared at first, but it turned out to be the best thing that could have ever happened.

When I knew how sick I was this time, I thought about calling you. To be honest, I thought about calling you the day Kaitlin died. You were the first person that entered my mind. I longed for my friend. That's when I understood what I had done to you. To us. I was too scared to call you all those years, but I should have.

Frank tried to comfort me, but it's not quite the same as having my best friend beside me. You, the woman I thought of as my sister for so long. I have so many regrets and losing you is one of the biggest.

I know you've told me I don't have to keep apologizing, so I'll try not to. I admire your ability to put aside my betrayal. I'm not sure why I ever thought having an affair with Jack was okay. I've analyzed it over the years and at the time justified it because I was "taking care" of Jack when you weren't. I let him use me and I deceived you and was beyond hateful.

With all that said, I can't imagine the strength it took for you to put all that behind you and treat me with the kindness I didn't deserve. You are a lovely person and I can never thank you enough for your help with Emma and for your gentleness with me. They say you can tell the character of a person by how she treats those who can do nothing for her. You, my dear friend, are the essence of this quote.

I am heartbroken I missed out on twenty years of fun with you. I regret not being there for you when you were suffering the loss of your beautiful girl. I sure missed you when I lost mine.

I'm grateful you'll be there for Emma. On one of her last visits here, I was showing her your picture and telling her to call you Auntie Katie. It turned into Auntie Cookie and no matter what I did or said, it's Auntie Cookie. So, don't be shocked if that's your name from now on. Regi and I laughed and laughed as we tried to get her to say Katie. Oh well, cookies have always been one of my favorite things.

I wish I could be here longer. I'd love to see Emma grow up, go to school, drive a car, go to prom, graduate, get married. I want it all. I try to concentrate on how much joy she's brought me in the short time she's been in my life, but it's hard to reconcile the thought of never seeing her sweet face again.

I trust you completely, Katie. I know you'll watch over her. I know you'll fill the void I leave behind. I couldn't have found better parents for her if I had ordered them myself. I'll be forever grateful for you introducing us to Regi and Nate. I don't know what I would have done if they had said no and I appreciate your role in finding her a home.

I can feel myself fading away. I don't think I'll make it to Emma's birthday this fall. Make sure it's a happy day for her. Her little grin reminds me of our girls and the photo we found. I commissioned a local artist to recreate the photo in a painting for you. I know how much you love it and I like to think of our girls together again. I hope it brings you joy.

There's so much more to say, but I don't have the words. Mitch is such a fine young man and a wonderful son. He loves you more than you'll ever know. I'm thrilled you and Spence found each other and are making a life together. He adores you and is the perfect match for you. I know he'll cherish and protect you. Most important, I know he'll love you. You deserve all the happiness in the world. You are surrounded by such a loving and caring group of friends on *this beautiful island. I can tell you're finally home, Katie.*

I leave you with my love and gratitude, my friend. I long for the day you can truly forgive me for all I've done. That would bring me great joy and relief. I hope you find it in your heart to do that—and that I'm still around to hear it. Life is shorter than you think, so spend your days in happiness. Tell the people in your life how much you love them and how much they mean to you, while you can.

I love you and will miss you, Maggie

Kate's eyes blurred with tears and she reached for a box of tissues as she read the letter one more time. She laughed when she recalled Emma at breakfast squealing about cookies. Now it made sense.

She cut open the box and slid out a framed painting. She smiled through the tears. The artist was one of the best and a favorite she featured at the shop. It was so lifelike. She marveled at the shimmer of light off the towheaded girls. He had done a wonderful job and captured the unburdened joy of childhood in the faces of the two girls. Subtle cherry blossoms were in the background and the rose colored chubby cheeks and smiles coupled with the bright eyes of the girls, conjured up the happy memory of the day.

She held it up to a couple of walls and noticed the small plaque at the bottom of the frame. "Together Again" was engraved on it and when she turned it over she saw, in Maggie's shaky hand, *Karen and Kaitlin, our beloved girls together again. With all my love, Maggie.*

She wiped her eyes and sat at her desk, where she glanced at the wall space. She contemplated and decided on a spot near the window at the side of her desk. She wanted to see those smiling faces as often as possible.

* * *

As the days marched on, life on the island became slower and more manageable. Lulu was happy to relinquish her days at Alexander's to Andi and spend her time spoiling her new granddaughter. She vowed to fill in whenever Kate needed help but had jumped at the opportunity to watch Emma while Regi worked. She spent her days pushing a stroller and treating Emma to picnics and trips to the park.

Izzy was helping full-time at the winery, getting ready for the harvest. Mia was still in school and showed no signs of quitting, which brought Izzy some peace. Kate spent her days at the store and was able to take Friday through Monday off, with Andi more than capable of handling the traffic in the store now that the tourist season was over.

Mitch had the approval to ditch his cane and was ready to head back to work after the festival at the end of the month. He was golfing each week with Max and they were organizing one more fishing trip before he had to leave.

Spence had another trial coming up and would be visiting the city again for a few days next week. Kate was glad Mitch was still here to keep her company. Dr. Westman had cut her therapy back to twice a month. The results had surprised Kate. She knew her final exam would come when Mitch did leave and when those important anniversaries related to Karen rolled around, but she was feeling stronger and more positive.

She had retrieved Maggie's ashes from the funeral home and installed her urn on the mantle. At Ellie's suggestion, she also had them use a small portion of the cremains to create two glass memorials. She selected two hearts, both on stands with lights, designed to be used as nightlights. She gave Emma one and would explain it was a way to remember her grandma when she was old enough to understand. She knew Maggie would love the idea of watching over Emma from her dresser. Kate kept the other one in her office under the painting from Maggie.

The mornings were crisp and the days were a bit shorter. Kate gripped the mug of warm coffee in her hand and snuggled deeper into the blanket as she waited for the sun to rise. She loved the upcoming season and the subtle changes in weather but knew it would mean her morning ritual on the patio would soon have to end. She rested her head against the cushion and sighed as the delicate light of morning breached the horizon. Today's started with soft blues under lighting the bank of darker clouds. As the sun rose, it looked like an artist had filled a brush with the perfect blend of pink and gold and swept it across the canvas. The brilliant glow from the rose gilded sun pierced the ribbons of color and created a gorgeous soft pink that illuminated the space between the dark blue clouds.

"Aah," she whispered. "What a beauty." She took a sip from her cup and thought of her old friend's letter. "You're right, Maggie. I'm finally home."

ACKNOWLEDGEMENTS

I always feel like I'm on a getaway with old friends when I begin to write a Hometown Harbor Novel. I hope it's as relaxing for you to read as it is for me to write. I love this area of the Pacific Northwest and if you have never visited, you must add it to your bucket list.

Kate is one of my favorite people in Friday Harbor. When I first introduced her I hinted at her backstory, but in FINALLY HOME the layers of her life unfold. While she is the main focus of this book's journey, there are also a few subplots concerning Ellie and Blake and another character I enjoy, Izzy.

My next project is a new Cooper Harrington mystery. I've got several ideas for new cases for Coop, so my focus will be on this series for the foreseeable future. As of now, I don't have plans in the works for another Hometown Harbor novel, but am toying with the idea of some short stories for the series, or possibly a special release for a holiday.

As always I'm thankful for my early readers, who are diligent when it comes to reading my manuscripts. Theresa, Linda, and Jana were kind enough to read my drafts and give me valuable feedback and ideas.

I'm working with a new cover designer at Alchemy Book Covers and am thrilled with Keri's design and work. She's a pleasure to work with and a talented designer. Jason and Marina at Polgarus deliver expert formatting and are always professional and accommodating.

I continue to be supported by wonderful friends and family as I pursue this second career of mine. I appreciate all of the readers who have taken the time to provide a review on Amazon or Goodreads. These reviews are especially important in promoting future books, so if you enjoy my novels, please consider leaving a positive review. Follow this link to my author page and select a book to leave your review at www.amazon.com/author/tammylgrace. I also encourage you to follow me on Amazon and you'll be the first to know about new releases.

I'd love to add you to my mailing list and you'll get free exclusive content just for joining. I use the list to keep you informed of news, blog posts, and periodically choose subscribers for free giveaways. Fill out the quick form here on my web page and you'll be part of my exclusive reader group.

Visit www.tammylgrace.com and sign up. Follow me on Facebook at www.facebook.com/tammylgrace.books to keep in touch—I'd love to hear from you.

From the Author

Thank you for reading the fifth book in the Hometown Harbor Series. This series is designed to be read in order since spoilers are revealed in subsequent books. If you enjoy the series and are a fan of mysteries, you'll want to try my Cooper Harrington Detective Novels. They're whodunits featuring a lovable private detective, his loyal dog, and a few other memorable characters. They feature a crime, usually murder, but are not overly violent and a bit on the cozy side. The first one, KILLER MUSIC, won the Gold Medal in Mystery in the 2016 Global E-Book Awards. They can be read as stand-alone novels, but I recommend reading them in order, as you'll learn and understand more behind the main characters in subsequent books.

I'd love to send you my exclusive interview with the canine companions in the Hometown Harbor Series as a thank-you for joining my mailing list. Instructions and a link for signing up for my mailing list are included below. You'll also find questions for book club discussions at www.tammylgrace.com. Be sure and download the free novella, HOMETOWN HARBOR: THE BEGINNING. It's a prequel to FINDING HOME that I know you'll enjoy.

Enjoy this book?
You can make a big difference

Thanks again for reading my work and if you enjoy my novels, *I would be grateful if you would leave a review on Amazon*. Authors need reviews to help showcase their work and market it across other platforms. I'd like to be able to take out full page ads in the newspaper, but I don't have the financial muscle of a big New York publisher. When it comes to getting attention for my work, reviews are some of the most powerful tools I have. You can help by sharing what you enjoyed with other readers.

If you enjoyed my books, please consider leaving a review

Hometown Harbor: The Beginning (FREE Prequel Novella)
Finding Home (Book 1)
Home Blooms (Book 2)
A Promise of Home (Book 3)
Pieces of Home (Book 4)
Finally Home (Book 5)
Killer Music: A Cooper Harrington Detective Novel (Book 1)
Deadly Connection: A Cooper Harrington Detective Novel (Book 2)

Thank you very much for taking the time to leave a review.

ABOUT THE AUTHOR

Tammy L. Grace is the award-winning author of the Cooper Harrington Detective Novels and the Hometown Harbor Series. You'll find Tammy online at www.tammylgrace.com where you can join her mailing list and be part of her exclusive reader group. Connect with Tammy on Facebook at www.facebook.com/tammylgrace.books or on Twitter at @TammyLGrace.

Made in the USA
Coppell, TX
16 June 2021